A PASSIONATE NEGOTIATION

He couldn't seem to take l... wild river child grown into thi... Any man in his position woul... make her his wife in every way...

"Perhaps we should make an agreement—here and now. So that each of us will know what to expect."

"An agreement?" she asked, her voice edged with suspicion. "What kind of agreement?"

"That's up to you," he said. He turned from her seeking eyes and walked toward the window that looked onto the front gallery and out toward the river.

"It isn't as if we have only one choice. We can try to make this a real marriage . . . or we can continue as we have in the past."

Lily frowned. Somehow this wasn't what she'd expected him to say. Nicholas was the kind of man she thought would storm into a woman's bedroom, sweep her up into his arms, and give her little choice about it.

"I . . . I don't know what to say."

"But surely you know what you want," he said, turning and moving quickly to her.

Lily couldn't move. He was so close to her now that she could see the faint stubble of his beard and the slight quirk of amusement on his sensuous lips. When his hand moved toward her, she tensed, making a quiet sound in her throat when he touched her. His fingers burned through the fabric of her gown, sending tingles along her arm as he traced his hand slowly toward her shoulder.

"Has any man ever touched you this way?" he whispered.

"No," she answered, her voice breathless. "Of course not." She found herself leaning toward him, wanting something she couldn't quite name.

He laughed softly, delighted with her response, and moved his fingers to the sensitive skin just below her collarbone. His breath mingled with her hair as he trailed his fingers downward and brushed the back of his hand against her breast.

Lily gasped and closed her eyes.

"You've become a beautiful, bewitching woman," he murmured, pulling her into his arms.

BOOK YOUR PLACE ON OUR WEBSITE AND MAKE THE READING CONNECTION!

We've created a customized website just for our very special readers, where you can get the inside scoop on everything that's going on with Zebra, Pinnacle and Kensington books.

When you come online, you'll have the exciting opportunity to:

- View covers of upcoming books
- Read sample chapters
- Learn about our future publishing schedule (listed by publication month *and author*)
- Find out when your favorite authors will be visiting a city near you
- Search for and order backlist books from our online catalog
- Check out author bios and background information
- Send e-mail to your favorite authors
- Meet the Kensington staff online
- Join us in weekly chats with authors, readers and other guests
- Get writing guidelines
- AND MUCH MORE!

**Visit our website at
http://www.zebrabooks.com**

WILD RIVER BRIDE

Clara Wimberly

Zebra Books
Kensington Publishing Corp.

http://www.zebrabooks.com

ZEBRA BOOKS are published by

Kensington Publishing Corp.
850 Third Avenue
New York, NY 10022

First Printing: May, 1998
10 9 8 7 6 5 4 3 2 1

Printed in the United States of America

Chapter 1

August, 1817
Natchez, Mississippi

Two women stood on the second-story balcony of a squalid ramshackle building that faced the street. On the tall bluffs behind them, the town of Natchez sat, its elegant houses pristine and white in the afternoon sun, a breeze stirring the green trees.

But here, Under-the-Hill, the air was hot and still, the scent from the muddy river especially strong and pungent.

One of the women wore only a skirt and chemise, her nakedness eliciting whistles and howls of glee from men passing in the street below.

The other waved a lace-trimmed but dingy handkerchief at the noisy admirers, although she glanced at them only briefly and with a quiet look of boredom.

"Lord, I hope they go on to Frannie's place," she sighed. "I'm dog tired, and it's too hot and late in the day to be thrashin' about in bed with some man who's been on a keelboat for a month."

"Money's money I always say."

The second woman only grunted, her weary, jaded eyes searching the greener ground beyond the row of dirt gray buildings that lined the streets.

"Lord have mercy, will you look at that."

She flipped her handkerchief toward the grassy strip along the river.

"It's Lily, ridin' that old plug of her pa's. Rides like a little demon, don't she? Wild as the old Mississippi, they say."

"Ah, she's a good girl. But since her pa died a couple of weeks ago . . ."

"Look at her—ridin' that old nag, that flamin' hair of hers flyin' in the wind. The girl's gonna ruin that fine white skin if she ain't careful. But still, she's gonna be a beauty when she grows up and adds a bit o' flesh to her bones. Can you imagine what she'd look like dressed up proper, ridin' a real fine horse?"

"Well, that ain't likely to happen. She's a river child, pure and simple, and she'll never be anything else. No matter how much her pa wanted somethin' better for her. More'n likely she'll end up here with us or down the river at Fran's."

"God, I hate to see that happen. She's a sweet girl, despite her wild tomboy ways."

"Well, it'll probably happen sooner than later. You heard that her maw's got the fever, too, didn't you? Fran's over there right now, tendin' the poor lady." She nodded in the direction of the small Gaines house.

"Yeah . . . it's a shame. The girl's mighty young to start workin' in a brothel."

"Why?" the second woman said, grinning wryly. "I was barely fifteen when I started. You too. It weren't so bad. Least we had a warm place to sleep and good food to eat. Besides, like you said, money's money, ain't it?"

"Girls," someone called from the balcony doorway. "Come inside . . . we got customers."

The two women turned to look at one another, rolling their eyes with resigned boredom. They grumbled beneath their breath before flashing bright, pasted-on smiles and turning to go back inside.

Lily Marie Gaines rode hard, trying to banish the grief and fear she felt. But despite trying to focus her attention elsewhere, she couldn't seem to stay away from their small house for long, and she hadn't been able to banish the memory of her mother's thin, pale face.

She couldn't believe this was happening. One moment her parents had been vibrant and alive and the next her father was dead and her mother so ill that it seemed she was destined to soon follow.

Yellow fever had raged through the small town of Natchez so quickly and so lethally that the Board of Selectmen had written a resolution appointing four men to guard the town day and night. A city watch, they called it, meant to isolate immediately anyone found on the streets in a stricken condition and get him or her away from the public as quickly as possible.

A quarantine hospital had even been built, two miles downriver from Natchez, at Bacon's Landing.

But that had come too late for her father. And Lily had managed to keep her mother's illness from the authorities because she had begged Lily not to let her die in a strange place.

When Lily rode back to her house and tied the horse to the fence outside, she was so lost in thought that she didn't hear the door open at first.

"Lily, dear, come inside. Mr. St. James is here to see your mother like she asked." The woman who stood on the front porch wrung her hands as she gazed with great sympathy at Lily.

Her garishly powdered and painted face and the faded, red-spangled dress that she wore told of her profession, as did the scent of cheap perfume and whiskey that always seemed to cling to her thin body.

But despite the woman's reputation, Lily had never seen Miss Fran Dupree as anyone other than a kind, loving neighbor who gave of herself and her time when anyone needed help.

Lily hurried into the house, stopping abruptly when she saw the tall man in the center of the room. His presence seemed to fill the small space—not only the size of him, but something else ... some masculine magnetism that even a girl as young as Lily could sense.

As if in a slow-moving dream, she allowed her gaze to wander over him, from the toes of his shining Blucher boots upward to the tightly fitted linen trousers that emphasized muscular thighs. In the excessive heat, he wasn't wearing a coat, but his ruffled shirt with full sleeves appeared freshly starched and the material quite costly. He looked decidedly out of place in the small, plain house.

He was looking straight at Lily, waiting for her to speak, she presumed. Or more likely waiting for her to come forward and properly acknowledge his presence.

She knew Nicholas St. James. He took her father's ferry often, traveling back and forth from his plantation across the river to his other house in the city. Oddly enough, over the past year, the two men had become unlikely friends.

Lily had always been uneasy around him; she didn't know why. And today he intimidated her as much as he ever did.

With that rather arrogant lift of his square chin and the appraising glint in those cool gray eyes, he always made Lily feel ragged and poor. He made her feel like a child.

But she wasn't a child. She was fourteen. An age when some considered a female a grown woman. Especially here beneath the hill, where men came every day from the passing boats, looking for female companionship. Lily knew what went on in the houses along the streets. Her mother had tried to shield her from all that, but she knew.

She pressed her lips together and walked past him to the small bedroom where her mother lay.

"You shouldn't be here, *monsieur,*" she said, using her most grown-up voice. "It's yellow fever that my mother has. And it's the same that killed my father, here in this very house."

"I'm told I survived the fever as a child. I'm immune," he said, with a casual lift of his broad shoulders.

The heat in the small room was suffocating. The house stood in the shadow of the bluffs and the interior was, like today, often so dark and shadowy that candles had to be lit in the middle of the day. The guttering luminaries, placed in bottles, and dented pewter candlesticks, made low, murmuring noises, like distant ghostly voices. It was the only sound, except for an occasional soft gasp from the woman who lay dying.

Lily walked to the bed and took her mother's hand, feeling the thin fingers tighten against hers. It was the first acknowledgment of anyone's presence that her mother had made in days, and Lily was so surprised that she fell to her knees beside the bed, leaning close and touching her mother's face. She brushed the dull strands of hair back from her pale skin. It saddened her seeing the life-lessness of the once lustrous locks. The red hair with glints of gold, so like Lily's own, had always been the her mother's pride and joy.

"Mother?"

Her mother opened her eyes, blinking slowly several times, as if it took all her strength to do so. Without moving her head, she turned her fevered gaze toward the man at the foot of the bed and lifted her other hand a few inches from the covers, then let it drop weakly.

". . . St. James," Her voice was a ghostly whisper in the quiet room.

He came immediately to kneel at the opposite side of the bed from Lily, seemingly indifferent to any inconvenience to himself, or any lowering of his standards.

Lily's mouth dropped open as she stared across the bed at him, surprised by what she considered an unusual display of kindness. He never seemed anything but cool and aloof in her presence.

"Thank you . . . for coming." Her mother managed to turn her head slightly toward the man. And now Lily could barely make out her words.

"I was so sorry to hear of your husband's death, Mrs. Gaines. I was at the plantation when word reached me. If I'd known—"

"No . . . no. No time. I . . . I must . . ." Her voice trailed away weakly, her breathing so labored that every one seemed to be her last.

"What is it? What can I do for you, ma'am?"

"Lily . . . my baby . . ."

Her name, coming so weakly from her mother's lips, sent a jolt of despair straight through Lily's heart. Despite her vow to be strong, a quiet sob escaped her lips, and she bent her head to touch her forehead against her mother's hand.

She had no idea why her mother had called this wealthy man to her deathbed. Lily had always been fascinated by his tall, dark good looks, and the elegant clothes he wore, but she had never understood why he would befriend her father.

But this was still a rather primitive settlement, her father would often say. And the very act of survival in such a place sometimes made strange and often lasting alliances.

She could barely make out her mother's whispered words to the man at her side. Even he had to bend his dark head closer to hear.

"It's time . . . do you remember . . . ?" Those odd fragmented phrases were all Lily could really understand. But they sent a cold fear rushing over her.

Was her mother asking this man to help place her in an orphanage?

Lily looked up and across the bed. Her eyes were troubled as they met and held his cool gaze. Yet for all his coolness, Mr. St. James seemed as troubled by her mother's words as Lily was.

She felt her mother's fingers grow limp and fall slowly from her grip.

"Mother," she said, her voice urgent and trembling with fear as she stood up and bent over the bed.

She heard the sound of her mother's breath gurgling softly in her throat and felt Miss Fran's hands on her shoulders.

"There, there. She's still with us, child," the woman said. "Why don't you come away for a while? Come outside where the sun is shining and the birds are singing. A new barge just pulled into the landing, and it's loaded with all kinds of exciting goods, they say."

"No," Lily said, clamping her teeth together. Tears sparkled in her eyes as she looked defiantly at the man watching her. "I can't leave her."

"Well, darlin', I can't stay right now," the woman said regretfully. "I fear I have an appointment. But if you'd come outside at least, I could keep an eye on you from my room across the way."

"It's all right, Fran," Nicholas said. "Let the child stay here if it's what she wants."

Lily cast a resentful look at the tall man. She wasn't sure if it was his soft, condescending voice or the fact that he called her a child that made her so angry.

"Lily . . ." Her mother's voice summoned Lily back toward the bed.

"Yes, Mother? What is it? Shall I get you some water? Some broth—?"

"Listen," she whispered. "You must do . . . as Mr. St. James asks. You . . . must. Promise me . . ." She gasped and began to cough.

Tears streamed from Lily's eyes as she lifted her mother's head to try to ease her breathing. At that moment she would have promised her anything.

"Yes ... yes," Lily whispered fiercely. "I promise, Mother. I promise. Whatever you want, I'll do."

Suddenly the room grew quiet. Lily thought she'd seldom seen such peace as that which descended over her mother's pale face. She smiled and closed her eyes, then nodded once.

The next moment she was gone.

"Mother?" Lily desperately clasped her mother's hands to her chest. "Mother!"

She was barely aware of the quiet sound of sobbing in the room behind her. Or of the hard hands that pulled her away from her mother's body. The taste of tears and the scent of newly starched clothes filled her senses as she was lifted to strong arms and carried to another room.

She couldn't fight anymore. She was so weary and weak. She had sat by her mother's bed for days now, without sleep and with hardly anything to eat. Suddenly, she felt ill and disoriented, as if she herself might be dying, too. And at the moment she didn't really care. If it was the yellow jack that descended upon her, then let it come. Without her mother, she thought she might even welcome its darkness.

When Lily woke, she didn't recognize her surroundings.

The room where she lay was warm with sunshine. Lacy white curtains covered the windows, and through their intricate patterns, she could see green leaves moving in the breeze. And the furniture was so beautiful it almost took her breath away. She thought it was the most beautiful place she'd ever seen.

She glanced down at her body, not recognizing the neat white cotton gown she wore, or the lace-edged sheets that covered her. She moved her feet and felt the cool smoothness of fine linens against her skin.

Her mother was gone. She remembered that much with a terrible wrench of her heart.

But where was she? Was this heaven?

The door to the room was open, and she could see out into a wide hallway, where a red-flowered carpet and the edge of gleaming wood floors were also splashed with sunlight. She thought from the waning light that it must be nearing dusk.

She heard voices and pushed herself up in bed, deciding by the dizzying spin of her head not to try standing just yet.

"Have you completely lost your senses?" a woman's voice said. "You can't really mean to go through with this."

"Oh? And why can't I?"

Lily recognized the second voice immediately. It was the deep, rather indulgent tone of Nicholas St. James's voice.

"Her father and I had discussed the possibility several times, and I was not averse to it. He was always concerned because a child here cannot inherit without being married. And even though they lived rather poorly, believe me, he had managed to put away a small fortune from his business. Uneducated or not, he was quite an astute businessman. As his friend, I can hardly stand by now and let the state take all that he worked for, while his daughter is sent away to an orphanage."

"But why you?"

"Why not?" Nicholas replied flatly. "There are no other relatives, and as a friend of the family, it's left to me. Mary, I don't understand your concern. Arranged marriages are not uncommon. It's only your romantic heart that makes it seem so impossible, my dear sister."

"It's just that you sound so nonchalant about the entire thing." Mary looked at her brother as if she could barely believe all she was hearing.

"Hardly. I have a few concerns. Of course I do. I'd be a fool not to under the circumstances."

"There's more to it than you're saying," Mary suggested.

"Perhaps." Nicholas shrugged his shoulders and gazed toward the double door at the end of the hallway.

"Do you care for the girl? Is that it?"

"Please," he scoffed. "She's a child. And a wild one at that. Still . . ."

"What?" Mary asked.

He shrugged again, frowning. How could he explain this to his sister when he hardly understood it himself? Why was he so willing to give up his freedom for this girl that he barely knew?

True, he'd made a promise to her parents, but no one would fault him if he failed to keep it. After all, what obligation did he really have to these river people?

Yet . . .

What was it about the girl that compelled him so? That spark of defiance he saw today in those emerald eyes? Her wildness that he found both pathetic and admirable?

He'd seen a glint of intelligence and spirit in her over the past year. Perhaps it was even the way she looked at him with such distrust sometimes. When he rode the ferry, he would often catch her watching him with that little look of skepticism in her eyes. He'd wondered what he had to do to make her smile, or to see a friendly look on her defiant little face.

But marriage? Perhaps Mary was right. Perhaps he couldn't do this.

He turned, rubbing his chin thoughtfully as he spoke.

"On the practical side, I'm twenty-five years of age and unmarried. It's time I began thinking about the future. And heirs for Live Oaks Plantation."

"My dear brother," Mary sighed, exasperated, "there are dozens of mothers in Natchez and the surrounding countryside who have made it well-known that they would like nothing better than to marry off their daughters to Nicholas St. James. You know full well that you could have your pick of any one of them."

"And *you* know very well that I'm not inclined to be led around by the nose. Nor do I intend to spend the rest of my life sitting by the fire, watching my wife do needlepoint or escorting her to every soiree in town. I'm much happier going my own way. This way, there will be no such expectations, and I can live just the way I always have."

"But if you marry this girl, you could be an outcast in this town."

Hearing the unseen woman's words, Lily frowned. The arrogant, handsome Nicholas St. James was getting married?

She heard his laughter, deep and cynical.

"Do you think I care a whit about that? Don't you remember hearing what the Natchez Nabobs did to our mother when she married Father . . . a man who dared to make his fortune in the lowly vocation of sawmilling?"

"That was a long time ago. And they accept us now as if we were born to the—"

"Exactly. Do you think I give a damn whether those hypocrites accept me or not?" Nicholas said, his voice booming loudly in the hallway.

"Is that why you're doing this?" His sister Mary gasped. "My God, Nicky, tell me you're not doing this to spite the gossiping old hags you think offended our mother. She forgave them. Why can't you?"

For a moment there was no answer. Lily saw a shadow in the hallway, and she slid back down into bed when she saw Nicholas St. James walk past the door, head down, hands in his pockets. The afternoon light gleamed against his dark hair and emphasized the darkness of his skin.

"You are a rebel. You always have heen," Mary huffed with exasperation. "You're too stubborn for your own good."

Only silence followed her accusation.

"And what about this girl?" Mary asked, her voice growing quieter and more patient. "She's only a child, Nicholas. Only fourteen, I understand. Surely you don't mean to—"

"All the better," Nicholas said. "A young wife is more likely to be sweet and pliable. Easily molded into the kind of woman I prefer to run my household and bear my children."

"That is insufferable. You can't mean it."

"Oh, but I do mean it," the deep voice drawled.

Lily's eyes narrowed and she frowned. He *was* insufferable. And she felt sorry for the poor girl he intended bending to his will and molding into his perfect wife.

"Besides," he added, "I promised her dying mother today that I would not abandon the plans I made with her husband. As the law is written, the girl is still a child and cannot inherit. Even her home, such as it is, would be lost to her. She'd be homeless . . . perhaps even forced to work at one of the places on the landing. And I liked and respected her father far too much to let that happen to the chit."

Lily felt a slight tingle run through her entire body. They were talking about her! Dear Lord, she was the girl they were finding so unsuitable!

She pushed herself back up in bed, forgetting about her previous dizziness. Forgetting everything except the odd feeling that raced through her body and set her heart to pounding.

"Guardianship, I can understand. But marriage, Nicholas?"

"More convenient," he said. "Fewer legalities. As a married woman, she will inherit everything, which of course I shall keep for her until she's older. Just one simple ceremony will take care of everything."

"But Nicky . . . darling . . . what about love? Surely you—"

"Love?" he grunted softly. "I have no need for love, Mary. It only gets in one's way. No, I much prefer a docile wife at home, and if I should happen to find love elsewhere, so much the better and much less complicated at that. There's always the option of annulment once the girl is old enough to be on her own."

"I can't believe you take marriage so lightly."

"I promise you, I don't take it lightly. Any more than I take giving my word lightly. If it will ease your mind any, once the marriage ceremony has taken place, I intend sending the girl home with you to Boston. That is if you and Theodore have no objections."

"Of course I have no objections, but—"

"I want her to have the finest education available before coming back to Natchez to live as my wife. By then, even you must agree, she'll be old enough to come to her marriage bed. If continuing the marriage is what I choose," he added with an indifferent drawl.

"At least you have enough decency to wait about that," his sister mumbled.

Lily realized that she was holding her breath. Listening and waiting. But for what? She already knew she was the one they were discussing. Wasn't that what her mother had called him to her deathbed for—so that her Lily would be provided for when she was gone?

"It's settled then," Nicholas said. He walked back past the doorway. "As soon as Lily is well, I'll explain the situation to her, and we will be married."

Lily was hardly aware of pushing the covers back away from her. Or of leaping down from the high four-poster bed. All she knew was that the cool arrogance in his voice infuriated her beyond all reason.

She came to the doorway in a rush, her gown whirling about her long, coltish legs. Her eyes were bright and stormy as she faced the man in the hallway.

Nicholas had not seen the girl since his sister and his housekeeper bathed her and placed her in the upstairs bedroom of his home. Earlier today in the dark, spartan, little house beneath the bluffs, Lily's hair had been in long braids. Now, loose and shining, the red-gold curls lay in a riotous mass about her face and shoulders, practically overwhelming her small, thin body. Through the cotton gown, he could see long slender legs and arms, and the outline of a woman's burgeoning body.

He actually felt a quick moment of sympathy for her. Even a hint of guilt that she had apparently overheard his seemingly cold and callous plans.

Until his gaze moved up to meet blazing green eyes that stared defiantly and angrily into his.

"I won't do it," Lily cried, her voice still husky from sleep. "I won't never agree to marry you, Nicholas St. James. I ain't to be bought like some broodmare for your plantation. Do you hear me? I won't!"

Lily felt her head spinning and her surroundings growing dark. She grasped the smooth surface of the door facing as she slid slowly to the floor, crumpling into a small heap at the feet of an astonished Nicholas St. James.

Mary knelt quickly beside the girl, grimacing as she looked up at her brother.

"Well, well, brother," Mary murmured with a touch of irony and more than a hint of pleasure. "So much for your sweet, pliable girl just waiting to be molded by your hands into a devoted wife."

Chapter 2

Nicholas cursed beneath his breath as he bent and scooped the feather-light girl up into his arms and carried her back to bed.

"Ask one of the maids to come up and sit with her, won't you?" He didn't turn as he spoke to his sister, but instead stood with his hands on his hips, gazing down at the girl on the bed. She looked so young and helpless in the huge four-poster. Surrounded by white and covered in white, she might have looked like an angel except for the fiery hair that lay spread about her face.

"Willful little chit," he murmured.

"Nicky," Mary said, moving quietly to stand beside him. "If you're having second thoughts . . ."

"More than second thoughts," he admitted, his voice quieter and more serious now. "But I made an agreement with her father, and I won't go back on my word just because the girl happens to be disagreeable."

"You think you can persuade her to come around?" Mary asked.

"Ah," Nicholas said, putting his arm around his sister's

shoulders. "That, my dear, is where you come in. You will teach her, influence her with your gentility . . ." He was grinning mischievously as he touched his sister's round nose. "And perhaps even convince her in the next few years that I'm not the high-handed ogre she seems to think I am."

"That," Mary said, smiling up at her only brother, "might be the harder task to accomplish."

Lily liked Mary St. James Claiborne. In the two days since she'd confronted Nicholas and told him she'd never agree to marry him, his young sister Mary had spent almost every waking hour with Lily.

She'd been extremely kind and sympathetic when telling her about her mother's burial.

"The fever you know . . ." Mary said softly. "There had to be a hasty burial. The Selectmen hope it will help stop the spread of the disease."

Lily nodded; she couldn't reply because of the aching lump in her throat.

"The doctor examined you that first day after we brought you here," Mary said, brushing back a tendril of flaming hair from Lily's face. "He told Nicholas that it's a miracle you haven't contracted the fever, but that some people seem to be naturally immune to the disease. Or he speculated that you might even have had a touch of it as a child, the way Nicky did. It seems that if a person gets the fever and survives, they can never have it again."

Lily's eyes grew dark at the mention of Nicholas St. James's name. He hadn't bothered to come and see her since that day she'd collapsed at his feet. And since she was still taking her meals in her room, she didn't see him at dinner either. But once when she'd heard the sound of clinking dishes coming from somewhere below, Lily had peeked over the upstairs balcony, hoping to see into the dining room. But she'd only been able to see the hallway with its brass chandelier ablaze with lights and a red-flowered carpet much like the one upstairs outside her own room.

Mary leaned over and took Lily's hand.

"He's really a very nice man, Lily," she said. "And I'd say that even if he weren't my big brother."

"But why does he want to marry *me?*" Lily asked, her eyes troubled and stormy.

"He's an honorable man. It was something he had promised your father because they were friends, and he had such great respect for him. And when your mother reminded him of that promise on her deathbed, well . . ."

"But I don't want to marry him. I don't want to marry anyone."

"I know," Mary said sympathetically. "But you're young. You'll feel differently about all that one day."

Lily let her gaze wander curiously over the young woman who probably wasn't more than five or six years older than she. The stylish white-muslin dress that Mary wore made Lily feel even more shabby and out of place than usual. And the young woman's dark hair, neatly fashioned atop her head with ringlets falling about her slender face, made Lily touch her own unruly mass of brass bright hair. She looked more like one of the saloon girls on the riverfront than a lady like Miss Mary.

"You're married yerself, ain't you?" Lily asked shyly.

"Yes I am," Mary said nodding. The question brought a different, warmer look to her face and she smiled.

"Theodore and I were married a year ago, and we moved to his home in Boston right after the wedding. This is my first trip home since then and oh . . . I do miss him so."

Lily turned her head slightly, noting the look of wistfulness in Mary's pale eyes.

"You love him," Lily said. It wasn't that she didn't understand love. She'd seen love between her own parents. Not romantic love exactly, but something warm and deep and abiding. Yet it was something she couldn't imagine for herself. Not with the likes of Nicholas St. James at least.

"Oh, yes . . . very much," Mary whispered. "I'm afraid I quite adore my husband." Then she laughed, a quiet delightful sound that echoed around the room and made Lily smile with her.

Mary bent toward Lily, looking into her eyes as she did.

"It's going to be all right, you know," she said. "Nicholas will take care of you and see that you never want for anything."

Lily twisted her lips disdainfully and crossed her arms over her chest.

"I ain't said I'd marry him yet," she growled.

Mary frowned. Best not to correct the girl's speech now. Not when she was just beginning to befriend her. That would come later and gradually. When she was in Boston and in school.

But Lord, the girl was willful and stubborn. It made Mary wonder anew what her brother was getting himself into. She was uneducated and awkward. But Mary had to admit, the child was also bright and potentially beautiful, with a strong, undeniable spark in her that was unusual for a girl her age. And if Mary had anything to do with it, that spark would remain, even after the refinement and polishing had been accomplished.

Yes indeed. A little spark, a little stubbornness, might be just what her brother Nicholas needed in a wife. Every woman he'd ever been involved with had fallen too willingly into his arms. Maybe it was time he encountered one who didn't.

"Lily," she said. "Listen to me very carefully, my dear. In England, there are thousands of marriages made out of convenience. Even here in this country. Some of them turn out to be better than marriages made for love. Sometimes friendship is not such a bad start between a man and a woman."

"Me and him ain't friends."

"Yes, I know," Mary said, sighing. "I only mentioned that as a possibility. But I'm going to be perfectly honest with you and I expect you to think about this very carefully. The one thing that bothers me about this . . . partnership . . . is that you might one day find yourself falling in love with someone else."

"I don't intend to fall in love with any man," Lily said haughtily. "Somebody to boss me around . . . make me have babies."

Mary smiled indulgently.

"You will, darling. Believe me, with that hair and those beautiful green eyes, men are going to be lined up to confess their admiration to you, whether you're married or not. And that might be a temptation to an innocent young girl like you. And when that happens, you'll find that being married will complicate things."

Lily frowned. Her brazen-looking hair and odd-colored eyes an asset? No one had ever said such a thing to her before. The only attention her bright hair ever caused on the riverfront seemed more negative than positive.

"No," Lily murmured in shy denial.

"Oh, but yes," Mary said, laughing. "And one more thing I must warn you of, dear." Her smile vanished, and her look turned more serious. "If Nicholas values anything, it's his pride and his honor. It would not be wise for you ever to tamper with that. Do you understand what I mean?"

"You mean I ain't to look at another man, but it's all right for him to have other women," Lily said.

Mary rolled her eyes toward the ceiling. This was not going to be easy.

"Well, that's not exactly what I meant."

"But that's the way it is, ain't it?" Lily asked. "Amongst the rich?"

"Not necessarily," Mary said, feeling exasperated. "At least not with everyone. Oh . . . fiddle, Lily. Why must you ask so many questions? Why can't you just marry my brother and do as he asks?" Mary laughed. "Don't answer that.

You must remain exactly the way you are." Mary looked at Lily's shabby dress and unruly hair. "Well, in some ways, at least," she added sweetly. "I'll help you choose which ones."

"That's the one thing I think I might like about this whole mess," Lily said, her voice low and quiet.

"What's that?"

"Going to Boston with you," Lily said. "Learning to be a lady like yerself."

"Well," Mary said, her eyes bright, "I must say I'm flattered. And encouraged. Then you'll do it? I can tell Nicholas that the wedding may take place? I don't mean to rush you, but Nicky wants me away from Natchez as soon as possible because of the fever. I've never had it, you see."

"Guess I ain't got much choice," Lily said. "If I don't marry your brother, I'll lose everything my father worked so hard to build. But you can tell him for me I ain't goin' to take no whippins!" She pressed her lips together into a hard, thin line. "I ain't gonna stand for a man what beats a woman."

"Good heavens," Mary said, laughing. "Of course Nicky would never beat you. Where do you get such ideas?"

"I've seen it happen before," she said, remembering the brawls and fights she'd seen along the riverfront. "Some men treat women like property, like something to be owned or to be brought to heel like a dog or a mule."

"Oh, Lily, your father didn't treat your mother that way? I'd hate to think you were ever subjected to—"

"Oh, no," Lily said. " 'Course not. My father was a kind, gentle man. He loved my mother."

Mary sighed with relief. There was no telling what the child had seen and heard, growing up where she did. And under the circumstances, she supposed it was no wonder she was such a cynical, mistrustful little baggage.

"Well, you can put that part of your life out of your mind. You'll be living in an entirely different world now." Mary leaned forward and put her arms around Lily. "I'm glad you're to marry Nicholas," she said. "You won't regret it, Lily. I have a feeling that someday you're going to be very happy you made this decision."

"I'm not so sure about that. But I promised my mother as she lay dyin'. And Mr. Nicholas St. James ain't the only one what believes in keepin' promises."

Mary viewed Lily's clenched jaw and proudly uplifted chin with skepticism. The girl seemed determined to make a battle of wills out of this unholy covenant between herself and Nicky. And between the two of them, Mary wasn't sure which one would emerge the victor.

The marriage ceremony took place that evening in the parlor of Nicholas's elegant home on Orleans Street.

There were no guests, no members of the Natchez ton to fuss over the bride and whisper behind their lacy fans about her credentials, or lack of them.

Besides the bride and groom, there were only Mary and Mrs. Lloyd, the housekeeper, and Father Benedict from Natchez's only Catholic church. Even though he knew Nicholas and Mary from childhood, he seemed deeply disturbed about marrying one of his flock to someone who had no proof that she was Catholic.

"She is," Nicholas said, squeezing Lily's hand, as if in warning.

"Yes, Father, I am," Lily nodded fiercely. "I just don't practice it much."

Nicholas cleared his throat and smiled at the priest.

"But she will, father. My bride will be going to Boston with Mary, where she'll study and familiarize herself with the laws and ways of the Church."

"I see," Father Benedict said, still frowning. "Some men prefer young wives, for a variety of reasons," he said, speaking low and only to Nicholas. "Not that I have any objections. But nevertheless, I'm happy to see that you are sending her away for an appropriate period of time."

"Yes, Father," Nicholas said, nodding solemnly.

"All right," the Father said. "Shall we begin?"

Lily's wedding dress of white brocaded silk had been put together rather hastily. Mary and Mrs. Lloyd had fashioned it using one of Mary's dresses and then constructing a covering chemisette of lighter silk which was tied with satin ribbons just beneath Lily's small breasts. Two young servant girls had made her bridal wreath of white roses attached to a simple tulle veil.

Mary looked affectionately at the girl, whose slender body seemed rather lost in the layers of silk. But Lily's eyes sparkled with pleasure as she ran her hand over the material. She was obviously pleased with the dress, and couldn't seem to stop touching it and admiring it. Neither its poor fit nor the fact that it engulfed her seemed to detract from the girl's joyous pleasure in it.

Mary couldn't remember a time when she herself had ever felt such complete and innocent joy from wearing a beautiful dress. Beautiful clothes had been her birthright. And she'd never given much thought to it until this moment, seeing Lily's sweet, guileless reaction.

"Nicholas ... take your bride's hand if you will," the Father said.

Lily felt faint and a bit ill as she placed her hand in Nicholas's larger one. He felt warm and strong, and for a moment she forgot her animosity toward him and simply welcomed his strength.

She was trembling, even leaning against him, as the priest droned through the words of the ceremony.

"It'll be over soon," Nicholas whispered, his voice not unkind.

His words caused Lily to straighten. She certainly didn't need his pity. She lifted her chin and stared straight ahead.

Nicholas felt the girl stiffen beside him and saw the defiant, stubborn look that moved over her face. He closed his eyes for a moment as he felt the same doubts the girl was obviously feeling.

Was this total madness? It wasn't the first time his honor had gotten him into trouble. Would this odd, tempestuous girl cause him one day to regret his decision to honor her dying mother's request?

"It's too late now," he muttered to himself.

Father Benedict stopped and stared at Nicholas.

The room grew completely quiet and Nicholas could feel the gazes of his bride and his sister upon him.

Damn, he hadn't meant to say the words out loud. Glancing down into the blazing eyes of his bride-to-be, he knew he had only given her one more reason to resent him.

"No, go on, Father. Please excuse me," Nicholas said.

Lily stared up at the tall man beside her who still held her hand tightly in his. In his grayish blue coat with its gilt buttons and white-silk waistcoat, he was as striking a figure as any man she had ever seen. She'd hardly been able to take her eyes off him when she and Mary came into the parlor and found him waiting with Father Benedict. The white stock tied neatly beneath his chin emphasized the darkness of his skin and hair and the strength of his jaw.

He was a powerful man. Not only physically, but in other ways as well. He was wealthy and important in Natchez, well thought of and respected.

Was he already regretting the marriage? Could she ever live up to his expectations as a lady and a wife . . . if she ever decided she wanted to?

As the Father uttered the final words of the ceremony, Lily glanced quickly at Mary. She couldn't imagine she could ever walk and talk with the easy confidence of her new sister-in-law. Or that she could learn to converse easily with someone as elegant and imposing as Nicholas St. James.

"Son . . . you may kiss your bride."

Lily heard the words and her body went stiff. It was as if she were frozen to the floor. She couldn't make herself turn. Couldn't make herself lift her lips for her husband's kiss.

She heard Nicholas's quiet mutter of impatience and felt his hand pulling her around toward him. His finger beneath her chin lifted her face upward and she found herself staring into those haughty gray eyes, filled now with annoyance and just the slightest hint of amusement.

She clamped her cold lips together and waited. And when she saw his dark head lowering toward hers, she closed her eyes, her body trembling with nervousness.

She was surprised by his humorous grunt and the feel of his warm lips on her cheek. Her eyes flew open, but he was already turning away from her, shaking hands with Father Benedict, then going across the room to the large silver punch bowl that sat on a sparkling crystal stand

He ladled pink liquid into two crystal cups and held one out toward Lily. As if in a dream, she found herself moving toward him, her hand outstretched.

She took the cup and turned, trembling, to face Mary and Mrs. Lloyd and others. The servants filled other cups and handed them around.

"Friends and family," Nicholas said with an air of resignation as he lifted his cup into the air, "please welcome my new wife to this house and to this family—Mrs. Lily Marie St. James."

Chapter 3

April, 1822
Boston, Mass

"Mrs. Lily Marie St. James."

Lily turned the ring on her finger as she murmured the words. They still sounded strange to her, even after all this time.

The woman who stood gazing out the second-story window of one of Boston's most elegant homes was not the same person Nicholas had introduced in his parlor almost five years ago.

Her hair held the same fiery glints of red, it was true. Sometimes Lily despaired that her riotous curls could ever be tamed. But with the help of Mary's expert hairdresser, it was now worn in a fashionable style atop her head. Lily still could not seem to tame the dozens of curls that escaped naturally no matter what she tried, nor could she believe that she had brought about a vogue amongst young Bostonian women. That they wanted to look exactly like the very popular young Mrs. St. James was still a mystery to her.

And though they'd probably never admit it, some now discreetly added rinses in shades of red to their own hair. Hoping, no doubt, to match the attention that the young woman from Natchez received at every social function she attended.

For Lily, who still sometimes considered herself just a shabby river urchin, had become the belle of Boston. Her beautiful clothes, fashioned by some of the world's most renowned designers, draped a tall willowy figure that was the envy of Boston society. When she entered a room, she stood a head taller than most of the women, and that alone was usually enough to draw every gaze in the place toward her.

But it wasn't her height that attracted men and women alike. Some, intending to flatter no doubt, declared that her intellect matched that of Boston's most scholarly males.

"And why shouldn't it?" she once asked, wide-eyed. For the life of her, Lily could see no practical reason to pretend ignorance just because she was a female. She had been amazed by her love of learning in the school her husband sent her to. She couldn't seem to get enough of books and ideas. And Mary still frowned at her when Lily couldn't seem to remember that it was fashionable to bow to the opinions of men in a social atmosphere.

One evening she'd found Lily in the men's parlor after dinner, laughing and espousing her opinion about America's recent purchase of Florida from Spain. Mary had been simply horrified.

Lily smiled and turned from the window. It was cool in the room this morning. Still wintry in Boston. She rubbed her hands over the sleeves of her pale yellow Jaconet muslin, trying to bring some warmth to her skin beneath the material.

Natchez would be warm now. The trees would already have turned green, and jonquils would be blooming en masse on the banks along the river, reflecting their bright buttery color in the water.

Lily went to the mirror and, with her fingers, fluffed up the puff sleeves of her dress which were drawn up by a narrow ribbon. The long sleeves were trimmed in the same pleats as the corded tucks and scalloped hems around the skirt.

Would her husband approve of her new look? Would he be pleased with her and the changes that had taken place over time?

It wasn't as if he hadn't seen her. But the last time had been more than two years ago. Lily had still been a defiant child then. Had still been struggling to become the young lady that Mary had tried so hard to make her.

The birth of Mary and Theodore's first child two years ago had kept Lily in Boston because no one was able to accompany her back to Natchez. And then last summer another yellow-fever epidemic had swept the Southern city, causing Nicholas to send word that they must not try to come.

"I hope," he had written in his letter, "things will have improved by spring. The magistrates have forbidden excavation in the city, hoping to prevent the unearthing of any old seeds of the disease. City lots are being drained of stagnant water and a new law has been passed that wells and cisterns must be covered. Below the hill, some boats carrying workers known to be diseased have been set adrift on the river, rather than being allowed to come ashore as usual."

But almost as soon as Nicholas had declared the city safe again, Mary had discovered that she was expecting another child. And now she wanted to delay Lily's return to Natchez even longer.

But her schooling was finished, and Lily had declared that she wouldn't stay in Boston for another summer.

"I'll go home alone if I must," she'd said last night at supper. "But I am going home."

"She's right, Mary," Theodore said, gazing sympathetically at Lily. "It's time for her to leave Boston, and you well know it. As much as we'd both like it, we can't keep her here with us forever." Theodore's smile had been warm and sweet, and it had caused Lily's eyes to fill with tears.

She did love him and Mary so. They had become her parents and her friends. The brother and sister she never had. And she would miss little Teddy so much that she couldn't even bear to think about that.

But she wanted to go home.

Mary had finally, reluctantly agreed. Lily would leave tomorrow morning, accompanied by an older woman they'd hired to chaperon her on the trip.

Oh, but she could hardly wait to see Natchez. To sit on the grassy banks along the Mississippi and hear the sweet plaintive song of the mockingbird. To breathe in the pungent muddy scent of the river and feel the warm breeze against her skin.

And oddly, she longed to see Nicholas.

She'd met many men in Boston. Handsome men, charming men, who danced with her and declared her the most beautiful woman they'd ever met. Men who said they could die gazing into her emerald eyes. Men who made her laugh and men who wanted to tempt her to forget the marriage vows made to someone she hardly knew, just as Mary had warned years ago.

Yet none of them held the mystique of Nicholas St. James. And none of them piqued her curiosity so much. Or her exasperation.

When he wrote, he barely acknowledged their marriage. He treated her more like a sister than a wife, signing his letters, "Affectionately."

Her first visit home had been a disaster, partly because she still resented Nicholas and his high-handed ways. And partly because he insisted on introducing her at the afternoon lawn party he gave for her, as if she were a child instead of his wife.

It still galled Lily remembering that party.

She'd felt so out of place in her prim little white dress. She'd been the only one with her hair tied back with a ribbon—the rest of the women wore elegantly coiffed hairstyles and some of them couldn't have been more than a year older than she.

Mary had taken Lily's side, declaring that it was time she at least looked the part of Nicholas's wife. But Nicholas had disagreed, and a terrible argument ensued in which he declared Lily an impudent brat who needed a spanking more than she needed a change of wardrobe.

Lily flushed even now thinking of her behavior that day.

She had been awful, flouncing out of the room and bounding up the stairs two at a time as Nicholas's guests watched with amazed speculation.

Lily had heard the whispers, seen the stares. Some of them had no doubt warned Nicholas that a marriage to such a poor, uncouth girl would never work. He had married beneath himself. And that day Lily gave them their proof of it. Not that she cared.

She had deliberately changed into a pair of ragged old britches and scuffed boots, then come downstairs, marching with deliberate contempt through the hallway, past the gaping stares of their guests and out the back toward the stables.

She'd expected Nicholas to follow her. She could hardly have missed the furious look he gave her as she made her defiant little march through the house.

But he hadn't.

And in the end, she had wound up feeling deflated and dissapointed. And completely foolish.

She had ridden until dark. And when she'd returned home, all the guests were gone and the house was calm and quiet. Mary's look of disappointment had sent an arrow of pain straight to Lily's heart. She had never meant to hurt her, or make her regret her faith in her.

And Nicholas? Well, his behavior had completely baffled Lily.

"Did you enjoy your ride?" he'd asked calmly.

"Very much," Lily replied through stiff, unyielding lips.

"Good. It's almost time for dinner." he said. "I suggest you change your clothes and meet us in the parlor. We'll go into the dining room together."

Lily didn't know why she'd always felt such anger toward Nicholas. She couldn't blame her behavior entirely on the fact that she still grieved for her parents. Or that she missed her home and felt alone and isolated in Boston.

No one had been kinder or more generous than Mary and Theodore. Their servants had treated her wonderfully, as had their friends. She had been welcomed into Boston society as if she were born to it.

Their love and patience had brought her to life, and the past two years had given her the kind of existence she could only have dreamed of as a child.

So why was she so restless? Why did she often have this underlying sense of dissatisfaction and longing?

It was only because she was homesick for Natchez, she thought.

She walked back to the window, her eyes clouding over as she remembered that last tumultuous time she'd been in Natchez two years ago. So different from the first visit. But then she'd been different, and she'd had time to grow and learn.

Yet despite Lily's belief that she had matured, Nicholas had spent most of the evening with a beautiful woman dressed in black taffeta. Even now, Lily could remember the way her dress rustled as the woman moved past. She'd seemed to float rather than to walk. The scent of her perfume had been exotic ... intriguing. Not the sweet innocent scent of lavender or rose water, but some heady, forbidden fragrance that was unforgettable. And the look in her eyes when she'd been introduced to Lily had been odd. Sympathetic almost.

Lily shook her head. She'd wondered about the woman many times since then. About the way she looked at Nicholas, the way she seemed to hang breathlessly on his every word as he bent his dark head toward her.

There had been a sense of intimacy between them. Something Lily sensed rather than knew.

Jeanette Mireaux. Still stunningly beautiful, though she was probably past thirty now, an age when some women were considered matronly. But her pale blond hair and sparkling blue eyes made her look incredibly young. She had skin the color of magnolia blossoms and a laugh that could capture the attention of every male in a ballroom and cause them to turn toward the sound. Jeanette Mireaux had made Lily feel like a child again. And a boy-child at that.

Lily frowned and bit her lower lip.

What was the woman to Nicholas? Was he in love with her? The thought brought such a pang of agony to her chest that she could hardly believe it.

She had asked Mary about the beautiful widow that night as they were going upstairs to bed.

"Oh, darling, she's just a friend," Mary said, putting her arm around Lily's shoulders. "Nicholas knew her husband very well. He feels sorry for her, that's all. And responsible for her, I'm sure, the way any honorable man would feel toward a friend's widow."

But Lily noticed that Mary hadn't quite been able to look her in the eye. And she'd quickly changed the subject, as if she didn't want to discuss the matter further.

Lily had lain awake that night for hours. Curious about the relationship between Nicholas and Mrs. Mireaux. And seething that he still treated her like a child.

She had been relieved to go back to Boston. Happy to be away from Nicholas and that smug, amused smile on his face.

When had all that changed for her?

Lily wasn't sure how she felt about her husband now. Or what would happen when she went home for good. Would he still treat her like a girl? Make arrangements for them to live separate lives? Annul the marriage perhaps?

Or would he take her to his bed . . . make her his wife in more than name only?

That thought and the images it evoked caused Lily to catch her breath unexpectedly.

She touched her fingers to her lips as her eyes grew warm and soft with curiosity.

She remembered something Mary had said to her long ago, that Lily was young and that she might feel differently about marriage one day.

Then, Lily had never imagined that day would ever come. Or that she would be having such odd, disquieting thoughts about the man she once thought she hated.

For some unexplained reason she'd seen him differently that last trip home. She had been jolted by his handsome appearance. Fascinated by his smile and flash of white teeth. Intrigued by the broad shoulders and muscular build and surprised by the graceful way he'd whirled Mrs. Mireaux across the dance floor.

He'd been in an especially good mood and when the music for the last dance had begun, much to her surprise, Nicholas had sought out Lily and danced her around the room while everyone watched, smiling their approval.

He had kissed her that night when the dance ended.

It had happened spontaneously, teasingly at first. But it had been a real kiss. His mouth had captured hers in a kiss that was as warm and soft as the Mississippi breeze. Lily had felt her knees weaken and begin to tremble. And when Nicholas pulled away and the room twittered and burst into a smattering of applause, he had looked into her eyes. For one brief moment, she thought she saw surprise, even pleasure warm those beautiful intriguing depths.

But just as quickly he had left her side to mingle with his guests and see them into the dinner buffet.

Lily had never been able to forget that kiss. Or the look she'd seen in his eyes.

Maybe Mary was right. Maybe now she didn't dread the thought of being married nearly as much as she once had.

"I'm coming home, Nicholas," she whispered. "Home to Natchez . . . and to you."

Chapter 4

"She's coming home. She should be arriving sometime tomorrow."

Dark fingers moved lingeringly over pale skin. The woman lying naked on the bed trembled and turned over to face the man above her. There was a slight pout on her luscious full lips and a frown line between fine brows as she pushed tousled blond curls away from her face.

"Well . . . you always knew this moment would come, Nicholas."

Jeanette Mireaux sat up in bed, seemingly unconscious of her nakedness, or of the way her full white breasts beckoned to her lover.

"Yes . . . I did."

She gasped as he bent his head and brushed a kiss across her skin.

Part of her wanted to push him away and discuss what they were to do now that his young bride was coming home. Another part, however, wanted nothing more than to plunge her fingers into his thick dark hair and pull his head even closer.

As usual, when she was with Nicky, the latter won out.

Sometimes she felt as if she didn't know this strange, compelling man at all. She'd never been touched as deeply by any man, never been moved as powerfully as she was by his skilled, passionate lovemaking. And yet sometimes she felt as if their heated sessions meant little to him except a release from some pent-up wildness that he managed to hide from the polite society of their outside world.

There were times when she looked into his eyes with undisguised longing. Times during the heat of their pleasure together when she wanted to see something besides desire in those cool gray eyes.

"What shall I do about you, chérie?" he asked, bending over her.

"What . . . what do you . . . want to do . . . oh, Nicky . . ."

How could she give any sensible answer when his hands touched and burned? When his lips sent her senses reeling and her body writhing with want and need? She wondered senselessly, not for the first time, how many women it had taken to give him this experience that drove her insane and made her forget everything except him and the way he could love her.

She had thought that this might be the night she would put aside her pride and tell him how she felt. That she loved him. Didn't he know it anyway? Would it really change anything if she told him how much she needed him . . . wanted him for her own?

Now with the subject of his young bride between them, she wasn't sure she should say anything.

The touch of his hands pushed all other thoughts away. Even the final reality that the young, virginal Lily would be coming back to Natchez to claim her rightful place in Nicholas's home. And most likely in his bed.

Jeanette groaned and pushed her slender white body tightly against his. Already his mouth and hands had aroused her, and the seductive words he whispered sent her drowning in a sea of desire.

"Love me," she whispered, her words a plea. "Please, Nicky . . . just . . . love me."

She gasped with pleasure as he answered her with his body. And for a while that pleasure blotted out all reason and lulled her into thinking that everything would be all right. That nothing could change what was between them or the way she felt when they were together.

Not even a beautiful young wife.

His lovemaking sent her head reeling, sent her body out of control time and again before he allowed himself to end it. His dark, muscular body glistened with perspiration when he moved beside her and took her in his arms.

Jeanette lay quietly against him, telling herself she must enjoy their last moment of such freedom. For when his wife came, even if Nicholas intended to continue this liaison, she knew it would have to be done in secrecy. And that was something that filled her with dread. She didn't want to lose him. She couldn't.

Suddenly her eyes grew misty, and she closed them tightly.

"Jeanette?"

She shook her head, refusing to open her eyes.

"What's wrong?" he asked. He reached out to brush the tears away from her fair lashes.

"Nothing," she said, her voice breathless. She opened her tear-filled eyes and gazed up at him, letting her hand trail over his handsome face and down to his chest.

"I always know when you're lying. What's bothering you? Is it Lily? Is that it?"

"Do you have no idea how I feel?" she asked quietly. "How lost I shall be without you?"

"This doesn't have to end," Nicholas said. "Not now. Certainly not because of Lily. We shall go on as before . . . until we both agree that it's over."

Jeanette shook her head and sat up, pushing him away.

"Everything is too easy for you, Nicholas," she muttered as she moved to the edge of the bed.

She glanced back once, regretfully almost, at the man who lay tangled in the white sheets. His body tempted her even now and the mouth that had lost some of its hardness made her take a deep breath. She reached for a silky robe and slid her arms into the sleeves.

"Don't put that on," he said.

"I am getting up," she said, turning to look into his eyes.

A slow smile moved over his handsome features and with a knowing, confident lift of his brow, he patted the bed beside him.

"No, Nicky, we need to talk."

"We can talk just as well with you here beside me."

"Are you not concerned at all that your wife is coming home?"

"You may call her my wife if you wish. But you know as well as I do that it's only a legality."

Jeanette sighed heavily, but she didn't return to the bed.

"She's a child, Jeanette," he said, pushing himself upright and frowning at her. "And hardly competition for a woman like you, if that's what you're worried about."

"Well, I am worried about it," she snapped, blue eyes flashing. "Any woman would be worried about it. She's grown into a beautiful young lady. And you, my dear Nicholas, seem to be the only one in Natchez who hasn't noticed that yet."

He frowned, then laughed.

"I haven't forgotten the kiss you gave her the last time she was home."

"What kiss?" he asked, rubbing a hand over his jaw.

"You know very well what kiss. At my party two years ago. You danced the last dance with her and then you kissed her. Everyone in the room saw how sweet it was, so don't pretend you don't know."

"I don't remember," he said, shrugging his shoulders and smiling flirtatiously with her. "I swear it."

"You liar," she said.

Jeanette crossed her arms over her breasts. She was breathing hard as she stared into his teasing eyes. He made her furious with his coolness sometimes. It was almost as if no emotion ever penetrated the surface of his very beguiling skin. As if he purposely didn't intend to let passion touch his heart.

"Come back to bed, love," he said, his voice low and seductive.

"You know I can't," Jeanette said, stamping her small bare foot against the floor. "Not until we've settled this."

"It *is* settled. My wife is coming home. I'll see her out to Live Oaks, then I'll come back here to the town house, where unfortunately business ventures will probably keep me away from her and the plantation for weeks. Perhaps even months.

"You are completely unscrupulous," she said.

"Thank you. Now, come here."

"You are only fooling yourself if you think any woman, even one as innocent as Lily, will put up with such treatment for long."

Jeanette thought that she envied the girl and pitied her at the same time. As his wife, this young woman would be privy to Nicholas's life in the most intimate of ways. Ways that she herself never could be. Lily would be the one to breakfast with him, discuss politics and social events with him at dinner, plan parties and stand beside him as hostess. Build a life with him, not just an afternoon or a night here and there.

And she'd be the one to have his children.

And yet, like every woman who'd ever loved Nicholas St. James, she, too, would soon learn that she could never completely claim him for her own.

"Look," Nicholas said, his voice growing impatient, "Lily knows this is not a real marriage. And I didn't send her to Boston and my sister's home for nothing. She will have learned by now how a lady behaves. Just as she has also no doubt learned that a good wife is discreet and does her husband's bidding in all things.''

Jeanette stared at him, an incredulous look on her beautiful face. Then she smiled and shook her head. Sometimes men were such fools. And if she didn't love this one so much, she might actually wish his young red-haired wife would be the one to teach him a valuable lesson.

"Oh, my darling," she whispered. She smiled wistfully before giving in and going back to his bed. "If you believe that, then I think you are in for a great surprise."

Lily was completely exhausted. It was very late when the carriage pulled into the bricked courtyard at the back of the Orleans Street house.

But she couldn't contain her excitement at seeing one light still burning in an upstairs bedroom. Nicholas's bedroom.

Was he waiting for her? Had some instinct told him that she'd arrive a day earlier than expected? That she'd urged the driver to go on well past midnight rather than stop at yet another inn for the night?

It was a few moments before one of the servants opened the carriage door. He was out of breath as he hastily tried to button the top buttons of his shirt.

Lily felt a twinge of guilt at rousing him from his bed. She smiled at him, hoping to soften her deed.

"Burton?" she asked, squinting through the darkness as she stepped down out of the carriage. "Is that you?"

Her legs ached and for a moment she felt as if she were still bouncing on the carriage's hard horsehair seats.

"Yes'm, Miss Lily," the older man said. "It's me."

One of the other servants hurried over to them, holding a lantern above his head and casting a light on Lily and the other, older woman who now stepped from the carriage.

"Burton, this is Mrs. Shimway. She'll be staying in one

of the guest rooms for a few days, until she's rested and
ready to go back to Boston.''

"And I swear, I can hardly wait to take to my bed this
night,'' the woman said.

"We . . . we wasn't exactly expectin' you tonight,'' Burton said, rolling his eyes back toward the upper story of
the house.

"I know,'' Lily said. She picked up the smallest of her
bags and started toward the house. "But I was so anxious
to be home. I simply couldn't face another night on the
road.''

She stopped, realizing that Burton and the other servants
weren't following.

"It isn't a problem, is it?'' she asked. "Mr. Nicholas is
here—he is expecting me, isn't he?'' She glanced up at
the second story of the house. From this vantage point,
she could only see the rear gallery, but a faint light glim-
mered from the upper hallway through the large glass-
paned double doors.

Burton looked up, too.

"Ain't no problem a'tall.'' he said. "But Mr. Nicholas,
he done gone to bed. He was real tired, ma'am, and I
don't think he wants to be disturbed. But we can get you
and Miz Shimway settled in your rooms right away. Yes'm,
right away.''

"But . . .''

"Jim . . . Marcus . . . take the ladies' bags upstairs, but
be real careful not to disturb Mr. Nicholas.'' Burton turned
back to Lily, his dark eyes shining. "If you'll just wait in
the downstairs hallway, I'll go up and make sure everything
is just right for you.''

"But . . .''

Despite Lily's beginning protest, Burton and the others
hurried her and Mrs. Shimway into the house and disappeared up the stairs with their luggage.

"I'm sorry about the delay, Mrs. Shimway,'' Lily said. "I

know you must be completely exhausted. It's my own fault for insisting we come home earlier than planned.''

"It's quite all right, my dear,'' the woman said. "I understood your eagerness to get home. Why, you could hardly sit still all day. Not that I blame you. This is a lovely home . . . just lovely. It's the first time I've traveled to the South, you know.'' Mrs. Shimway moved down the hallway, peeking into the darkened rooms and letting her gaze trail over the beautiful rosewood tables and gold-framed French mirrors.

Lily tapped her foot and bit at her lower lip. It was a beautiful home, but she would enjoy it much more if she could see Nicholas tonight.

She took a deep breath and shook her head slightly.

Patience was a virtue. It was one of the many things the Sisters had tried to drum into her head, probably because she was one of their most impatient students.

She smiled at her thoughts and felt her tensed muscles relaxing a bit. She was home. That was all that mattered now. Did it really make a difference that she would see Nicholas in the morning instead of tonight?

For now, she would have a nice warm bath and sleep in his house. *Her* house, she corrected with a smile.

In an amazingly short time, she was in her room, almost asleep as she lounged in the long copper bathing tub, her neck against the headrest at the back. Her hair, pinned atop her head, fell in damp tendrils down her slender neck. She stretched out her long legs the full length of the tub, breathing in the scent of lavender bubbles as her movements stirred the water.

She glanced around the unfamiliar room. She'd been surprised when Burton had put her here at the back of the second floor gallery, rather than the room she usually had at the front, across from Nicholas.

"A leak from a recent storm, ma'am,'' he'd said. "We'll have it fixed right straight any day now.''

"This room is fine,'' Lily said.

Lily smiled as she moved her hands in the warm water.

Burton and the others seemed nervous, eager to please her, and it made her feel welcome. As if she truly were the mistress of this beautiful house.

She lazed in her bath until the soapy water grew cool. Then, feeling weary and relaxed, she finally stepped out of the water and dried on soft towels before the fire. She let her mind wander dreamily, wondering and imagining what might happen if Nicholas came in.

She walked about the room and glanced into the mirror above the fireplace mantel as she dried her skin, letting her gaze move over her slender body. Her small breasts were erect and firm, her skin soft and smooth. Yet Lily still felt as if her body were too slender, her legs too long and coltish to be feminine. She often longed for a petite, curvaceous body, as was more the fashion.

But she had changed and matured, and she couldn't help wondering what Nicholas would think of her now. Would he be pleased by what was reflected in the mirror?

The warmth that suddenly moved over her caught her by surprise, leaving her unsettled, her skin tingling with some odd sensation that she didn't quite understand.

Had it been the long trip? Today's even longer day of travel and now the warmth of the bath that caused her to feel this way?

Her eyes darkened as she stared at her image in the mirror.

Or was it the imagined vision of dark hands touching this flesh, of cool gray eyes turning warm with desire when they looked at her?

"Dear . . . heavens . . ." she whispered, turning quickly away from the mirror. She moved to the bed to find her nightgown and slip it quickly over her head. "What on earth . . . ? Are these feelings wrong? Is this part of what Mary told me about? Feelings of love and intimacy that women must share with their husbands?"

Lily moved restlessly toward the one long window that

overlooked the courtyard. As tired as she was, she wasn't sure she'd ever be able to sleep now that she was finally here in the city and the house she'd so often dreamed of.

As she stood gazing down, she saw a movement out of the corner of her eyes, near the steps in the courtyard below. She couldn't quite make out who it was. But then the figure stepped out into the light that fell from the doorway.

It was a woman. She wore a dark, hooded cape that covered her petite figure from head to toe. But when she turned back toward the porch, and lifted her head, Lily saw her face and gave a little gasp of surprise.

"Widow Mireaux?" she whispered, her voice catching in her throat. No, surely she was mistaken. Why would the woman be here at such a late hour, especially if Nicholas had already retired?

The obvious answer struck her like a blow. Lily closed her eyes and stepped back from the window as an unexpected ache began somewhere down deep in her heart. She knew instinctively that this was something she didn't want to see. Something she didn't want to know.

But unable to stop herself, she opened her eyes and stepped back to the window again. Her fingers moved automatically to catch the quick gasp that came from her lips when she saw a man step out of the shadows of the house and take the woman in his arms.

There was no mistake about who he was. The tall, powerful form, and the dark head that bent toward the beautiful woman was the same one that had been etched in Lily's mind for years.

Nicholas.

When the woman's hood fell back, revealing pale blond hair, Lily groaned. It *was* Jeanette Mireaux.

Nicholas wrapped her in his strong arms, holding her in a kiss that seemed to go on forever. One so heated and passionate that Lily felt the touch of it like a blow to her heart, even from the distance that separated them.

Tears welled up behind her lids, and yet she couldn't seem to pull her eyes away from the scene.

Well, what did she expect? Had she really expected Nicholas, experienced and sophisticated, to spend his days and his nights alone? Lily's instincts had told her from the very first moment she met Mrs. Mireaux that something was going on between them.

But she had pushed those suspicions away. And she had allowed herself to dream that Nicholas would one day want her. Love her even. Like a silly child reaching for the stars.

"You're a fool," she whispered. Fiercely she wiped the tears from her eyes and turned away from the window. "Did you really think you could fit into his world . . . his life so easily?"

She fell across the bed and with clenched fists flailed helplessly against the soft pillows.

"A blind, stupid fool."

Chapter 5

It was almost noon when Nicholas pushed open the door to Lily's bedroom and stepped inside. The curtains had been drawn against the light, and the room felt cool and still.

For a moment he stood at the door, breathing in the sweet scent of lavender that permeated the room. A woman's scent, he thought with a wry smile. Did the child imagine herself a woman now that she was nineteen?

He stepped to the bed, letting his gaze rest on the tangle of bright hair that lay spread upon the pillow. Without thinking he reached forward and picked up a lock of the hair, testing its soft texture between his fingers.

Lily opened her eyes and sprang up in bed, pulling the sheets up in an instinctive movement as she pushed herself back against the pillows.

Nicholas took a step backward, the lock of hair tugged free from his fingers as he gazed with amusement into flashing cat eyes.

Her fists clutching the sheets were small, and he noted the delicate bones and feminine shape of her nails. Then he blinked and slowly let his gaze wander back over her again.

She was different, despite the defiant look that still lit those brilliant eyes and the undeniable pout on her mouth. It was a mouth that was full now and ripe. No longer a little girl's.

Nicholas frowned and turned to walk across the room with his hands behind his back.

He didn't know exactly what that niggling little feeling was that sat just in the back of his mind. Surprise? Perhaps. Pleasure?

He grunted softly and rubbed his chin as he turned to look at her again. As if he might have been mistaken about what he saw.

"I'm sorry I wasn't awake to greet you when you arrived last night," he muttered.

Lily lifted her chin. Her mouth quirked disdainfully as she stared at his broad shoulders and the long legs clad in buff-colored trousers.

"It doesn't matter," she said, careful to use her most cultured tone. "I was exhausted and so was my companion, Mrs. Shimway."

"Ah, Mrs. Shimway," he said, stepping closer to the bed. "A delightful woman. I'll admit I was skeptical when Mary said they were hiring a companion to chaperon you on the trip to Natchez. But the lady seems quite responsible and careful about protecting the reputation of a young woman traveling alone."

"Of course she's responsible," Lily replied. "Mary and Theodore love me. Do you think they would see me off with someone they couldn't trust?"

Nicholas, hearing the irritation in Lily's voice, gazed at her for a moment. Her eyes were red, and they looked swollen. She still clutched the sheet tightly beneath her chin, staring at him with accusing eyes as if she feared he might leap at her any moment.

Mary had written often, telling him how anxious Lily

was to return to Natchez, and warning him in the process to be open and kind. So he knew it wasn't a reluctance to be here that made her so skittish.

Was it him? Was she frightened of him?

He couldn't understand why the idea should irritate him so.

"I was only making conversation," he answered, keeping his voice infinitely patient. "Would you like to have breakfast now? Or would you prefer having the noonday meal . . . with me?"

"Neither," she said, scooting down farther into the bed. "I'd prefer staying in bed for the rest of the day."

Nicholas bit his lip, forcing himself to restrain the words that were on the tip of his tongue. He felt an urge to pull the covers away from her and demand that she get out of bed. If she insisted on behaving like a willful child, then he had no compunction about treating her like one.

He couldn't understand how Mary could write in her letters about Lily's progress when the girl still seemed as stubborn as she was when she left here four and a half years ago.

For a moment they stared into each other's eyes, hers sparking defiance, his cool and indifferent.

"As you wish," he said finally, turning on his heel and walking to the door. He stopped at the open doorway and turned, almost smiling at the look of astonishment on her face. Clearly, she'd meant to provoke an argument.

"If there's anything you need, Mrs. Lloyd and the servants are at your disposal."

When Nicholas softly closed the door behind him, Lily clamped her lips tightly together and stared at the ceiling.

Now what was she to do? She really wasn't sleepy anymore. And actually she was quite hungry, although she didn't intend going into the dining room and admitting that to Nicholas.

Her cheeks burned, remembering the way he had looked

at her. Those eyes of his always seemed so knowing, so damnably superior.

She'd learned by listening discreetly that Nicholas had quite a reputation in Natchez. Not so bad as some, but he wasn't known to be exactly virtuous where women were concerned.

He gambled, too, they said. Dueled, even.

Lily threw the covers back and swung her long legs over the side of the bed. Lily St. James didn't intend to let her husband's reputation, or his crude behavior affect what she did. Not for one moment. She'd just have to avoid her husband until after he had lunched, then she'd manage to find something for herself to do.

In the meantime, she intended to see the house and all its beautiful furnishings. It was hers now. Finally, she had a home of her own and elegant clothes to wear. A life ahead of her that once she could only have envied. And she told herself that for the moment, all those things would be enough.

Later, only when she learned that Nicholas was out riding, Lily went to the kitchen. Two young servant girls, peeling vegetables, scrambled about, springing up from their seats and curtsying.

"Oh," Lily said. "You mustn't do that . . . not to me."

It was only a moment before Mrs. Lloyd came bustling into the kitchen to see what was going on.

"My dear, there's no need for you to come out here," she told Lily. "Just ring the bell in the dining room and someone will come to take your request."

Once she might have backed away and let Mrs. Lloyd have complete rein of what she did and how she behaved. But not now. She was no longer a schoolgirl, but a competent woman, ready to assure her duties as mistress of Nicholas's home.

She might have to remind herself every moment of that

fact. But it wouldn't do to remind her housekeeper more than once if she expected to command any respect. And she knew this was the time.

"Oh, but I wanted to make the kitchen one of my first visits," Lily said. "I want to meet everyone and to see where the meals are cooked. I'm quite interested in what kind of food will be served and how it's prepared."

"Oh," Mrs. Lloyd said, with a lift of her brow. She glanced at the cook, a big-boned woman with skin the color and patina of mahogany. "I see. Well."

Mary had already warned Lily that it would be hard for Mrs. Lloyd and some of the others who had known her since the beginning, to accept her now as mistress. And as Nicholas's wife.

"Mrs. Lloyd," Lily said, keeping her voice soft and kind, "I assure you, I don't intend taking over any of your responsibilities. I know Nicholas depends on you for so many different things and of course so will I."

The cook rattled a spoon in a heavy, iron cooking pot, rolling her eyes toward Lily and then Mrs. Lloyd.

"I hope that will be all right with you and with Clemmie."

"Well," Mrs Lloyd began. She seemed not quite so troubled as she had been only moments ago. "Clemmie is used to running the kitchen the way she sees fit . . ."

"Of course," said Lily. "I thought perhaps you and I would confer as to the menus and so forth."

"Well, then," Mrs. Lloyd said, with a nod of her head, "I guess it's settled. You are, after all, Mr. St. James's wife." The woman laughed, seeming to feel rather awkward. "But if you don't mind my being perfectly honest . . ."

"Of course," Lily said. "I want you to feel free to say whatever you wish to me."

"It's just that . . . you were a child last time we saw you. And now you've come home this beautiful, woman . . ." Mrs. Lloyd's dark eyes sparkled as she let them move over Lily's fashionable dress of green *gros de Naples* and the mantelet of black lace that she'd pulled around her shoulders against the cool spring air. "I . . . I hardly even know how I should address you."

"You will call me Lily, of course," Lily replied, smiling at the woman's discomfort. "It's what you've always called me."

"Oh, but things have changed," Mrs. Lloyd said. "It wouldn't be seemly of me to address you in such a casual way. No, I'm afraid I shall have to address you as Mrs. St. James."

Lily laughed and took a piece of fruit and a slice of fragrant nut bread from the counter.

"If it's what you wish," she said. "But I must warn you, it might take a while for me to answer to the name."

Lily was still smiling when she went outside. At least things were off to a good start with the household. She hesitated a moment as she stood outside the kitchen door nibbling bread and fruit. And though she hadn't intended to eavesdrop, the sound of her name made her listen.

"Miz Lily St. James gonna be the talk of this town," Clemmie was saying. "Yes, ma'am, you just mark my words, Miz Lloyd . . . the talk of this here ole town."

"Indeed, she shall," Mrs. Lloyd agreed. "I only hope and pray that Mr. St. James has the good sense not to flaunt that brazen Widow Mireaux in the poor girl's face."

Lily stiffened, by now unable to make herself leave if she'd wanted to.

"Lordy, but I don't know 'bout that. Can't keep a man from bein' a man, Miz Lloyd," Clemmie said.

Lily clenched her teeth and moved her gaze resentfully back toward the house. She was very close to the spot where Nicholas had kissed his mistress good-bye last night.

"Men will be men, will they? Well, we'll just see about that." Lily pulled her mantelet snugly about her shoulders and walked toward the house. "Mr. Nicholas St. James is going to learn that he's no longer married to a poor senseless child without a mind of her own. I'm no longer that naive little girl who once lived Under-the-Hill."

She stepped inside the house into the second room of the double parlor—what was called the women's parlor at the back of the house. There she finished her breakfast, then wandered about the room, letting her fingers trail over the rosewood piano and the more delicate pieces of furniture. She stepped to a golden harp near the fireplace and was plucking absentmindedly at the strings when she heard someone enter the front door of the house.

Keeping out of sight, she moved to the door and peeked toward the entryway. She saw Mrs. Lloyd escorting a young man into the library.

"Mr. Nicholas will be here any moment," she heard Mrs. Lloyd say. "He's just ridden into the stables."

"Thank you, Mrs. Lloyd."

Lily waited until the housekeeper had gone upstairs, then she stepped into the hallway and made her way quickly to the library.

"Jared?" she said, stepping to the door. "Is that you?"

The man turned toward her. His face, set in a polite smile, changed immediately when he saw her.

"Lily?" he whispered, staring at her as if he saw something he couldn't quite believe.

Jared St. James looked very much like his cousin Nicholas, except that he was not as tall. And he'd always affected a cynical, rather jaded manner that never sat well with Lily. But he was fun and he was young, much nearer Lily's age than Nicholas.

"As I live and breathe" he said, coming forward. "Let me look at you." He took Lily's hand and turned her around, his eyes taking in every inch of her willowy figure. "My God, but you've grown into a stunning creature. Absolutely stunning."

When Lily met his eyes, there was something in their depths that made her a little uneasy. She didn't think she'd ever met a man whose gaze told her so blatantly that she was a desirable woman.

She pulled her hand away and took a step backward.

"Don't," he said quickly. "Please . . . don't go. I didn't mean to be so forward with my remarks." Still, the look in his eyes belied his words. "It's just . . . well, God, I'm surprised, that's all. Last time I saw you, you were all legs and arms topped by a mass of wild hair. And now you've become this breathtaking creature I hardly know."

Lily laughed. She couldn't help it. Despite the discomfort felt for a moment, Jared had a way of speaking his mind that was both funny and charming.

"Well . . ."

When Lily heard the deep voice from the doorway, she didn't have to turn to see the disapproval on her husband's face. She could hear it.

"Cousin Jared," he said, strolling into the room. "I see you've reacquainted yourself with my wife." Nicholas's gaze fell on Lily, moving over her green dress and black mantelet in a look that made her catch her breath. "And I see you decided to leave your bed after all, my dear." he said to her, his voice dripping with sarcasm.

Lily didn't reply. When she glanced at Jared, she saw his look of surprise and the way his brow lifted with speculation. Undoubtedly he felt the tension between her and Nicholas just as much as she did.

"If you'll excuse us, Lily," Nicholas said, "Jared and I have some business to discuss."

"Of course," Lily answered, thankful for an excuse to leave the awkward situation.

Before she could go, Jared stepped forward, catching her hand in a move that seemed to surprise Nicholas as much as it did Lily.

"I'm so pleased you're home," Jared said. "I'd be most grateful for the opportunity to show you around Natchez. That is if my cousin has no objections."

Lily lifted her chin and turned to Nicholas, giving him a dazzling smile and a questioning little shrug of her slender shoulders.

"Nicholas?" she asked, letting her voice carry only a

hint of challenge. "You have no objections . . . do you?" she asked sweetly.

She didn't miss the glint of irritation in those steely eyes, or the grim look of disapproval on his handsome face.

"I'm not sure there'll be time for that," he said, his voice steady. "I had intended to take Lily to Live Oaks tomorrow."

So you'll have more time for your mistress? she wanted to shout.

"Oh, I don't know," she said instead. "Will you be staying there as well?" she asked, her voice innocent.

"No . . ." he said, watching the play of emotion on her face. "I'm afraid business will keep me in Natchez for several more weeks."

"Oh, that's too bad," Lily replied. "Then, of course I wouldn't think of staying at Live Oaks while you are working so hard here in the city. I'll stay here, too. So, Jared . . ." she said, dismissing Nicholas and turning to smile at his cousin. "I'd love to accept your invitation, since my husband will doubtless be too busy to escort me himself. Would tomorrow at two be convenient for you?"

"More than convenient," Jared murmured, bending to place a kiss on her hand.

Lily smiled at Nicholas, ignoring the look of cold fury on his face as she excused herself from the room. She had barely stepped out into the hallway when the door thumped loudly behind her. But she could hear Nicholas's voice through the thick wood and walls.

"What is it this time, Jared? Have you run through your monthly stipend so quickly?"

Jared's response was low, more cajoling and level, and Lily couldn't quite make out what he said.

She smiled as she walked away. Her friendliness to Jared seemed to have angered her husband.

"Good," she muttered to herself.

Chapter 6

Lily found Mrs. Shimway in the garden.

"Oh, my dear, I've never seen such lushness," the woman said. "It must be the heat and the moisture that moves in from the river, but everything in the garden is just bursting with greenery and color. Why, back in Boston, the trees were still bare . . . remember?"

"Yes," Lily said, taking a seat on the bench beside her. She took a deep breath of air, closing her eyes as she took in the familiar rich fragrances.

Natchez in springtime. There was no other scent like it, she thought. It was the smell of the earth and the air, of flowers and grass and trees. And perhaps Mrs. Shimway was right, perhaps it was even the odd, pungent warmth that blew in from the great river as well.

She leaned her head back and opened her eyes, letting her gaze wander through the limbs of the huge live oak above them. Birds twittered and sang. Squirrels chattered and rustled among the leaves as they jumped from limb to limb. The sky above was a brilliant blue with delicate white wisps of clouds—mackerel clouds, her father used to call them.

Lily couldn't resist laughing out loud.

"Oh, it's so good to be home," she said, almost to herself.

"I met your husband this morning," Mrs. Shimway said.

Lily turned and looked into the woman's plump face, noting the twinkle in her pale eyes.

"Yes, he told me."

"Oh, yes indeed. Such a charming man. There's nothing quite like the charm of a Southern gentleman, you know. And handsome . . ." Mrs. Shimway's look was faraway and wistful. "Really quite handsome. Even though he does have that look about him."

"Look?" Lily asked. "What look?"

"Why the look of the rogue, don't you know," she said, laughing self-consciously as she met Lily's skeptical look. "Oh yes, my dear. I definitely see a touch of the brigand in your husband's eyes. That dangerous kind of look that makes one think he might sweep you off your feet and spirit you away to a pirate ship."

She was practically twittering with excitement, and Lily found it rather irritating.

"Isn't it odd that so many women are attracted to men like that?" Seeing Lily's frown, Mrs. Shimway seemed to be trying to restrain herself a bit. Or at least to regain her usual conservative composure.

"Are they?" Lily asked, gazing into the distance. "I suppose I hadn't noticed."

But she had noticed. Woman always flocked to Nicholas at gatherings. They teased and flirted and begged prettily to sit by him at dinner. Even Lily had to admit there was something wildly masculine and dangerous about him. Even this morning, as angry and hurt as she was, she had felt an undeniable attraction when she looked at him.

"Oh, bother," she said, jumping up from the bench. "I just remembered something I have to do. Will you excuse me, Mrs. Shimway?"

"Of course, dear. Perhaps we could have tea together this afternoon?"

"Yes . . . tea," Lily said as she moved along the walkway. "Why don't you tell Mrs. Lloyd we'd like to have tea served in the ladies' parlor at four."

Lily had to get away. Away from Mrs. Shimway's fluttering hands and ardent conversation. Away from the house and the memory of Nicholas in the courtyard last night.

What was wrong with her anyway? It wasn't as if this marriage meant anything to either of them.

She wandered for a while in the gardens, letting her mind clear as she touched the spring flowers and breathed in their scent. And as always, the river seemed to draw her toward it and she found herself at the edge of the yard where the bluffs overlooked the Mississippi.

From here she could see the curve of the river to the north, and where the channel widened, several barges that were slowly making their way downriver. But she couldn't see any of the buildings beneath the hill or the docks where the various boats landed.

Suddenly she was filled with such a strong sense of longing. Something she hadn't felt in ages.

She remembered so vividly how it had been riding with her father on the ferry, listening to his deep voice as he conversed with the many passengers and welcomed them aboard. Sometimes Lily would sit where the breeze could blow in her hair and against her face. The passengers' chatter and the lapping sound of the river would soothe her and almost lull her to sleep.

Going across she'd keep her eyes on the little house where they lived, watching it until it was small and distant. Sometimes her mother would be on the porch, sweeping. And when the ferry moved out into the river, she would stop and lift her hand to shade her eyes. Then she would wave, and Lily would wave back.

It was a silly little ritual that never changed. Just as the greeting from her mother never changed when Lily and her father returned home late at night.

"Well, how was old Mr. River today? Was he easy, or did he give you a hard time?"

Lily's father would always laugh and tell her about their day and relate stories about his passengers. He often mentioned Nicholas in those stories, and his admiration of the man had been evident. But Lily had never dreamed that her father had approached him about marriage to her. Her father had been a cautious man, always worrying about money and Lily's future. And though he probably had made enough money to move them up to a house on the bluffs, he never wanted to leave the little house on the river.

"I don't belong there," he would say when her mother urged him. "Ain't no amount of money ever gonna make me belong up there. But now, Lily here . . . that's another matter. Someday I'd like to see her settled down, maybe married to a fine Natchez businessman and living in a home up there like a real fine lady."

"I guess you got your wish, Papa," Lily whispered. Her chin trembled, and she bit her lip to keep from crying. Why was she crying? She had everything her parents had ever wished for her.

She wondered often about the ferry. Nicholas had written to her in Boston that it was still in operation and doing well. He had wanted to sell the little house and deposit the money in her account, but Lily had asked him not to. Somehow she hadn't been ready to let the house go. In fact, she supposed it was still there and that it still belonged to her. Nicholas had never mentioned selling it again after that.

Lily straightened her shoulders and wiped her eyes.

Perhaps she'd ride down there one day. See how things were. See if any of the people were still there that she knew from her childhood.

She might even ask Jared to take her there, for she had

a feeling that Nicholas would not approve if she asked him.

Somehow, just thinking about it made her feel better. She spent the afternoon reacquainting herself with the house and gardens, then met Mrs. Shimway in the parlor for tea.

"I'm sorry I won't be joining you and your husband for dinner tonight," Mrs. Shimway said, placing a dollop of butter on a hot, steaming scone. "But I've decided to leave tomorrow, so I'm going to retire early."

"Oh, but you've hardly had time to rest," Lily protested. She had grown fond of the kindly woman on the trip to Natchez and she regretted feeling irritable with her earlier. "You can't leave so soon."

"Well, you know, I have a cousin in Georgia whom I've not seen since childhood. She has a lovely home in Savannah, and she's asked me time and again to come visit her. I've decided this would be a good opportunity to spend some time there with her." Mrs. Shimway looked around the elegant room. "I think I'm growing quite fond of this part of the country, and I want to see more of it."

"I understand; nevertheless, I shall hate to see you go," Lily said.

They said their good-byes and Lily went upstairs to change for dinner. She told herself that it didn't really metter what she wore, but she couldn't deny that she wanted to look her best, if for no other reason than to surprise her husband and see that half-hidden look of admiration she'd seen in his eyes today.

She chose a dinner dress of emerald green silk, with sleeves caught up in ribbons and trimmed with blond lace. The lace-draped bodice was cut low, exposing Lily's shoulders and dipping in a vee between her breasts. The skirt was caught up on each side in a graceful drape of the same blond lace and ribbon trim. She knew it was rather an elegant choice for only a casual dinner, but something made her want to prove to Nicholas that she was no longer the river child he remembered.

The lace-trimmed fan that Lily carried was more to keep her hands occupied than anything else.

When she stepped into the dining room, she could feel her heart pounding in her throat.

Nicholas was there, gazing steadily down at her, his eyes narrowed and assessing. In his dark evening jacket and dazzling white shirt, he was so handsome he took her breath away.

For a moment as he looked at her, Lily thought the dress had been a mistake. His gaze seemed to undress her as he looked her over from head to foot. It was almost as if by dressing this way she had given him a right to see what lay beneath her elegant clothes.

"The dress becomes you," he said. "It matches your eyes."

When Nicholas reached out his hand to her, Lily's heart was beating so hard that she feared she might actually faint.

With a lift of her head, she ignored his hand and glided past him, opening her fan and waving it in front of her face in a movement she had learned from Mary.

Nicholas gritted his teeth as he felt Lily's rebuff, and he watched her move by. An invisible cloud of lavender followed, causing him to frown and shake his head.

He could hardly believe his eyes, or senses.

When had the chit grown up? And how had she suddenly turned into this cool, elegant creature with skin the color of alabaster and dark-lashed eyes that emitted such bold sparks?

He had seen the evidence of her transformation in Jared's greedy glances today. It had surprised him. And it had angered him. And Lily's complete inability to see what Jared was up to had frustrated him even more.

It was, after all, his duty as her guardian to protect and advise the girl, wasn't it?

When Lily turned to sit at the other side of the table, Nicholas looked into her eyes before his gaze moved down instinctively to the bodice of her lace-trimmed dress. Her breasts rose and fell softly, and the lacy fan she waved caused her hair to move in intriguing wisps about her face, one of them catching just at the corner of her mouth.

With a swift intake of air, Nicholas frowned, surprised by his body's response to her. He could feel the heat stirring his blood, and for a moment it took all his strength not to reach out and touch her. To move the wisp of hair away and taste those full pink lips for himself. He almost groaned aloud before he was able to stop himself.

God's grief, what was he thinking? This was Lily . . . the child he'd promised to protect.

But that promise had been easier to keep when she was a scrawny, defiant tomboy.

"My sister served you well, I see," he said, intending to distract his disquieting thoughts. "Her choice of clothes is excellent as always."

"I chose this dress myself," she said, her voice cool and defensive. "In fact I've been choosing my own clothes since I was sixteen."

Seeing that haughty little lift of her chin, Nicholas cleared his throat and walked around to pull out her chair. The air in the room was so heavy with tension that he actually felt relief when the servants finally came into the room carrying the first course.

Nicholas sat at the end of the table with Lily on his right. As the servants placed the soup before them, he watched Lily's gaze moving with interest about the room.

Nicholas picked up his soup spoon, motioning with it toward a cherrywood étagère at the end of the room.

"You seem interested in my mother's china," he said.

"It's lovely," she said. "I looked at it earlier today. Old Paris china is one of my favorite patterns."

"You know, it's been years since anything in the house

was redone," he said. "Probably since before my mother died. So if there's anything you'd like to change . . ."

"No," she said. Lily sipped from her spoon. "Except for my old room. I'd like it back. I like being at the front of the house so I can see the river."

Nicholas stared at her as if he didn't quite understand.

"Burton said it was being repaired?" She knew from the look on his face that he had almost forgotten her unexpected arrival and Burton's need to tell her something to keep her away from Nicholas's room. And his mistress.

"Oh, repaired. Yes, well, I think it's finished now. I'll ask Burton to move your things tomorrow."

Even though the dinner was delicious, they moved through it rather awkwardly. Lily found herself longing for it to be over so she could go to her room and be herself again.

They were just being served dessert when Ncholas turned to her with a serious look in his eyes.

"There is one thing, Lily," he said. "I feel I should warn you about my cousin Jared."

"Indeed?" Lily said with a lift of her brows. She couldn't seem to help growing cool with him. It was just as Mary had predicted all these years ago. Nicholas was to have his way, but Lily would be expected to remain the ever-virtuous, obedient wife.

"I'm no longer a child, Nicholas, to be lectured about which friends I choose."

"I can see that you're no longer a child. And that is precisely the point I'm trying to make."

"And what is there to warn me about?"

Nicholas recognized the rebellious tone of her voice and the way her mouth was set in that sullen little way.

"I hardly think that you are as naive as you pretend. I think you know perfectly well what I mean."

"Why don't you make it clearer to me?" she said sweetly.

"All right," he said, leaning back in his chair and smiling. "If you insist. Jared is a notorious rake. He has no money of his own, and, quite frankly, he's never expressed any ambition for doing anything about it. Working for a living is beneath him, it seems. He depends solely on me for funds, and if he weren't my only living male relative I'd have cut him off long ago. Are you aware that he has been known to take advantage of young women such as yourself?''

''Such as myself?'' she asked, her eyes clear and sparkling.

''I'm speaking of young women with money,'' Nicholas said through clenched teeth. ''Everyone in Natchez is aware of what happened to your parents. Some of them even know that I've set up a separate account from what you inherited. And from the ferry business that continues to run. The money has grown, and you've become a very wealthy woman in your own right, Lily.''

''Oh.'' Lily's cheeks burned, and her eyes felt hot. How humiliating to know that everyone in town was aware that their marriage was a farce. That he had only married her at the request of her dying parents. She was a charity case, and he was the kind benevolent benefactor. ''I see.''

''Look, this isn't something I'd intended talking about tonight. One day soon, I'll have my lawyer come in and we'll sit down and discuss all of this. What I'm getting at is that Jared is well aware of your wealth.''

''And you assume that a man would only be interested in me because I'm rich?''

Nicholas cursed quietly, then rubbed his hands over his eyes.

''No, dammit, that's not what I'm saying. Why do you always make everything so difficult . . .'' he muttered.

''You mean, why can't I be a sweet, complacent child who hangs on your every word?''

Nicholas banged his hand on the table, making the crystal dishes in the silver epergne jingle and causing Lily to jump. He rose from his chair and slammed the door to the hall as Lily watched him in wide-eyed wonder.

"What do you want from me, Lily? Let's have done with the games and just tell me, for I swear I have no earthly idea what would please you or take away this childish anger you seem to feel toward me."

He stood with his hands on his hips, watching her, his eyes dark with anger and impatience.

"I'm not used to being told what to do," she snapped. "I don't like it."

"Oh," he drawled, sliding back into his seat. "You don't like it. Well, miss, like it or not, you are going to be told what to do as long as you are under my protection. I will not see you engaging in inappropriate behavior with Jared or with anyone else."

"I beg your pardon! I haven't engaged in anything, inappropriate or not."

"You are talking foolishness," he said, sighing heavily.

"I want to be able to come and go as I please. Is that so foolish? Or wrong?"

"Yes, it is," he declared. "A woman has no freedom in these matters, you know that. Her will is her husband's."

"Ha!" Lily stood up, almost turning her chair over as she did. "*My* will is certainly my own. And might I remind you that we are husband and wife in name only."

Nicholas leaned back in his chair. Now he let his eyes move deliberately over Lily's breasts and up to her flushed cheeks.

"That, my dear, can be remedied very easily."

"You . . . you wouldn't dare," she whispered.

"Woudn't I? You seem to hold me in such vile disregard, what makes you think I won't take you upstairs this moment and put an end to these foolish notions you seem to have about what I can or can't do?"

As she stared into his glittering eyes, her lips parted in amazement. And for some reason, she was finding it difficult to breathe properly when he looked at her that way.

She swallowed hard and started toward the door. But Nicholas was quicker. He stood up and reached for her,

grabbing her arm and pulling her around to face him. He
was breathing as hard as she was as his eyes bored into
hers.

"Let me go," she whispered. She could feel the warmth
of his hands through her dress, smell the clean scent of
his clothes and the tangy scent of shaving soap. He made
her forget her argument and even the reasons for them.

"You are my wife, Lily," he said, his mouth very close
to hers. "In every way except one. And when I decide that
one last barrier shall fall, then fall it will. So be careful of
your flirtatious little games, my sweet. You're a woman
now, as you seem so fond of reminding me. And don't
forget that I can make you mine anytime I wish."

Lily jerked away from his hands. She was so angry that
tears sparkled in her eyes as she faced him. She made
herself remember Jeanette Mireaux and the pain and
humiliation she'd felt when she saw them together. All
Nicholas's posturing and lecturing was simply a matter of
pride and possession. It had nothing to do with genuine
caring or concern.

"You are a cruel, arrogant man," she bit out. "And no
matter what you do to me, you can't make me like it,
Nicholas. Not ever."

Chapter 7

That night as Lily lay in bed, she heard the clock in the downstairs hallway strike one, then two and three. She tossed and turned, even lit the lamp and read a while. But no matter what she tried, she couldn't sleep.

And she couldn't banish Nicholas's face from her mind.

How intense he was. Not like the laughing, carefree young men who had danced and flirted with her in Boston. He was different, frightening even, and yet she couldn't seem to banish the allure he held for her.

Why should she keep thinking of him when she found his words and his manner totally overbearing? Not to mention what she thought of his liaison with the beautiful Widow Mireaux.

There had been times tonight when she imagined she caught the scent of a cigar or that hint of leather and soap. Times when she might have drifted off to sleep if it weren't for the possibility of his nearness. Then she'd open her eyes and stare into the darkness, wondering if he was outside her door, or even hidden in the shadowy corners of her room.

For a moment her heart would pound wildly. She could never be sure if it was fear she felt, or something else entirely.

"Oh, this is ridiculous," she said, finally bounding out of bed for what seemed like the hundredth time.

She walked to the door just to assure herself it was locked. Then she went to the window. The same window where she'd watched him with Jeanette Mireaux.

"I must find my own way here," she whispered. "Somehow I have to find a way to live my own life. Despite Nicholas . . ."

Nicholas stood at the southern end of the upper gallery, watching the moonlight glimmer on the river. He had walked the width of the porch a dozen times, each time stopping at the door leading into the upper hallway and gazing toward the room at the back of the house where Lily slept.

He couldn't seem to get her out of his head. Or the reality of what a beauty she'd become, with that proud, haughty look of hers and her beautiful hair afire with golden glints from the candelabra.

He didn't know why, but he found himself wanting to bend her to his own will. Wanting to force her to admit that he was her husband, wanting to hear her say that she would do as he asked.

Dammit, why *couldn't* she become the quiet, respectable wife he expected?

Yet despite all her proud defiance of him, there was still that little-girl helplessness in her eyes that made him want to take her in his arms and promise his protection. She had an innocent sensuality about her that he doubted she even knew she possessed. And Nicholas had decided she was far too beautiful and seductive for her own good.

And for his.

Suddenly he cursed softly and stalked back across the

gallery. He thought he heard the muted sound of the clock downstairs striking three.

She made him so angry. Made him want to shake her and put her away from him. What in God's name had he done, taking on a young girl as his wife the way he had? What had possessed him to marry her instead of simply being her guardian? Even if she couldn't have inherited her father's money, he could at least have looked into other possibilities of controlling her monetary interests until she came of age.

Legal expediency, he'd told Mary. And himself.

But being perfectly honest, he had to ask himself—was that really it? Or was it because of these odd disquieting feelings he felt every time he looked at her? This odd blending of protectiveness and desire that he couldn't remember feeling for any other woman.

Marriage had been simple and quick, and after all, nothing had ever managed to stop him from doing as he pleased, when he pleased. Why should he expect marriage would make any such difference? He'd even had the notion that a wife would put an end to the machinations of those silly, giggling debutantes and their mothers. She'd bring respect and peace into his life. Restore the grace and stability that had been missing from the household since his mother died.

Nicholas laughed, a humorless bark that caused the crickets momentarily to cease their chirping.

"Grace and stability indeed," he said mockingly.

For a moment he considered going out to the stables, saddling his horse, and riding to the other side of town where Jeanette's small, elegant home stood. Tomorrow morning he could wake up in her bed and in her arms, feeling a release from tension that only a night of lovemaking could bring.

But somehow that thought didn't bring the same satisfaction it always had before.

Damn the girl if she hadn't spoiled everything.

He'd have to find a way to deal with her. Somehow, he'd simply have to decide what he would do and what part she was to play in his life. This battle of wills had to stop.

Perhaps he'd speak with Jeanette in the morning, ask her advice. If anyone in Natchez knew the ways of a woman, it was certainly his mistress.

The next day, Lily had breakfast sent up and sipped her chocolate. Jared was waiting in the library when she came downstairs.

She didn't see Nicholas and didn't ask where he was. She was only relieved that she didn't have to deal with him this morning.

When she stepped into the library, Jared came to his feet. His eyes glinted with approval as he let his gaze move over her dress of white Indian muslin with its stripes of fine drawnwork.

"You are a vision," he murmured, taking her hand and bringing her fingers up to his lips.

"Why, thank you, Jared," she said with a slight curtsy. She couldn't help smiling at his warmth. How refreshing it was after Nicholas's cold arrogance. "Shall we go? I'm most anxious to see Natchez. And I have a special place I'd like you to take me."

"Anywhere," he said, causing Lily to smile again. "Your every wish is my command."

"Oh. Jared," she said, glancing at him from the corner of her eyes. Walking to the mirror over the fireplace, she smoothed her hand over her hair. "Please, don't be so serious. Although I do appreciate your enthusiasm, you must remember that I am a married woman. What I need most is a friend . . . not a suitor."

His eyes grew wide, and for a moment he seemed taken aback. She knew he hadn't expected her to be so outspoken. Most men didn't. But she was relieved to see a small shake of his head as he returned an agreeable smile.

"Then friend it shall be," he said, motioning her through the door.

If Jared seemed surprised by her request to go down to the river, he didn't show it. Only later, as they drove along Silver Street, did he say, "I'm afraid this area has grown even more disreputable since you left. If Nicholas learns that I've brought you here, he won't be pleased."

"Oh, Nicholas," she said. "What he doesn't know won't hurt him. I certainly don't intend telling him. Do you? Oh, look, Jared," she said. "There it is . . . there's the house where I used to live. Stop there in front . . . please."

The look he gave her was one of skepticism, but he did as she asked. The front yard was so small that he was able to pull the carriage almost to the front porch of the little white house. The place looked clean and apparently well tended, but the windows were curtainless and there was obviously no one living there.

He made a quiet murmur of protest when Lily scrambled down from the carriage, not even waiting for him to come around and attend to her.

"Lily . . ."

"I want to go inside," she said.

"I'm not sure that is wise." Jared glanced around at the varied mingling of people passing on the street. Some of them stared with open curiosity at the fine carriage.

Lily hurried up the steps and put her hand above her eyes, pressing her face against the window, peering inside like a child.

Jared sighed and followed her, turning the doorknob and pushing the door open as Lily gave a small gasp of surprise and stepped inside the house.

She stood for a moment, gazing into the empty but freshly painted rooms and breathing in the cool, closed-off scent. The furniture was gone, and the windows had been stripped and cleaned to a sparkle. The paint was nice, but unfamiliar. The house had not been painted when she lived there.

Yet despite the emptiness and the changes, there was such a familiarity to it that it brought an unexpected pang to her heart, and she felt her eyes filling with tears of nostalgia and loss.

Hesitating, she stepped to the doorway of the bedroom where her mother had died, while Jared waited at the front door. When she made a quiet sob and put her hand to her mouth, he came immediately to her side.

"Lily?" he murmured. "Lily, if this is too much for you, we will leave."

How could she explain? How could she tell this man who barely knew her how it felt standing here in the room where she last saw her mother?

She hadn't had time to grieve. She'd been whisked away to the elegant house on the hill and married before she knew what was happening to her. She had not come back to this house again. Her mother's burial had taken place so quickly that Lily had not even had a chance to say a proper good-bye. Sometimes, in Boston, she'd managed to convince herself that her mother wasn't really gone, and she would write letters to her, then throw them into the fireplace before anyone could see them.

She'd gone to Boston, where nothing was familiar. Where she was forced to forget Natchez and this little house on the river. She loved her life with Mary and Theodore and she wouldn't change that. She loved learning and wearing fine dresses. And it pleased her to have people look at her with a respect and admiration that she'd never known before.

But for all the happy moments, there had been just as many melancholy times when she wished she could recapture those days of her childhood, when there had been laughter in this little house. When her life had been filled with peace and security and a certainty about who she was.

The finality of knowing that could never be again hit her like a blow, and she found herself trembling.

"Dear Lily," Jared murmured, moving toward her.

He turned her around and took her in his arms and despite her earlier skepticism and Nicholas's warning about his cousin's sincerity, she let him hold her.

"It's all right," he said, whispering against her hair. "You mustn't cry. You don't have to live in squalor like this any longer. You have a new life now. You're a new person."

Lily stepped away from him and wiped her eyes.

How could she expect someone like Jared or Nicholas to understand, when their lives had always given them anything they wanted? Jared completely misunderstood why she was crying.

"Hello?" The voice that shouted greetings came from the porch outside.

Lily took a deep breath and pulled away from Jared, going to the front of the house and looking outside.

"Yes?" she asked, seeing the woman standing on the porch

She was obviously one of the transients who wandered the streets here along the landing, making a living as best they could from the passengers and crews of the ships. Her dress, once elegant and bright, was now ragged, the skirt's hem dark with filth and dirt.

A small pushcart, piled high with pots and pans, sat in the street, just past the small yard's sparse patch of grass.

"You be movin' in here, miss?" the woman asked. Her smile revealed teeth that were stained, some of them even missing.

For a moment Lily felt sickened by the sight and rancid smell of the old woman. She even felt a bit nervous, having such a person approach her. Then she remembered where she was. And who she was.

"No," Lily said, forcing herself to smile at the woman. "I was just looking inside. I . . . I used to live here."

"Eh?" the woman said, cocking her head to one side. "Live here you say?" Her rheumy old eyes moved with obvious curiosity over Lily's bright hair and beautiful gown, then past her to the elegantly dressed man who stood in the doorway watching her with a hint of disgust on his handsome face.

"Miss Lily?" the woman asked. "This can't be our little Miss Lily?"

Lily's face changed, and her eyes grew wide as she stared into the face she should have recognized if not for the heavy ravages of time.

"Miss Fran?" Lily whispered. She stepped forward, staring into the woman's pale eyes. "Oh, Miss Dupree, it is you," she whispered. She opened her arms, but the old woman moved away, cringing away from Lily.

"Naw, now ye don't want to be huggin' the likes of me. I'll spoil your beautiful dress."

"I can't believe it's you," Lily whispered. "But what . . . how . . . ?" She didn't know quite how to express her concern about the old woman's state. She certainly didn't want to insult her.

"A woman what's old is of no use here," Fran said with a twist of her mouth.

"But . . . but you aren't old," Lily protested.

"It ain't so much the years that age you here, child," Fran said, her eyes filling with sadness.

"Lily," Jared said behind her. She felt his hand at her elbow. "We really should leave here."

Lily shook him away, not bothering to turn and look at him. She knew what she would see—the same look that Nicholas no doubt would have. One of disgust and disapproval that Lily would lower herself to speak to such a dirty creature.

She glanced out toward the cart on the street and saw a man approaching, a man who was as ragged and dirty as Fran herself. He was glaring toward the house.

"Fran?" Lily whispered, nodding toward the man.

"Oh," Fran said. The fear that moved over her face sickened Lily and made her want to step between the woman and the approaching man.

"Oh, dear." Fran said. "Now I've done it."

"What the hell you doin'?" the man roared. "This don't look like work to me. Standin' here gabbin' and wastin' the best part of the day. Didn't you see the keelboat what just pulled into shore? They be needin' some cook pots, old woman. Now git!"

"Yes . . . yes," Fran muttered, turning to leave the porch. "I'm comin'."

"Wait," Lily said, beneath her breath. "I can't let you go with him."

"Have to," Fran said, her breath coming in frightened gasps. "I have to go."

"Lily, just let her go," Jared warned behind her.

"Sir." Lily said, calling to the grizzled old man in the street. "I was just buying some cookware from this lady. If you could wait only a moment."

Hearing Lily's words, the man's face changed, and though he was still frightening-looking, he seemed less inclined to do anything to Fran.

Lily opened her lace reticule and pulled out several coins pressing them into Fran's dirty, wrinkled palm.

"Here, take this," she whispered. "And put some of it away for yourself if you can. I'll come to see you again when I can . . . just to make sure you're all right."

"Oh, Miss Lily," Fran whispered, gazing up at her with dampened eyes. "You don't worry about an old hag like me. You're an elegant lady now, and you shouldn't even be down here in this part of town." Fran glanced at Jared, her look skeptical and slightly disapproving now. "This ain't your husband," she said.

"No, this is my husband's cousin," Lily said.

"Frannie!" the man in the street roared. "Git the money and come on."

"I'm comin'!" Fran yelled back. "Don't come back

here," she said, turning back to Lily. "You hear? Don't come back."

Lily's shoulders slumped as she watched Miss Fran shuffle out to the street. She clamped her teeth together when she saw the old man take Fran's wrist and pry the money from her fingers, then push her toward the cart.

She didn't protest when Jared took her arm and pulled her toward their carriage.

"She's right, Lily," Jared said. "This place is hardly suitable for a lady like you. If Nicholas finds out I brought you here . . . Hell's bells, I hate to think what he might do."

"But this was my home," she said. "Just because my circumstances have changed, it doesn't mean I don't still have feelings for the people we once knew . . . like Miss Fran."

"She is a ragged old witch," he proclaimed. "She used to be a woman of the streets, for God's sake."

"She was our neighbor," Lily said, clamping her full lips together. "And she was kind to my mother."

"It isn't the same now, Lily," he said, his voice cajoling and more sympathic again. "You don't belong here. And you never will again."

Chapter 8

Leaving the riverfront area, Jared drove back up to Natchez, pointing out places of interest, or the houses of people that Lily might know.

But her heart was no longer in it. She couldn't keep her mind on anything except Miss Fran and the pitiful way she now lived.

Jared had dismissed the incident so quickly and so lightly. She wondered if people like him and Nicholas had no feelings at all for such people. Did they feel no responsibility for the homeless? No compassion for the poor?

"There's a small tearoom nearby," Jared said. "Would you like to stop and rest? Have a pot of tea?"

"Yes," Lily said, nodding distractedly. "That would be nice."

She tried to make herself concentrate on the houses and the beautifully kept lawns. When they turned onto High Street, she gave a murmur of genuine pleasure as they passed one particular small white house. It was simple, but elegant, with brilliant white paint and dark green shutters. The garden was filled with roses in a well-kept yard.

It was the kind of house she might have chosen for herself if she had been allowed to live her life alone.

She glanced back over her shoulder as they passed, frowning when she saw a buff-colored horse tied beneath a holly tree at the side of the house.

Seeing Lily's glance back, Jared slapped the reins lightly against the horse's back and hurried on down the street.

"Jared," she said, frowning to herself. "Whose house was that?"

"Which one?" he asked.

"The white one . . . back there on the corner. The neat one with green shutters."

"Why, uh, I'm not sure I remember."

"Jared, don't lie to me," she said, touching his arm. "Not even to try and spare my feelings. After all, Nicholas and I might be husband and wife, but everyone in Natchez knows it's a marriage of convenience only. There's hardly any attachment of emotion."

"If I'd been more thoughtful, I would never have driven down this street."

"It's the home of Jeanette Mireaux, isn't it?"

"Lily . . ."

"Well, isn't it?"

"Yes," he said quietly.

"That was Nicholas' horse tied beneath the tree."

"Really, I don't know . . ."

"It's all right," she said, shrugging her slender shoulders. "I can assure you, it bothers me not in the least. Now, where is that delightful tearoom you mentioned earlier?"

Jeanette Mireaux lay on a silver-and-maroon-striped chaise in her small, but elegantly appointed bedroom. She had purposely selected a new gown of silk *peau de soie,* in a blue that Nicholas had once said matched her eyes.

But today he hardly seemed to notice. He barely even said hello when he came in.

Instead, he began pacing the room, as he was still doing, while she watched him from her reclining position. He cursed quietly and muttered, his hands alternately waving in the air, then being thrust into the pockets of his dove gray trousers.

She thought he was still the most beautiful man she'd ever known. When her husband was killed, Nicholas had been so kind, so giving. At first, they had been friends. And then gradually, lovers.

She had never known such ecstasy as she'd found in Nicholas's arms. Not even her husband, as much as she loved him, had satisfied her the way Nicholas did.

She thought it had been a mutual eventuality, their love affair. But even now, after all this time, Jeanette knew that Nicholas did not love her. Not the way she wanted him to.

Oh, he cared for her. He would do anything for her. But love . . . that was another thing entirely for this proud, mysterious man.

"What in hell am I to do with the little vixen?" Nicholas asked. He raked his hand over his face, closing his eyes for a second. "I swear, Jeanette, sometimes she makes me want to strangle her."

"Why, chéri?" Jeanette asked quietly.

"Why?" He glared at her. "Because she's obstinate and pert. She seems to think she can come and go as she pleases. And she has little regard for my reputation, or her own, for that matter. Today, she's being escorted around Natchez by none other than my indolent cousin Jared."

"Oh," Jeanette said. "Indeed?" She repositioned herself on the chaise so that she was sitting. Her eyes grew bright with curiosity as she watched the man she loved ranting and raving about his young wife.

Something wasn't quite right about the entire scene. Or about Nicholas's overreaction to something Jeanette found quite trivial.

"You know what I think of Jared," Nicholas continued. "He takes after his father. I don't know what would have become of Jared's mother if not for my family. When Jared's father died, I couldn't for the life of me understand how anyone could let his own mother live in poverty while he was out spending his small inheritance as if it were a fortune."

"You were good to her, Nicholas," Jeanette said. "You did the right thing, finding her a place to live, seeing that she was cared for. I'm sure it gave her a great deal of peace before she died."

"I hope so. God knows, Jared never gave her any peace while she was alive."

"Some men might not be so forgiving as you've been," Jeanette said.

"Forgiveness has little to do with it," he growled. "I'd like nothing better than to let the scoundrel starve. What I do, I do in the memory of my aunt. She was a good, kind woman who deserved better than she got in life."

"Perhaps Jared will mature in time."

"He's reckless and irresponsible. In the past few months he's been involved in matters that are, to say the least, questionable."

"Yes, there was the duel last year as I recall," Jeanette said.

"That, and his continuous gambling. The boy's sole purpose in life seems to be spending money and trying to bankrupt the St. James estate."

"Oh, Nicholas," Jeanette said, laughing softly. "That would take some doing. With all your wealth? Why, I've heard the ferry alone brings in enough to assure an entire new fortune for you."

"The ferry is not mine. You know that. I'm only tending it for Lily."

"But she's your wife," Jeanette said, frowning. "What belongs to her belongs to you."

"I didn't want that," he said. "The reason I agreed to

take her in was because she couldn't inherit her parents' estate. Now that she's of age and a married woman, it's hers now, free and clear.''

"Does she know that?"

"Why?"

"Well, perhaps she'd like to see to the running of it. After all, I understand she worked with her father as a child. And Lily does seem to have a good, practical head on her shoulders.''

"That's out of the question," Nicholas said, turning to pace the room again.

"Nicky, darling . . . please stop your pacing. You're making me quite dizzy.'' She hoped he would take the hint and come to her side. She had thought of little else but having him in her arms since the night she was spirited away from his house because his bride arrived too early.

But he hardly seemed to hear her.

"Why is it out of the question? If you're so miserably unhappy with the girl and she with you, wouldn't that be the perfect solution? You've built up such a business that she never need want for anything. Even if there is no divorce, you could buy her a separate house—it isn't unheard of." Jeanette waved her hand languidly about the room. "Living alone is not so bad," she said, smiling. "Not so bad at all. No one to tell me what to do or where to go. I can stay up all night if I wish and sleep until noon. I can have as many lovers as I wish with no one to tell me otherwise.''

"Oh," he said, finally taking the bait and coming to stand beside her. "And how many lovers do you have, m'lady?'' he teased.

"Only one, darling. Only one. But he is quite enough, believe me.'' Her eyes sparkled up at him, and her lips parted invitingly.

He bent to kiss her, opening her mouth and letting his lips capture hers completely until she was straining upward, wanting him closer. Wanting him undressed and in bed with her.

"Oh, Nicky," she whispered when he pulled away. "Please, can't we just forget Lily for the moment?

But he had moved to a nearby table and picked up his gloves, pulling them on as he gazed thoughtfully into the distance.

"Nicky," she asked, frowning at him. Did he intend just to leave her here like this? Her body fully awakened by the look of him and the touch of his warm mouth on hers? "Nicky, you can't be leaving." She swung her legs over the chaise and stood up, purposely letting her silk gown swing open to tempt him. She moved behind him and wrapped her arms around his waist.

"Hmm, my love?" she murmured, pressing her breasts and pelvis seductively against him.

He turned, smiling at her in that cool way of his. She knew he wanted her; she could feel it. He was an insatiable lover, leaving her sometimes in complete and delicious exhaustion. And yet he could turn away from her as if it meant nothing to him.

He kissed her lightly on the lips and put her gently away from him.

"Some other time, love," he said. "Right now, I have an appointment with my lawyer, to discuss exactly what my options with Lily are."

Jeanette pouted her lips prettily at him.

"Some other time indeed," she said. "Well, I just might not be here when you decide to come back."

Nicholas made a quiet noise of amusement and pulled her into his arms, kissing her thoroughly until he felt her body begin to tremble.

"You know, Jeanette, one of the things I like most about you is that you behave in a liberal, mature way. We have a mutual understanding. I know what you want, and you know exactly what I want. No commitments, no expectations and nothing to tie either of us down. So don't pout, chérie. I have enough of that childishness at home."

"But . . ."

He touched her face and let his eyes move with pleased amusement down her bare breasts and her rounded belly beneath the revealing silk robe.

"You're not going to change on me now, are you?" he asked.

She wanted to tell him that she had already changed. What she wanted was different now than when he first came to her bed. She loved him deeply and completely. Couldn't he see that? She wanted to be able to be seen with him by the entire world. She wanted to be his wife. Not Lily. Not that child who had no idea how to please a man like Nicholas. Yet she couldn't seem to find the words to tell him at all. Not when he looked at her that way and spoke with such coolness.

"No," she whispered with the slightest catch in her voice. "No, I'm not going to change. Just come back to me soon, Nicky . . . will you?"

"You can count on it," he said, his voice low and seductive as he kissed her again, then turned to go.

"And let me know what happens with Lily," she added, as he went out the door.

He waved his hand above his head as if to signal he heard her. Then he went across the porch and bounded down the steps as if she were already forgotten.

Jeanette bit her lips and walked into the parlor to pour herself a small glass of sherry. Taking it back to the bedroom, she stretched out on the chaise again.

Something was wrong. She could feel it.

She'd never known Nicholas to be as distracted as he was today. Oh, he had a quick temper sometimes, especially when someone insulted his pride or questioned his masculinity. But all men were that way, weren't they? But normally, Nicholas was coolheaded and deliberate in his decisions. Self-controlled and imperturbable in his daily life.

So, how was it this girl managed to make him so angry and so frustrated?

Unless he wanted her. Unless he saw her, not as a child any longer, but as a beautiful desirable woman.

"Could that actually be it?" she whispered. "Could Nicholas be thinking of making love to her . . . making her his wife in every way?"

"My God," she muttered, coming up from the chaise, her eyes troubled. "And he doesn't even know it."

For a moment she felt tears stinging her eyes as her dreams of a life with him whirled and teased about in her mind.

She laughed, a sad, melancholy sound that barely moved past her lips and was muted by her tears. Then, with deliberate steps she went to the gilded French armoire, pushing her hands through the dresses until she found just the right one.

"I have to see this girl," she muttered as she flung her silk robe across the bed.

For a moment she gazed into the mirror at her white body, her hips and breasts rounded to feminine perfection. So Nicholas always told her. She'd learned how to use this body. How to make men happy. And she received pleasure as well. She was older than Nicholas, and now she wondered if, at her age, her beauty was finally fading. Was the pleasure Nicky found with her growing old for him at last? It was something she'd always feared and dreaded.

She had to see this girl for herself. Surely she couldn't have changed so much in the past couple of years that Nicholas could now be taken with her.

Perhaps the look on Nicholas's face when he spoke of Lily was something else. Not passion, but something closer to hatred. That would certainly make more sense, wouldn't it?

"Yes, of course," she said as she fumbled in the dresser for her lacy underthings. She would find out. Somehow she thought if she could see Lily for herself, she could judge the measure of this girl's appeal to a man.

Chapter 9

Less than an hour later, Jeanette Mireaux arrived at Nicholas's house on Orleans Street. As she hurried through the front gate and up the brick walkway she smoothed her hand down the skirt of her blue shot-silk dress. The bonnet of straw-colored satin was almost the same color as her hair and was tied beneath her chin with a wide blue ribbon that matched her dress.

She was confident she looked her best as she went to call on Lily. After all, in the matter of taste and fashion sense she need not feel inferior to anyone.

She knocked on the front door and was greeted by Burton, who allowed his tired old eyes to move suspiciously over her before he went down the hall to fetch Mrs. Lloyd.

The housekeeper hurried to the door, the keys at her waist jangling stridently as she walked. Her face as she approached Jeanette was set in a mask of disapproval, her thin lips drawn tightly together.

"Mr. St. James is not at home, ma'am," she said, her voice dry and emotionless.

"I know that, Mrs. Lloyd," Jeanette said, employing her

most polite voice. "I haven't come to see Nicholas. I'm here to call on Lily."

Mrs. Lloyd practically snorted, and her eyes darkened with displeasure.

"I'm not so sure Mr. St. James will be approving of that," she said, almost to herself.

"May I come in, Mrs. Lloyd?" Jeanette asked with an impatient sigh. "I assure you I have no intention of being indiscreet or of saying anything that might upset Lily. I simply want to call on her so that we might reacquaint ourselves before the party in her honor."

"What party?" Mrs. Lloyd asked suspiciously.

"Why, the one I intend to give for her," Jeanette said with a satisfied smile.

"Mr. Nicholas doesn't know about this, I take it."

"No, but he will. Just as soon as Lily tells him about it. Then he can hardly say no . . . can he? Well . . . are you going to let me in, or are you going to leave me standing here until Nicholas comes home?"

"Miss Lily is not home either. But we're expecting her any moment. I suppose you can come in and wait if you've a mind to."

"Why thank you, Mrs. Lloyd," Jeanette said, brushing past the woman and moving down the hallway to the door of the ladies' parlor. "I'll just wait in here if that's all right. It's always been one of my favorite rooms in this glorious old house."

Mrs. Lloyd rolled her eyes and went back into the dining room, clucking her tongue as she picked up her polishing cloth.

Jeanette was walking around the room when she heard a carriage at the back of the house. She went to the window, breathing a sigh of relief when she saw that it wasn't Nicholas, but Lily and Jared who emerged from the carriage in the courtyard.

They were laughing heartily when they came up the back steps and into the hallway of the house.

"Oh Jared," Lily said breathlessly. "You've had me laughing all day. Please, you must stop."

Jeanette did not make herself known right away. She couldn't. The sight of Lily St. James had left her quiet speechless.

The young woman's dress was of the finest Indian muslin and the elegant drawnwork pattern was fashionable and obviously expensive. But it wasn't the dress so much that captured Jeanette's attention. It was Lily herself—everything about her.

Her gleaming mass of hair and creamy skin made a breathtaking combination. And her unusual height and lithe figure was something Jeanette could only ever have dreamed about.

The thin, awkward river child was gone. And in her place was a beautiful, composed woman.

She was absolutely stunning. And she was young.

Jeanette felt her heart skip, then begin to beat again just as Lily turned toward the parlor and saw her.

"Oh," Lily said, her eyes growing huge with surprised speculation. "It's you."

Jared touched Lily's arm and moved closer. Jeanette didn't miss that protective little gesture, and she wondered at it. Why would he feel a need to protect Lily from her? After all, the girl had no way of knowing about her affair with Nicholas. Still shaken by Lily's transformation, Jeanette forced herself to smile graciously and move forward.

"Lily, my dear, how wonderful you look. It's so good to see you. I wanted to welcome you home."

"Thank you, Mrs. Mireaux," Lily said. She didn't move. She couldn't. All she could seem to focus on was the woman's timeless beauty and her classic elegance.

The very nerve of her. The beautiful widow had just come from a rendezvous with Lily's husband. And whether the marriage meant anything or not, there was a certain amount of pride involved, Lily told herself. Did this brazen woman think she could just come in here with her cheeks aglow from her recent assignation and pretend that nothing was wrong? Even welcome her back home as if she really meant it.

She saw Mrs. Lloyd move into the hallway, and for once Lily was glad to see her.

"Shall I bring tea, Mrs. St. James?" Mrs. Lloyd asked.

Lily could heard the protectiveness in Mrs. Lloyd's voice, and it made her want to smile and to hug the older woman. Instead, she forced herself to remain composed.

"Jared and I just had tea. At that quaint little tearoom not far from where you live, I believe, Mrs. Mireaux. But if you'd care for some, I assure you it's no trouble."

"No," Jeanette said. It was one of the few times in her life that Jeanette had ever felt awkward and out of place. "Thank you, but I really must be going soon. I only wanted to stop by and ask if you might approve of my giving a garden party in your honor."

"Thank you, Mrs. Lloyd," Lily said, dismissing her housekeeper with a grateful smile. She turned to Jeanette with a lift of her brow. "A party? In my honor?"

"Yes. Of course, we'd have it here, since my house is so small."

"I don't know. What do you think, Jared?"

"I think that the entire city would be captivated by you," he said. "I think it's a splendid idea."

"Isn't he a dear?" Lily asked, smiling at Jeanette's look of bewilderment. "Why don't we go into the parlor and discuss it?" she asked.

"I believe I'll leave the discussion of parties and costumes to the ladies," Jared said. "I really must be going."

"Oh, but you will be back tomorrow, won't you?" Lily asked. "There are so many other places I'd like to see. And you are such a thoughtful escort."

"It will be my pleasure," he said, taking Lily's hand and bringing it to his lips.

Jeanette could only stare. It was obvious that the young man was completely smitten with Lily. And she seemed to be enjoying his attention tremendously. Perhaps that was the key to the entire matter. A way for Jeanette finally to have Nicholas for herself.

After Jared left, Lily waved her hand toward the elegant silk-damask settee near the fireplace.

"Please, have a seat," she said, her voice the epitome of grace and good manner.

"Well . . ." Jeanette said as she sat down. She spread her voluminous skirts carefully, posing elegantly, as Lily sat down across from her.

"We haven't had a good party in ages," Jeanette said. "And I thought, what better reason than to celebrate Lily's homecoming."

"How kind of you," Lily said. As she gazed at the woman, who was more than a decade older than she, Lily had to admit that she was still quite beautiful. The kind of woman, she imagined, a man would be proud to claim as a mistress. She couldn't seem to control the thoughts that whirled in her mind.

Had Nicholas made love to her today? Had he taken her in his arms, kissed those pouting full lips? Told her he loved her?

Lovemaking was a mystery. Something Lily couldn't possibly understand. But sometimes, when she thought of Nicholas, she had the most provocative images. Forbidden, sensual fantasies that went against her pride and her heart.

How could she ever think of being attached to a man who was involved so completely with another woman?

"Lily?" Jeanette asked.

"Oh," Lily said, shaking her head. "I'm sorry. Just daydreaming, I guess. It's been quite a day, and I suppose I'm tired."

"Certainly, you must be. And I won't keep you. But please, just let me know if you will agree to such a party. I do so hope you will consider it."

For a moment the two women looked into each other's

eyes. Jeanette was the first one to look away. And for the smallest fraction of a second, Lily felt sorry for her.

Did she love Nicholas? But of course, she must. Pretending, for someone like Jeanette Mireaux, must be very hard. She didn't seem like the kind of woman who would enjoy being whispered about or having to live in the shadows of polite society.

"I will think about it," Lily said, standing and walking toward the door with Jeanette. "Have you mentioned the idea to Nicholas?"

Just then they heard the front door slam. They looked up at the same time and saw Nicholas standing in the hallway. The surprise on his face flickered briefly, then was gone. Covered quickly, Lily thought, by his rather cynical smile.

"Mentioned what idea to me?" he asked.

"Nicholas," Jeanette said, her voice breathless. She hurried to his side and turned, as if expecting Lily to have followed.

Instead Lily stood alone at the end of the hall, facing Nicholas as if challenging him, watching the emotion on his face and in his steely eyes.

He wasn't pleased. She was certain of that. But was it Jeanette's presence or her own that made him so irritable?

Lily's eyes glinted with curiosity, and she lifted her brow, silently taunting Nicholas to respond.

"I was just telling Lily how much I would enjoy giving a party in her honor. You know it's been—"

"That's out of the question," Nicholas said. "I'm sure Lily isn't completely recovered from her trip."

"Nonsense. But of course I am," Lily said. "I'm hardly an old lady, Nicholas, to take to my bed for so small a thing as a trip from Boston."

Nicholas frowned, glaring at Lily.

"I was only thinking of your well-being," he murmured, between gritted teeth.

"Yes, I'm sure you were. And what a thoughtful husband

you always are," Lily said, practically simpering. "But I do believe a party would be just the thing. I could reacquaint myself with your friends—perhaps meet some people my own age." Seeing Nicholas's glower, she couldn't help smiling.

"Now that I think of it, yes . . . I think it would be just the perfect distraction."

She saw Jeanette's eyes grow wide as she watched the sparring between Lily and Nicholas. Her smile was rather nervous, as if she weren't quite sure she should be celebrating just yet. Quickly her gaze moved from Lily to Nicholas.

"Nicholas?" Jeanette asked quietly. "Is it all right? I . . . I don't want to make you upset with me."

For a moment Nicholas's face remained set and hard. But then he turned and looked down at Jeanette and smiled.

"Of course I'm not upset with you. It's very kind of you to think of a welcome-home party for Lily. I should have thought of it myself."

"Then it's all right?" Jeanette asked, glancing first at Nicholas, then down the hall where Lily still stood with her arms crossed as she leaned against the doorframe.

When Nicholas glanced her way, Lily lifted her hands as if none of it mattered much to her.

"Yes," Nicholas said. "It's all right. Whatever you wish."

Lily continued standing there after Jeanette left, and Nicholas turned back to face her.

"What was that all about? Did you invite her here?" he asked.

"She was here when I returned home," Lily said with an innocent look.

Just then Burton came into the hallway.

"Excuse me, Miss Lily," he said with a little bow. "But we've moved your things back to the front bedroom upstairs, just the way you asked.

"Thank you Burton," she said. "I think I'll go freshen

up before dinner." Burton left, and Lily moved toward the stairs.

Nicholas caught her arm just as she was going up the steps.

"Jeanette seemed a bit upset," he said. "Did you say something to—"

"No," Lily said, She turned to him, her face different now. There was no longer any need for pretense, for a polite smile or cool look of disinterest. That was something she had feigned for Jeanette. But now, Lily's eyes sparked angrily at him.

"No, Nicholas," she repeated. "I didn't say anything. I was very polite. There's no need to worry—she didn't say anything either. I expect she's much too discreet and well-bred to come right out and tell me all the sordid details of your relationship with her."

She pulled away from him and hurried up the curving stairway, but he caught her again at the first landing.

"And just what do you mean by that?' he asked, pulling her against him.

"Really, Nicholas, let's not play these games," she hissed. "I'm not a fool. So please . . . don't take me for one. I will continue your little charade, if you like. But only to a certain point. I will not, however, be made a laughingstock in my own home. You are not the only one who has pride, you know."

She watched his eyes change, saw the spark of disbelief and dawning realization. Had he thought her so dense she wouldn't be able to see what was going on right under her nose?

"I'll ask you to explain that," he said. He held her against him and she could feel his hard chest pressing against her breasts. She'd never noticed the flecks of blue in his eyes before.

"Do you have to hear me say it out loud?" she asked, with a lift of her chin.

"Yes, dammit, I do. If you have an accusation to make—"

"All right, if you insist. I know that you're lovers," she said with an indifferent shrug of her shoulders. "She didn't have to tell me. Although under the circumstances, I can't really understand her reason for pretending such kindness to me. I assume the party is just her excuse to be near you, my dear husband."

Nicholas stared hard into her eyes. She seemed so cool and unaffected. But were her eyes brighter than usual? Was that the slightest tremble he saw at the corner of her mouth?

Her vulnerable, very tempting, mouth.

He shook his head and stepped away from her as if her touch had scorched him.

"Lily," he said, his voice quiet and apologetic.

"No," she said, lifting her hand toward him. "Don't insult me further by trying to explain. There are no apologies necessary. After all, we mean nothing to each other. Our marriage is only a sham. It is nothing, I assure you. You must go your way, and I, of course, shall go mine."

She turned and hurried up the steps. Away from his dark, troubled gaze. Away from the strength of him that was sometimes so overwhelming and distracting.

She had no right to ask him for anything. He had, after all, given her a life she never would have had except for his kindness and generosity. Why should she expect anything more?

And why, she wondered, did admitting that hurt so badly?

Chapter 10

Lily somehow managed to get through dinner alone with Nicholas. Their conversation tended toward polite, inane matters. And this time, neither of them mentioned Jeanette or the proposed party.

It was much more difficult later in her room. For there, alone with her thoughts and just across the hallway from Nicholas, she was acutely aware of his presence. She could hear him walking about in his room, and once she thought she heard him go out onto the front gallery.

She had expected him to storm out of the house, to seek solace at Jeanette's cozy little house. But he hadn't. He came, instead, to Lily's room.

She knew it was him as soon as he knocked at the door. Lily whirled around, facing the door, aware that her entire body had begun to tremble ever so slightly.

"Yes?" she managed.

"Lily . . . it's me. May I come in?"

She hadn't locked the door, and she was glad because she wasn't sure she'd be able to walk across the room to open it. Instead she stood with her hand on the back of a stately, brocade-covered chair, lifted her chin, and made herself reply in a voice that sounded surprisingly calm and self-assured.

"Yes . . . come in."

Lily thought she'd never seen Nicholas the way he looked when he stepped into her room. It wasn't his casual dress—she'd often seen him without a coat and with his shirt opened at the neck.

It was more his manner, the way he dipped his head toward her almost apologetically as his eyes moved quickly over her champagne-colored dressing gown and up to the curls that swept over her shoulder and down over her breasts.

His arrogance seemed to have disappeared, and Lily opened her eyes wide, unable to believe that she was seeing an almost-humble Nicholas.

He cleared his throat and clasped his hands behind his back as he looked directly across the room into her eyes. His look was serious, but she had to admit that his virile male confidence was still intact. Still, he seemed different.

"I've been thinking," he said. His voice, quiet and low, rumbled in his chest. Lily thought she could feel the vibrations across the room. "We seem to have started our new life together on a bad footing. And for that, I hold myself responsible."

Lily lifted one brow and clenched her teeth together. What was he up to?

She said nothing, but stood waiting.

The truth was, Nicholas did feel responsible for their bad beginning. But more than that he found himself surprised by the way he was feeling about his beautiful, disturbing wife. Even stranger still, he found himself thinking of her at the oddest moments and wanting to know more about her. Something he could never remember experiencing with any other woman.

In her presence, he couldn't seem to take his eyes off her. When had his wild river child grown into this stunningly sensuous woman? Any man in his position would already have taken steps to make her his wife in every way. And he had to admit it was something that he thought about more and more as each day passed, especially when he saw her dressed as she was now.

The silk dressing gown clung to her lithe body, emphasizing small, perfectly formed breasts and the outline of slim hips and long, elegant legs. She looked so proud and haughty with her head held so regally, as she stared boldly into his eyes. Just the way she had in the dining room the night he threatened to claim his nuptial rights.

That had been a mistake. He'd known it the moment he saw the flash of fear and vulnerability in her eyes.

The same vulnerability he saw now. And no matter how much she might deny it, he'd seen the same hurt in her eyes when she'd confronted him about his liaison with Jeanette. That had caused him to admit something he never thought to admit—he felt like a monster for hurting her, and, truth was, this was the only way he knew how to make amends.

So why was he finding it so hard to bridge this barrier that lay between them?

He wondered if she had any idea how tempting . . . how completely desirable she was. Or how much that fact bewildered and confused him.

"Earlier, you said something," he said. "Something I thought might be worth discussing."

"What?" she asked.

"About our meaning nothing to each other . . . that our marriage is only a sham." Nicholas's eyes darkened, and he took a step farther into the room.

Lily felt her heart skitter crazily and begin to pound hard at her throat.

"Perhaps we should make an agreement—here and now. So that each of us will know what to expect."

"An agreement?" she asked, her voice edged with suspicion. "What kind of agreement?"

"That's up to you," he said. He turned from her seeking eyes and walked toward the window that looked onto the front gallery and out toward the river. He rubbed his chin thoughtfully before turning back to face her.

"It isn't as if we have only one choice. We can try to make this a real marriage . . . or we can continue the guardianship just the way we have in the past. It was what your parents wanted. I chose marriage for expediency. Friendship would be a pleasant bonus, don't you think? Something we can continue to work on together?"

Lily's lips parted, and she frowned. Somehow this wasn't what she'd expected him to say. Nicholas was the kind of man she thought would storm into a woman's bedroom, sweep her up into his arms, and give her little choice about what she wanted.

"I . . . I don't know what to say," she said.

"But surely you know what you want?" he asked, turning and moving closer to her.

Lily couldn't move, and she couldn't seem to pull her gaze away from the intensity of his eyes.

"I . . . I suppose the one thing I've always wanted is a family. Like Mary and Theodore." She saw an immediate spark flare deep in his eyes at her words, and she wondered if she'd been too bold again.

"Children?" he murmured.

He was so close to her now that he could reach out and touch her if he wished. He stared down at her, his dark head bent. She could see the faint stubble of his beard and the slight quirk of amusement on his sensuous lips.

"I . . . well, I suppose."

"With me?"

"I . . ." Lily could feel her cheeks beginning to burn.

"Is that question so hard to answer? Or is it the prospect of getting with child that makes you hesitate?"

When his hand moved toward her, she tensed, making a quiet sound in her throat when he touched her. His fingers burned through the fabric of her gown, sending tingles along her arm as he traced his hand slowly upward toward her shoulder.

"Has any man ever touched you this way?" he whispered.

"No," she answered, her voice breathless and quiet. "Of course not." She found herself leaning toward him, wanting something she couldn't quite name.

He laughed softly, delighted with her response, and moved his fingers to the sensitive skin just below her collar-bone. His breath mingled with her hair as he trailed his fingers downward and brushed the back of his hand against her breast.

Lily gasped and closed her eyes.

"You've become a beautiful, bewitching woman, Lily," he murmured, pulling her into his arms.

He took her lips in a kiss that was both sensuous and unrelenting. She hadn't known what to expect. But it certainly wasn't this bittersweet assault on her senses. She felt the intimate invasion of his tongue, and she pulled away, breathing fast and hard.

Nicholas's eyes had grown languid and warm and as he looked into her face, he seemed puzzled and a bit amused.

"You've never been kissed before," he said, his words an assumption.

"Not . . . not like that," she stammered, backing away from him and the confusing warmth of his body. She couldn't seem to pull her gaze away from his mouth.

"Oh," he said teasingly. "But you *have* been kissed. As your husband, should I be jealous, or offended? Should I send detectives to Boston to discover who the culprit is?"

Lily blushed and shook her head, knowing he was teasing her, and yet unable to make herself smile.

Suddenly Nicholas grew very still, and his teasing demeanor changed. His eyes narrowed, and he leaned toward her, placing his fingers beneath her chin and forcing her to look at him.

"Or perhaps I have to look no farther than my own

house for the answer." His voice was cold and his gray
eyes even colder.

Lily frowned at him, uncertain at first what he meant.

"Oh," she said. "You mean . . . you mean Jared," she
whispered, her eyes growing bright.

"That's exactly who I mean." he said, his teeth clenched
together. "Well?"

He was so changeable. One moment he was kissing her,
touching her. Making her feel as if she were the only
woman in the world he wanted to be with. And the next
he could be cold and overbearing, his beautiful mouth
twisting sarcastically, his eyes hard and unrelenting.

How foolish she was to think he might change for her.
That he would change any part of his life just because she
had come into it.

Lily took a deep breath and pulled away from him. She
walked toward the fireplace, to put as much distance as
possible between them.

"I hardly think that you have the right to ask me such
a question, under the circumstances," she said.

"Under the circumstances?"

"Does this agreement you mentioned include the right
for you to continue seeing your mistress?"

She saw Nicholas's fists clench and his eyes narrow. He
reached toward the chair that separated them, and, for a
moment, she thought he actually meant to fling it across
the room.

He stared at her, his eyes burning with heat and anger,
his body taut and still.

Lily found herself holding her breath. Waiting . . .
expecting to feel his wrath in some way.

"Don't make the mistake of underestimating me, Lily,"
Nicholas said. His voice, in the quiet room, sounded omi-
nous and threatening. "The question here is not about
my conduct, but yours. I won't sit quietly by while my wife
and cousin—"

"There's nothing going on between Jared and me," Lily

said. "I made it clear to him from the beginning that I neither wanted nor needed a lover."

He seemed stunned by her frankness.

"Have there been lovers?" he asked.

Nicholas gritted his teeth. He'd never considered the possibility that Lily might already have found love. God, but no one had ever made him more furious or more frustrated than this girl.

Lily wanted to slap him for his rude assumption. But something . . . some deep instinct warned her not to. She could feel the tension in him, see it in his eyes. He reminded her of a wild animal, waiting to spring, and she sensed that he needed only one word to send him over the edge into some primitive state that made her shiver even to think about.

"I don't intend to answer that," she said. She slipped quickly past him and opened the bedroom door, holding her body behind it as if it might protect her from his wrath.

"By God," he muttered, "you are an impudent little . . ."

He started toward her before catching himself and taking a long, deep breath.

They stood staring at each other like two old enemies. Cold gray eyes meeting emerald fire.

"Well," he said, his voice danaerously soft, "we seem unable to reach an agreement in even the simplest terms."

"I'm not your property," she said, sounding much like that young girl who faced him all those years ago outside this very room. "I'm afraid you made a mistake thinking I couldn't see through this agreement. Did you think I'd be willing to smooth the way for you to continue seeing your mistress more openly? No, Nicholas, I'm afraid you'll just have to sneak around."

He stood for a moment, his eyes boring into hers. That wasn't the reason he wanted an agreement. He knew, even if she couldn't, that it was even more selfish than that.

He wanted Lily. Wanted her in his arms and in his bed.

He wanted to possess her physically and emotionally. Sometimes, God help him, he thought he wanted her very soul.

Without a word he walked through the door, and Lily slammed it hard behind him, setting the wall sconces rattling and sending an echo throughout the house.

Halfway expecting him to barge back through, she quickly locked and bolted the door.

"Damn you," she whispered. "Damn you."

Lily thought she'd never felt so alone or so unwanted.

For one brief moment, he had made her feel like a woman. A wanted, desirable woman. And in an instant he took it all away.

It had been a trick. Just a cruel, heartless trick to make her feel secure so he could continue his trysts with the beautiful Widow Mireaux while his dutiful wife remained silent.

She couldn't hold back the tears of humiliation any longer. And as the tears came, she slid to the floor, feeling the coolness of the wood floor against her hips and legs. Then, like a child, she lay down with her knees drawn up, her sobs muffled against the silk of her dressing gown.

The next morning Lily avoided Nicholas altogether until Jared came to call for her. She was trying to leave the house quickly when Nicholas appeared out of nowhere, obviously still in a brooding, confrontational mood.

"So . . . you are intent on doing this, even though you know I don't approve?" he asked coldly, glancing at Lily, then Jared.

Jared shrugged his shoulders, the smile on his face disappearing as he realized Nicholas's anger.

"There's no reason for you to be rude to Jared," Lily snapped. "He is merely being kind to me by showing me the city."

Nicholas focused his gaze back toward Lily, taking in

her stylish butter-colored gown and the way it clung to her slender waist and rounded breasts.

"We'll be riding in an open carriage. Surely you can't find fault with that?"

"I don't like it," he said, glaring at her.

"Really? Why, my dear husband, I should think at your age, you must have found many things you don't like. Just as I have. But that doesn't mean you can change them. We must simply learn to endure. Patience is a virtue—that's one of the most important things I learned from the Sisters in Boston."

Nicholas growled in frustration. He never thought the expensive education he had procured for her would be thrown back in his face in such a saucy manner.

"I can see you've already made up your mind," he said.

"Yes . . . I have."

"Then I must insist that today be the last foray the two of you make together for a period of time. Do you understand my meaning, Jared?"

"Completely, cousin," Jared drawled.

"I'm sure you'll agree that an everyday thing will only cause talk."

"You should know," Lily said beneath her breath.

"What?" Nicholas asked, glaring at her.

"Nothing," she said, with a toss of her head.

"There's one other thing," Nicholas said.

"Yes?" Lily said, rolling her eyes with impatience.

"I heard that you and Jared visited your old home under the hill."

"That's right," Lily said. "He was kind enough to take me, although he warned me that you might not be pleased." She glanced briefly at Jared, smiling at his look of discomfort.

"You're right. I am not pleased," Nicholas said. "You are not to go there again, under any circumstances. Under-the-Hill can be a very dangerous place."

Lily stared into his eyes before slowly letting her lashes

dip and close. She could see from his stance and the glint in his eyes that Nicholas was aching for another argument. And she didn't intend getting into another one. Certainly not in front of Jared and where the servants were bound to hear.

"Shall we go, Jared?, she said, taking his arm. "I swear, I can hardly wait to be out in the fresh air."

Nicholas stood in the hallway, clenching and unclenching his jaw as he watched them go. When he heard Lily's laughter from outside, he whirled and stalked into the library.

"Dammit," he growled, slamming the door behind him.

Outside Lily and Jared waited while one of the kitchen girls brought a basket and placed it in the buggy.

"Well," Jared said, glancing at the cloth-covered container. "A picnic. You didn't mention that we were going on a picnic."

"We aren't," Lily said. "We're taking these things down to the riverfront . . . to Miss Fran."

"Lily," Jared said, turning toward her with a start, "you can't. You heard what Nicholas just said."

"Nicholas will learn that he cannot tell me where to go. Now, if you don't wish to take me, I'll understand. Just say so now, and I shall drive myself." Her eyes were steady and cool, giving away none of the turmoil she felt inside. She wasn't about to admit to Jared how unnerved Nicholas made her feel. With his growling, blustering ways, he made her feel like a child. But if she admitted that, she knew Jared would not take her for sure.

Her bluff worked. Finally, Jared looked away, grumbling beneath his breath as he moved to help her up into the carriage.

"Mon Dieu," he muttered as he slapped the reins against the horse's rump. "I can't believe I have let you talk me into this yet again.

Lily laughed and reached over to tweak Jared's cheek.

"You like it—you know you do," Lily said. "You enjoy the adventure as much as I do," she said.

Jared turned, his gaze growing warm as he let himself finally take in every luscious inch of her. Was she so innocent that she had no idea what her smiles and laughter did to him? What the touch of her hand against his face made him want to do?

Or were these games she played meant to tell him exactly the opposite?

Nicholas didn't deserve a woman like Lily. She needed a man to laugh with, not a father figure who would stifle her spirit and trample upon her sensitive heart.

Chapter 11

Before going down the hallway, Nicholas watched them leave. Slamming the door to the library, he stalked across the carpeted floor like a caged animal. He pulled book after book from the shelves, finally dropping one onto the floor and cursing as he bent to retrieve it.

The door opened, and he turned to see Mrs. Lloyd watching him with an expression of concern.

"It isn't my place to intrude," she said.

"But you probably will anyway," he said wryly, not bothering to look up from the book in his hand.

"Well, you must admit, sir, we've had more door-slamming in this house the last week than we've had in a lifetime."

Nicholas sighed and walked to the desk.

"Come in, Mrs. Lloyd."

There was a certain look of self-satisfaction on the housekeeper's face when she closed the door quietly and came to sit in a chair near his desk.

Despite his earlier anger, Nicholas couldn't help smiling. Mrs. Lloyd had been here since he was a boy, and her attempts to convince everyone that she wasn't a busybody didn't fool him at all. She'd always been interested in every aspect of his and Mary's lives. And Nicholas knew it was because she cared about them so deeply. She'd never had children of her own, and even though he and Mary were adults when their mother and father died, Mrs. Lloyd had willingly taken on the task of mothering.

Nicholas sighed.

"I never thought I'd admit this," he said, with a self-deprecating smile, "but I'm afraid I've run up against something here that I don't quite know how to handle."

"Miss Lily," she said with a wise nod of her head.

"Yes indeed," Nicholas said, leaning back, propping a booted foot on the clesk. "Miss Lily," he added tiredly. He rubbed his fingers against his forehead where an ache had started the moment he saw Jared waiting for Lily.

"She's had a hard life," Mrs. Lloyd said softly.

"I know that," Nicholas said, frowning. "All I've done is give her a home that any woman would envy, renovate the ferry and her old home, and ensure that no matter what happens she need never want for anything."

"You're a good man, Nicholas St. James. You take after your poor sainted mother, you do. But your goodness is not in question here."

For a moment he glanced at her with raised brows, Then, despite himself, Nicholas grinned and slid his foot off the desk. He propped his elbows on the smooth walnut surface and leaned toward the woman sitting across from him.

"And what is in question here, Mrs. Lloyd? I wish someone would kindly tell me."

The woman's eyes widened innocently, and she shrugged.

"Come on," he said. "Out with it."

"I just happen to think you might catch more flies with honey than you can with vinegar," she said.

"Ha," he said, whirling around in the chair and standing up with a quick restless energy. "I'm afraid it's going to take more than honey for this one."

"And another thing—if you'd married the daughter of one of the Natchez Nabobs, you might have a wife who would look the other way while you're traipsin' around town with that Widow Mireaux. They grow up thinkin' that's the way life's supposed to be. But this girl, now, she isn't like that. She was raised up in a God-fearing household to believe that when a man and woman marry they cleave only to one another."

Nicholas's hands were at his hips, and he was staring with disbelieving eyes at Mrs. Lloyd.

She bit her lips and looked up sheepishly at him from beneath her lashes.

"If I've said too much, then I'm sorry," she muttered. "But that's just the way of it. I hate to see the two of you makin' such a mess of things, that's all." Her eyes flashed feistily at her employer.

Nicholas muttered something beneath his breath and waved his hand toward her.

"It's all right," he said. "There's nothing wrong with speaking your mind. Not that you've ever been shy about doing that before," he added with a grin.

"And while I'm at it, if you've any sense at all left in that head of yours, you've got to get her away from Jared. The boy is no good for anything except makin' trouble. He's lazy and spoiled. I don't know why you've put up with him all these years anyway."

"Believe me, sometimes I ask myself that same question," Nicholas said. He rubbed his chin and walked across the room to stare out the front window. "But he's family, so I don't have much choice in the matter."

But Mrs. Lloyd's words troubled him. They were the same things he'd been telling himself. The same he'd tried to tell Lily. Only she wouldn't listen. Hell, he didn't know what it took to get the chit to listen to reason.

But he was going to find out.

"Oh dear," he heard Mrs. Lloyd say behind him. "Now I've gone and said too much. You're upset with me."

"No, not with you, Mrs. Lloyd," he assured her. "I'm grateful for your concern. Sometimes during the course of the week, the only people I see are cotton brokers, lawyers, and people like Jared, all of them trying to see what they can scrape from the St. James barrel. It's refreshing to have someone tell me the truth for a change, especially when I know they're doing it because they care about me."

Mrs. Lloyd blushed and stood up, brushing her skirt self-consciously.

"Thank you," she murmured.

"No," he said, taking her arm and walking with her to the door. "Thank you, Mrs. Lloyd. You know, I think perhaps I'll take your advice about catching those flies with honey. I'll be back this afternoon."

When he walked down the hallway, he was whistling.

By the time he reached the waterfront area and the empty house beneath the bluffs, he was not quite so optimistic. He was certain he'd find the carriage that Jared and Lily were in, but it was nowhere to be seen.

"Where the hell are they?" he wondered aloud. He'd known by the innocent look on Lily's beautiful face that she had no intentions of obeying his orders about staying away from this place. But where was she?

Lily stood in the buggy, clapping her hands and squealing with delight as she watched the horses race around the well-kept Pharsalia Course, which lay just outside town near St. Catherine's Creek.

Jared's gaze took in the blush on her cheeks, the excitement in her slender body, and the way her eyes lit as she watched the sleek animals reach out with their powerful legs.

"You enjoy the horses," he said. "I knew you would. That's why I wanted to come here before we take the basket to your friend."

"Riding was one of my biggest joys as a child and also later in Boston. I'm so glad you brought me here, Jared.

I've never seen such beautiful horses. And the course is simply splendid."

"You should enjoy yourself more," he said, pulling her down onto the seat beside him. "Stop being so serious. Just because old Nicholas is that way doesn't mean you have to be."

"I don't want to talk about Nicholas," she said with a determined shake of her head. "Not today. Not here beneath these beautiful old trees with the sounds of the crowd cheering the horses on."

"Good," he said. "Then we shan't." He waved to a passing waiter, who carried trays of drinks among the crowd. He removed two glasses, handing one of them to Lily.

"The track is owned by the Jockey Club," Jared said, sipping the champagne and gazing with narrowed, interested eyes at Lily. "Its members are composed of some of Mississippi's most aristocratic families."

"I used to watch men race Under-the-Hill," she said. "But it was never like this."

"I would think not," Jared agreed with that faint air of superiority. "Those *mule races* can hardly be equated with what takes place here. Pharsalia has the most skillful horsemen in the South. And the fastest thoroughbreds."

Lily sipped her champagne quickly. Too quickly. She found it went straight to her head, and she giggled as she leaned toward Jared.

"You know what I'd like?" she asked, her eyes shining brightly with enthusiasm.

"What?" he said. "Whatever it is, I swear, I'd love to be the one to hand it to you on a silver platter."

The bubbling drink had dulled her instincts a bit. She hardly noticed the gleam in Jared's eye or the intimate, almost-seductive tone of his voice.

"I'd love to race." She turned to him, and the excitement on her face could hardly be contained.

"Race?" he asked. "You mean bet on a race, or—"

"No, silly," she said, laughing. "I mean *ride* in the race."

Jared laughed. "Oh, no," he said, shaking his head. "That would never be allowed. No females and no Negroes allowed." With a teasing lift of his brow, he added, "Now there are events afterward where commoners and free Negroes can race their horses and mules."

"Oh, you men are so certain of your superiority, aren't you?" She crossed her arms beneath her breasts and leaned back to gaze through narrowed eyes toward the racecourse. "I could do it, you know," she mused thoughtfully. "I'm tall enough to pass for a man. And slender enough so that I might disguise myself."

"Lily," Jared warned, sitting up straighter. But his eyes glittered with interest. "You can't be serious. Can you imagine the scandal it would cause if anyone ever discovered—"

"No one need ever know," she said. "Except you and me. And of course I'd never want Nicholas to know. He has enough complaints against me as it is."

As she spoke, her eyes twinkled at the prospect of playing such a trick on the snobbish horse-racing aristocrats.

"Forget it," Jared said. He reached for the reins, preparing to drive away.

"You could help me," she said, pulling at his arm. "You know everyone here. All you have to do is find someone who needs a rider. Perhaps pay one of the grooms and slip me in just before the race starts."

"No, Lily," Jared said, maneuvering the carriage through the crowd.

"Please," she said. She clasped her hands around his arm, leaning against him as she looked up into his face with a teasing smile. "Please, please! please. It would be ever so much fun if those old spoilsports knew their well-trained jockeys had been beaten by a woman."

Jared glanced toward her, enjoying the feel of her hands on his muscles and loving the look of excitement that danced in her emerald eyes.

She excited him. Made him want to do anything she asked. Just to see that look in her eyes.

"Well . . ."

"You'll do it?" she squealed.

"It might be arranged," he said, finally, once they were out on the main road and headed back toward Natchez. "But what about Nicholas? He's bound to hear about it sooner or later. Everything that happens in this town has a way of getting out. And believe me, he won't be amused."

Lily shrugged. The champagne was beginning to wear off, and she felt a quick stab of apprehension. It was one thing to goad her husband and to talk boldly to him about his mistress. It was quite another to make a spectacle of herself in front of his neighbors and friends. She would be treading on dangerous ground.

"Well, I can at least think about it, can't I?" she asked, her expression growing thoughtful.

Nicholas was just at the top of the bluffs, intending to head back home, when he saw the carriage coming. Neither Jared nor Lily was looking his way, but seemed deep in conversation.

Without really knowing why, he pulled his horse into a stand of trees at the top of the hill. When the carriage moved by and turned down toward the waterfront, he clasped his fingers tightly on the reins, causing his horse to move and quiver in anticipation of his master's next move.

"By God, I was right," Nicholas swore. "She would defy me again, and in broad daylight."

He didn't stop to reason or to think. As his impatience at not finding her had grown, he'd quite forgotten all Mrs. Lloyd's wise advice and his own intention to be reasonable and calm.

But the sight of Lily's bright head so close to Jared's and the murmur of their laughter when they passed was more than he could take.

He pulled his mount around and back toward the hill.

Chapter 12

Nicholas rode slowly along Silver Street, being careful to maneuver his horse behind buildings as he went. There was no sense tipping his hand until he was ready for Lily and Jared to see him. He stopped at the boardwalk in front of a storefront with a sign reading Cheap Cash Store. Lily's house was on a corner lot across the way.

For a moment he lounged beside the door, mingling with other men who wandered in and out of the saloons and stores. But he needn't have worried about being seen—Jared and Lily seemed too intent on their own conversation to suspect that someone was watching them.

Nicholas clenched his jaw tightly when he saw Jared reach into the back of the carriage and lift out a heavy basket covered with a dainty linen.

A twinge of anger and frustration nagged at him. And he felt something else, too. It was disappointment that slammed hard in his chest. Disbelief that Lily had actually lied to him about her relationship with Jared. Somehow, despite her blatant dislike of Nicholas, he had believed her when she told him that nothing improper was going on between his cousin and her.

What he was seeing certainly looked like more than friendship. To Nicholas, who was an expert at arranging quiet, out-of-the-way assignations, it looked very much like the perfect place for a secret afternoon rendezvous.

A growl rose up from his throat, causing several passersby to turn and stare, then hurry into the safety of one of the stores. Nicholas didn't notice. All he could see, all he could think about was Lily's deceit. By God, she intended making a cuckold of him with his own cousin while she lied straight to his face. Almost daring him to do something about it.

"Then do something, I will," he growled. He took the boardwalk along the storefront in three long strides, and when he hit the dusty street he was running.

Lily heard the sound of footsteps behind her and turned to see Nicholas's face in a blur. The next thing she knew she was being lifted forcibly from the carriage and swung up into his powerful arms.

Her quiet cry and the sound of his heavy breathing mingled together in one loud rush.

"Nicholas! What . . . what are you doing?" she squealed, flailing against his chest and shoulders. "Put me down!"

"Is this the way you repay my trust?" he asked, shaking her until tendrils of fiery curls fell over her eyes, causing her to blink in amazement.

Nicholas was already furious, and the look of guilt on Jared's pale face made him want to do something desperate. It was a feeling not exactly foreign to him. He'd been involved in enough fights and duels to recognize this heat within him—the boiling blood brought on by pride and masculine ego.

"Now, Nicholas," Jared began, placing the basket on the porch. "This isn't what it seems. Lily here . . ."

"I don't even want to hear my wife's name on your lips," Nicholas barked. "At least be man enough to take responsibility for what's happening here."

Lily pushed at his shoulders, but his arms didn't budge.

"This is still my house," she managed, her voice breathless from her struggles. "And you aren't welcome here."

"Everything you have belongs to me," he said, staring straight into her face. "Or have you forgotten that small detail? You're coming home with me."

Lily had never seen him so angry. This was no teasing game he played. He was deathly, dangerously serious.

She swallowed hard, glancing around at Jared, and saw by the look on his face that he was as worried as she was.

"I . . . I will not," she whispered, her eyes wide and anxious.

She heard Nicholas's muttered expletive and felt his big body tense. Then, as quickly and as efficiently as a cat catching a mouse, he had turned her over and hauled her up over his shoulder as if she were a sack of cotton.

Lily screamed and grabbed the back of his shirt. He was walking quickly, and the sight of the ground moving swiftly beneath her made her dizzy.

Her squeals of outrage attracted quite a large crowd of men, most of whom obviously enjoyed the sight of Nicholas St. James carrying his very beautiful young bride down the street.

There was raucous laughter and a few shouts of encouragement to Nicholas as he continued resolutely down the street toward his horse.

"That's the way to do it, Mr. St. James," someone shouted. "Got to show 'em who's boss right from the beginnin'."

"Nicholas . . ." she groaned. She felt as if her ribs might actually crack. "You . . . you devil," she screamed, kicking at him. "Put me down."

But he only tightened his arm around her thighs. She couldn't believe it when she found herself being flung over the saddle of a horse.

"No!" she screamed, kicking. "Please, Nicholas," she

added finally. "You can't mean to make me ride home in this position."

"Will you behave yourself then?" Nicholas stood in front of her, holding her in place and letting her legs dangle across the horse. He was breathing heavily, and there was fire in his eyes. "And stop fighting me?"

"I hate you," she hissed, staring straight into his glittering eyes.

"Well, then I guess that answers my question," he said, starting to swing himself up into the saddle behind her.

"Wait," she said. "Wait . . ."

"Yes?" he drawled.

"All right . . . I promise . . . I won't scream anymore. And I'll explain everything. Just let me ride in the carriage with Jared back to the house."

"You can't be serious," he said coldly, pulling the horses's reins into his hands. "Do you really think I would let you climb back into that carriage with Jared here in front of all these people? You may ride behind me on my horse, or you may ride the way you are, slung over the saddle like a sack of feed. I assure you I don't care which method you choose."

"Damn you and your insufferable pride," she muttered, struggling to a sitting position.

"Uh-uh," he said. "I'm sure the Sisters in Boston would not approve of such language."

Jared drove by in the carriage, glancing defiantly toward Nicholas. His smooth cheeks were stained crimson and his eyes glittered with resentment.

"Take the carriage home!" Nicholas growled. "I'll speak with you later."

"Did you leave the basket?" Lily called to Jared.

"Yes," Jared replied. "Although someone will probably steal it."

Nicholas swung Lily around behind him and pulled his horse's head back toward the hill and town. There was still a great deal of laughter and speculation among the men

in the streets, and a few snickered remarks here and there.
Nicholas ignored them, but Lily buried her head against
his back, feeling more humiliated than she had ever felt
in her life.

She noted that Nicholas seemed in no hurry to get home.
He probably wanted to avoid seeing Jared and was giving
his cousin plenty of time to leave the carriage and be gone.

She shivered. What would he do to the young man? She
knew Nicholas had a certain reputation. But surely he
wouldn't challenge his own cousin to a duel over such an
insignificant matter? And surely not when she explained
why she had defied him.

Instead of letting Lily off at the back steps, Nicholas
rode the horse into the stables. Two stableboys were there
cleaning stalls, but one quick order from Nicholas sent
them scurrying outside.

He reached up to help Lily down, and as soon as her
feet touched the ground, she backed away from him.

"You will not defy me again, Lily," he said. He stood
with his hands on his hips, glaring at her.

"I warn you, I am not one of your pretty young Boston
bucks, willing to put up with anything just to have you
near."

The entire experience had left Lily shaken. And though
she didn't want Nicholas to know it, she was near tears as
she stood facing him, her hair disheveled, her beautiful
new gown twisted and wrinkled.

"And I will not be humiliated," she said, her breath
coming in quiet little gasps. "Damn you, I will not."

"I've warned you, Lily," he said. "Shall I also resort to
washing your mouth out with soap?"

"I won't let you do this to me," she hissed.

His grin was filled with arrogance and contempt. It sent
sparks of fury rushing through every inch of Lily's body.

With hardly a thought to the consequences, Lily hurled
herself at him, fists clenched as she tried to pummel him.
It was something that no amount of high-class Boston

schooling could wrest from her soul—that childhood instinct to defend herself. On the waterfront it had been a necessity.

Her blows glanced off Nicholas, and he caught her in his arms and crushed her hard against him, quickly rendering her helpless as he pinned her arms behind her.

"Is this what you want?" he asked. "Do you smile and flirt and chase after my cousin for this?"

Lily gasped when his mouth closed over hers in a hard, searing kiss. And for the briefest moment she couldn't resist kissing him back.

Lily could feel the fire of his lips burning like molten steel. The heat reached down deep into her chest and stomach and caused her legs to grow weak and shaky.

It ended just as abruptly as it had begun, but not before she looked up into Nicholas's eyes and saw that he was well aware of the way it had affected her. And that made her even angrier and more frustrated.

He smiled. Only the slightest hint of a smile. But one so meaningful and knowing that Lily found herself wanting to run from it.

He released her and stepped slowly away. There in the dimness of the stables, they glared at one another, like two wary cats.

"You are my wife . . ." he said, his voice quiet in the gloom.

Lily shivered as the sound of it rippled over her skin. He made the words sound like a threat—as if she were his possession.

". . . and you will do as I say. Have I made myself clear?"

She lifted her head and even as tears glittered in her eyes, she would not let herself look away.

"Abundantly clear," she said through gritted teeth. "You've proven that you can haul me through the streets and humiliate me. And I suppose you've proven that a man can force his wife to do anything he wishes. But he can't force her to like it. And I think that's what makes you so angry . . . and so mean."

She whirled around, skirts rustling against the straw-covered floor. With her head held high, she rushed out of the stables as Nicholas, open-mouthed, stared after her.

He closed his eyes and sighed heavily before slamming his fist against the side of a stall.

"Dammit," he muttered. "Damn this sorry thing called marriage to hell."

Chapter 13

By midafternoon it had begun to rain, a heavy, drumming rain that pounded against the rooftop and blew across the outside gallery floors. The wind came off the river, bringing with it the scent of fish and wet, muddy earth.

Lily spent the rest of the day in her room, alternately watching the rain and sewing on a sampler that she had begun in Boston. For a moment she wished Mrs. Shimway had stayed. At least there would be someone else in the house she could talk to.

She had halfway expected Nicholas to seek her out after her stormy exit from the barn. She was quickly learning that her husband usually had the last word.

His kiss, so unexpected, so intense, had shaken her. She couldn't forget that kiss, or the way he held her so tightly, as if he could force her to his will.

He could; she knew that. He was bigger . . . stronger.

Sometimes, Lily wondered why he hadn't already forced his way into her bedroom. He had threatened it. And he certainly seemed intent on letting her know just how easily it could be done.

Without remorse. Without emotion. Without love.

Lily sighed and pushed her needlework aside. She rose for what seemed like the hundredth time and walked to the windows to watch the wind dashing rain against them.

In Natchez, the rain could stop tomorrow, or it could go on for days. When she was a child, rainy days were spent repairing cables and rotting boards at the ferry, or inside the house quilting with her mother or putting up food supplies for the winter.

"Oh, Mother," Lily whispered. She leaned her head against the cool glass pane. "What shall I do? How I wish you were here to tell me what I should do about this predicament I find myself in. It was your wish for me to be with him, yours and Papa's, but I swear, I cannot see how you could put me in this man's hands."

She wished she had some friends. She had so many friends in Boston that she rarely ever spent an afternoon alone. And there were often young people in Mary and Theodore's home from dinner until midnight.

But now she was a wife. Things were different. Life was different here.

Aimlessly she walked about the room, stopping to open the armoire door and trace her fingers over the various materials of her gowns.

Perhaps now would be a good time to have a new wardrobe made. And since the date for the summer party had been set for next week, she could decide on a dress for that as well, although she had no idea what color she would choose. As Nicholas's returning bride and the guest of honor, she knew she would most likely be the center of attention. And no doubt, of much speculation. She wanted to be comfortable, but more than that she wanted to look presentable.

She turned to her desk, intending to sketch a couple of ideas when she heard the door across the hall open and close. She thought she caught the slightest hint of cigar smoke and heard muted footsteps on the hall carpet, then heavier steps as someone ran down the stairs.

She knew by the way the back door slammed that Nicholas was still in his dark mood, and she knew it was because of her.

Quickly she hurried out into the hallway and toward the back gallery, making certain to keep behind the curtains so that he would not see her watching him.

She felt a little tingle of pain and apprehension in the pit of her stomach as she watched him walk out into the rain and stand for a moment gazing up at the dark, turbulent sky. He seemed to welcome the rain, actually to accept the wind and storm that swept over him and tousled his dark hair.

Lily could see a bottle in his hand that hung by his side, and she could see wreaths of smoke encircle his head from his cigar.

She closed her eyes and breathed deeply as the smoke spiraled upward toward where she hid. Then it faded away, leaving only the pungent odor to tease her nostrils and throat.

When she opened her eyes, Nicholas was walking toward the stables. She squinted through the darkness and the rain and saw one of the stableboys bring his horse out.

The tawny-colored horse, obviously eager for exercise, whinnied and turned when Nicholas pulled himself up into the saddle. They made a handsome pair, those two, she thought. Two strong, well-muscled specimens. Each filled with such life and energy that it was almost palpable.

The horse galloped out the brick-lined driveway and through the gate. Nicholas waved the liquor bottle high over his head, and Lily thought she actually heard him shout something.

Suddenly, all the anger and resentment she'd felt earlier drained from her. She felt lifeless . . . hopeless.

He was going to Jeanette. She knew it with every inch of her body and with every instinct she'd ever felt.

"I don't know why it should matter to me," she said, hurrying back down the hall to her bedroom. She slammed the door behind her and was surprised to feel tears burning behind her eyes.

"And why should I be crying?" she fumed, angrily wiping her eyes. "It isn't as if I want the odious man. I certainly don't care who he goes to," she added with a toss of her head, "as long as he leaves me alone."

Jeanette wasn't expecting Nicholas, although she hadn't stopped hoping he would come. Every night she would go through the same ritual—bathing in various, expensive bath oils, having her personal maid style her hair, then picking out a special dress that Nicholas had admired, or even one of the new ones she'd just had made.

But he hadn't come. She'd sat alone waiting and fuming, sometimes crying. But it hadn't brought him to her, not since that day when he paced her floor, wondering aloud what he was to do with his high-spirited young wife.

And now he was here. Looking masculine and dangerous and causing her insides to quiver when she looked into his fierce eyes.

He stood in the doorway of her bedroom with one hand braced against the doorjamb, the other holding a bottle that appeared almost empty.

"Nicholas," she managed finally. She hardly knew what to make of his condition, or of the terrible dark look in his eyes.

"I hope I'm not intruding," he said with a polite nod. "I realize it's been a while."

"No . . ." she said, walking across the room to him. "You could never intrude here, you know that. My home is yours—I've told you that many times."

"Yes," he said. "You have."

Why was there such sadness in his voice when he said those words?

Jeanette moved closer to him, her movements causing the edges of her dressing gown to fall away from her breasts.

Nicholas didn't speak. She had learned long ago that he was not a man of pretense. He came here for one thing and both of them knew what it was.

The look in his heated gray eyes confirmed that. And it sent a spiral of pleasure rushing through her entire body.

He reached out lazily and with one finger caught at the edge of her gown just where her breasts came together.

Jeanette shuddered and leaned toward him.

"I'm so glad you came," she whispered.

It took no more than seconds for his skilled fingers to touch and torment her trembling body into a state of liquid heat.

His own arousal was obvious, and when he dropped the bottle to the floor and pulled her into his arms, she welcomed the feel of him through her silken clothes. She could taste the liquor on his tongue.

Jeanette knew how to please a man. It was the one skill she had with which to fight his beautiful river bride. And tonight, she intended to make full use of that knowledge.

She reached anxiously to the buttons of his shirt, her eyes hungry as she slid the material away from his broad shoulders. Then she deliberately pressed her full, aching breasts against his bare chest.

Impatiently, Nicholas smoothed his hands down her waist to pull her hips against him. His kiss was hard and hungry. Angry almost.

For a moment Jeanette pulled away, looking up into his eyes with a questioning gaze.

"Nicholas?" she asked. "What is it? Is something wrong?"

"Nothing," he growled, picking her up in his arms and carrying her toward the bed. "I want you, that's all. Right here . . . right now."

She couldn't repress the ripple of pleasure that raced through her at his words. He might never have said he loved her. But his intensity, his hot eagerness gave her such hope. A man couldn't possibly feel this and not love the woman just a tiny bit, could he?

"Yes," she whispered. "Oh yes." Snuggling her face against his neck, she let her tongue touch his ear and laughed when she him felt shiver. She had to make him forget that wild river child he had married. It was her last hope.

He took her with no gentle words of love, with no preliminary caresses or teasing as he sometimes did. He was like a man possessed as his body took hers again and again. For hours he tortured her with pleasure until she quite forgot that it was she who had intended doing that to him.

And when it was over, he swung his long muscular legs over the side of the bed and walked to retrieve his clothes.

Jeanette watched him lanquidly for a moment until she realized his intention. Then she sat up in bed, her eyes wide and puzzled.

"Nicky?" she asked. "You can't be leaving? Not yet?"

"I'm restless, *chérie,*" he said, not bothering to turn and look at her.

"Restless?" she said, her voice disbelieving. "After what just happened between us?"

He turned back, his eyes dispassionate as he pulled his shirt back on. For a moment his features softened, and a faint smile pulled at his sensuous lips.

He walked to the bed and bent to place a light kiss on her mouth.

"I'm sorry," he said. "It has nothing to do with you. You were quite bewitching, as usual."

"Then what?"

"I don't know," he said, shrugging his shoulders. "Just a bad mood. I'm not fit company for anyone tonight. You go to sleep. I'll see you soon."

"But . . ."

He grabbed the empty bottle from the floor, placing it on a table as he walked toward the door. The bottle rocked back and forth as he went through the house and out the door, like a murmuring little ghost reminding her of his absence.

The sound filled the room, until it was all Jeanette could hear besides the sound of her agitated breathing. She covered her ears, then leapt from bed and picked up the bottle, turning and flinging it with a crash against the marble fireplace.

Outside, Nicholas walked quickly to where he had tied his horse. Then he stopped and leaned his head back, taking a deep gulp of the fresh rain-scented air. The drops that hit his face felt cool and soothing. But inside he felt sick and disgusted with himself.

He'd used Jeanette. Not in the way they had always used each other, for pure, uncomplicated physical pleasure. He had used her selfishly, to try to escape his uncomfortable feelings.

It hadn't worked. He still felt just as restless, just as tense as he had before. And he knew the reason why. Jeanette wasn't the one he'd wanted to hold. To kiss. He had used her body as a substitute for the one he really wanted.

Lily. His beautiful, seductive bride, Lily.

He could no longer pretend it wasn't true.

"What the hell are you doing?" he asked himself.

His horse whinnied and turned its head back toward its master.

He patted the horse and shook his head. "It's me. Somehow I've lost sight of what it is I want. I thought I knew."

He glanced back toward the small white house, still aglow with lights.

"Everything seemed so simple once," he whispered. "I thought I could have it all. Instead, I seem to have nothing. Absolutely nothing."

Chapter 14

The rain kept Lily awake most of the night. She wouldn't even permit herself to think it could be something else haunting her sleep. That she might be awake because she was listening for the sound of Nicholas's footsteps in the hallway.

She couldn't be sure if he came home at all. She certainly didn't remember hearing him. And as curious as she was, she had no intention of asking Mrs. Lloyd about it.

The next morning, she left the house early, calling out to Mrs. Lloyd that she'd be at the dressmaker's most of the morning.

In town she left the carriage and hurried along the street toward the small, exclusive dress shop. Rain still peppered the streets, and the wind blew her hair about her face, snatching curls from beneath her straw bonnet. It was a miserable day, fit for neither man nor beast, but somehow Lily reveled in it.

She loved Natchez in the spring. And this spring storm held all the scents and the sounds that she remembered so well from her childhood.

All morning long she'd been filled with an odd sense of longing. While usually that wouldn't bother her, today it did. She was tired of feeling out of sorts. Tired of being angry and frustrated. Today she'd like nothing more than to spend a few hours laughing and talking with friends, the way she had in Boston. She'd been so anxious to return to Natchez. And now that she was here, she couldn't believe she was actually missing Boston and all its familiar possibilities.

Inside the dress shop, Lily was met by Madame Duvall, the proprietor and designer. She'd made dresses for Lily before, but Lily's size and shape had changed since then.

"Ah, Mrs. St. James," the petite woman said. Mrs. Duvall lifted a gold-rimmed lorgnette to her sparkling brown eyes as her assessing glance moved over Lily's figure from head to toe.

"Charming," she murmured, walking around Lily. "Absolutely stunning. Creating something for you is going to be a joy. Not like some of the others," she said, with a toss of her graying curls toward the rooms at the back. "So many young women your age seem to care more about the sweets table than they do about keeping a perfect figure."

Lily shrugged her shoulders and smiled, not sure what she should say. Her figure, if it was pleasing to anyone, had little to do with what she ate or what she wanted. It just was, and she supposed she should be grateful that she had inherited her mother's slender lines and fine bone structure.

As Madame Duvall motioned her toward the back of the shop, Lily could hear giggles from the other rooms. A curtain covered a doorway that led from the dressing room to a salon that she remembered as having panels of mirrors and gilded French chairs.

The dressmaker hustled Lily into one of the dressing rooms, handing her a gown of simple, unadorned material. "Put this on my dear and we shall go from there. I need to get new measurements for you, then we'll look at materials and patterns. I understand there's to be a party in your honor. Will you be needing something for that?"

"Yes, I suppose I will," Lily said.

"*Trés bon,*" the woman said. "It shall be my honor to comply, with pleasure." Madame Duvall stepped out of the dressing room. "Girls. Come quickly. I need you to pin up the waist and hem for Mrs. St. James."

One of the young seamstresses came into the room with Lily, nodding her head shyly, but not speaking as she helped her undress and slip the fitting dress over her head. Then without a word, she began to pin the fabric about Lily's waist.

Lily could hear Mrs. Duvall talking to other customers in the next room. There was the sound of giggling and an older woman's lower voiced reprimand.

"Stand still, Claudia, and let the girl finish the hem. This dress absolutely must be ready for Mrs. Mireaux's soiree. There will no doubt be several eligible young men there, and I certainly want them to see you looking your best."

"Oh, Mother," the girl said, her voice whining slightly. "I don't know why you insist that I go. You know full well I'm not interested in marrying. I'm having far too much fun for that." The girl was giggling. "Besides, the most interesting man in Natchez is already married.

The mother hissed and lowered her voice.

"Stop that this moment! It isn't funny to joke about such things, especially when I know the man you mean is Mr. St. James. And indeed taken."

"Very well taken," the girl said, giggling even louder. "Considering he has a wife *and* a mistress."

Lily felt her face burning and looked down to see the young seamstress's quick glance upward at her. But she was powerless to do anything to stop the conversation that continued next door.

"Claudia! A girl your age should not know about such things, much less discuss them in public."

"Well, it's the truth, Mama," she girl said. "Do you think we girls don't discuss such things when our mothers aren't about? Besides, I hear that his new wife is so gauche and wild that it's no wonder he still visits the Widow Mireaux. A fair little hoyden, they say."

"Well, I can tell you, you're wrong about that."

Lily recognized the voice defending her as Madame Duvall's. At the woman's protective tone, she felt a lump forming in her throat.

"I know Lily St. James, and she is far from being a hoyden. In fact, she's here in the shop, so I'd advise you to keep your voices down. She is a beautiful, gracious young woman who just returned from a very prestigious school in Boston. And if I don't miss my guess, she's going to turn Natchez on its ear . . . just the way she did Boston's high society, I hear."

The seamstress was in front of Lily, and now she glanced up at her with a sweet, encouraging smile.

Lily heard the mother's snort of displeasure and the girl's slightly nervous laugh. Then she could hear them moving about as if they were leaving.

"The dress will be ready day after tomorrow, Mrs. Gray," Madame Duvall was saying.

"See that it is, Madame Duvall," Mrs. Gray replied.

Obviously, the modiste's quiet reprimand and her defense of Lily had not sat well with the woman, and Lily was sorry about that.

She hated this. She hated having to please everyone and prove herself to Nicholas's snobbish friends.

She supposed it was that moment of feeling like an outcast that helped make up her mind about one thing. She would tell Jared to proceed with plans for her to race at Pharsalia racetrack. She would show these pretentious highbrows that she would not be dictated to by their beliefs and ridiculous standards.

And if, at the same time, she caused Nicholas St. James embarrassment, what did she care? Could he be any more embarrassed than she was at this moment?

The girl finished the dress, and Lily stepped out into the salon to meet Madame Duvall. The petite woman turned Lily all about, muttering beneath her breath as she placed more pins in the material.

Then, as her workers brought bolts of beautiful colorful material, spreading them about on tables and chairs, Madame Duvall thumbed through a catalog and magazine before bringing the pictures to Lily.

"Here," she said, pointing at one dress in particular. "This is how I envision you at the summer party."

Lily caught her breath. The black-silk gown, trimmed with red roses, was simple and elegant and completely feminine. The dress was quite seductive, unsuitable perhaps for a virtuous young woman—but then how could Madame Duvall know? The entire community might know that her marriage was one of convenience, but there was no reason for anyone to believe she was still a virgin.

"Of course it's your decision," Madame Duvall said. "You might have your own preference. But believe me, child, I've been in this business long enough to know which will be the dress of the evening." The woman looked through her lorgnette and winked. "And this is it."

Lily smiled, still considering the dress.

"And don't forget, I have the advantage of knowing what almost every other woman in Natchez will be wearing."

Lily hadn't been sure until that moment if she should let the woman know she'd overheard the conversation next door.

"Thank you for defending me earlier . . . I couldn't help overhearing."

"Oh," Madame Duvall said, frowning. "I'm terribly sorry that you were put in such an embarrassing situation here in my shop."

"It's all right. You were very kind," Lily said.

"Girls," Mrs. Duvall said, waving her hands and shooing her young helpers from the room, "I'll call if we need you."

"My dear," she said, addressing Lily, "you must pay little attention to the mutterings of such an ignorant young woman as Claudia Gray. She is a terrible gossip, only because she knows she has neither the bloodlines nor the looks to attract any man worthy of her mother's ambitions. Now . . . what do you think about the dress?"

"Oh, Madame Duvall, I do love it. It's absolutely beautiful. But I'm not sure . . ."

"With your hair and coloring, it will be perfect. The black is so sensuous and the red roses add just the precise touch of contrast, don't you think?"

"Yes," Lily said, laughing. "I suppose you're right."

"Of course I'm right. Madame Duvall is always right!"

Suddenly the older woman grew still, looking into Lily's eyes in all seriousness.

"I know how you feel," she said, her eyes filled with empathy and just the slightest hint of pain. "My father was a poor man, a blacksmith, who had little to give to his only daughter. If I had been one of my six brothers, I might have received some land, or at least a horse. But my father considered a female a poor investment. My only hope, he said, was in finding a good husband. I can well remember being the subject of the wealthier girls' ridicule. I didn't dress well, and I didn't speak well."

"But you . . . you've become so successful," Lily said. She could hardly believe this attractive, seemingly educated woman had ever been the way she described.

"Oh, yes," Madame Duvall said, sighing with pleasure. "Quite successful. But I wasn't above using a man to get what I wanted. Not that I didn't love my husband. He was a kind and generous man. Much older than I. But now that he's gone, and I have my own money, I would never put myself in the position of having to depend on a man again." She removed her glasses and tapped them against

Lily's shoulder. "Not that I'm recommending the same to you. Nicholas St. James is quite possibly the best catch in the territory. And if I'm not mistaken, he will soon be smitten with his young wife. If he isn't already."

The last remark was more a question than anything.

Lily murmured and turned away, letting her fingers move over a bolt of beautiful white-taffeta material.

"Hardly," she replied.

"Forgive my asking such a personal question," Madame Duvall said, "but do you want him to be?"

"I . . . I haven't really thought about it," Lily said, frowning. She couldn't decide why she was hesitant to say the words out loud. Sometimes she wasn't sure what she wanted.

"Then I think you *should* think about it," Madame Duvall said kindly. "And I'm going to make sure this dress is so exquisite that he can't help but notice. Who knows, perhaps this little party is the perfect place to begin.

"Perhaps," Lily said, her eyes sparkling.

Perhaps the woman was right. Perhaps it was time to put all their differences aside and try to live as husband and wife. The thought sent a thrill of anticipation racing along her spine.

But how could she possibly even consider such a thing as long as her husband was in the arms of another woman?

Chapter 15

By the time Lily chose other patterns and material for her summer wardrobe, it was raining harder than ever. She left Madame Duvall's dress shop, opening a small umbrella and hurrying to where her driver and carriage sat waiting.

As she passed a small restaurant, she glanced inside and was surprised to see Jared sitting with several other people at a table. He glanced up just as she passed, and his eyes immediately lit with interest. She was struck by how incredibly much he looked like Nicholas, and yet he was so much more open and accessible.

Lily hardly knew how to react when she saw Jared leave the table. She knew he was headed outside, and she wasn't sure if she should go on to the carriage as if she hadn't seen him, or wait without pretense.

She was concerned about him after yesterday's fiasco. And she was terribly curious to know if Nicholas had reprimanded Jared.

"Lily . . . wait . . . please," she heard Jared say.

She turned to him with a look of misgiving.

"Don't look so worried," he said, coming to her. His eyes as he gazed down at her were tender and warm. "Surely your husband can't forbid our speaking to one another on the street if we happen to meet."

"No . . ." Lily said quietly. "I . . . I don't suppose . . ." She shivered as the rain drizzled from the small umbrella and dripped on her shoulders, soaking the material of her dress through to her skin. She glanced rather longingly through the window where the patrons of the café seemed warm and content as they ate their meals or sipped tea.

"I'm terribly sorry about yesterday, Jared," she said. "I shouldn't have put you in such a position with your own cousin."

"It isn't your fault. Nicholas has long resented me, though I swear, I've done nothing to deserve it."

"I'm so sorry," she murmured.

"Here, you're getting wet," Jared said, stepping forward. "And cold. Come inside. Just for a moment to dry off," he added, seeing her look of reluctance.

"I . . . I don't know."

"We won't be alone," he said. "The restaurant is full as you can see. I'd like you to meet my friends, and one of the young ladies has brought her mother with her, so we shall be properly chaperoned." There was a twinkle in his eyes, perhaps even a challenge as well, she thought.

"Well . . . I suppose . . . just for a little while," she said, shivering as another rivulet of water ran beneath her collar and down her back.

As Jared escorted Lily toward his table, they were met with looks of curiosity, not only from Jared's friends, but from the rest of the patrons as well.

Lily knew they'd heard of her and for a moment, that thought made her clamp her teeth together in furious defiance.

Let them think what they would about her. And that included Nicholas.

At the table were three women and one other man. He

rose as they came nearer, his dark eyes moving over Lily in a way that made her wonder if she had made an unwise decision.

She'd never been introduced to a man quite like this one. There was something disturbing about him, something in his appearance that indicated he was not of the Natchez ton.

His clothes, though obviously expensive, were ill fitting, the colors gaudy and flashy. He must have realized that his jacket was much too tight across the shoulders and the tan trousers embarrassingly revealing. But if he did, he certainly seemed not one wit put off by it.

Lily glanced at Jared, and was somewhat reassured by his familiar smile.

"Lily, I'd like you to meet Charles Lydell, a breeder of some of the finest thoroughbreds in the South. Charles, this is Lily St. James, my cousin's wife—the young lady I told you about," he added, lowering his voice slightly.

Jared's remark caused Lily to frown slightly, but then she curtsied as the raffishly dressed man bent low. She was a little surprised that this was the man Jared had chosen to help her.

Jared held her arm and whispered so that she alone could hear. "If you're still interested in horse racing, this is the gentleman who can set things in motion."

At least now she understood a little more clearly why the man seemed so different and so out of place in Jared's company. She'd found in Boston that people in the horsy set were eccentric. They liked to dress in the brightest, most noticeable clothes imaginable. Nevertheless it was a bit surprising that Jared would be seen in public with such a man. She had a feeling that Nicholas definitely would not approve.

She turned her attention to the ladies at the table as Jared began the introductions and was surprised to find herself facing the very people who had just been discussing her in Madame Duvall's shop.

"Claudia Gray and her mother, Mrs. Prudence Gray."

Lily tried not to appear surprised. As Madame Duvall had said, Claudia was very plain, and the ruffled, beribboned pink dress she wore only emphasized her frizzy brown curls and heavy, rather masculine features.

Mrs. Gray and her daughter smiled pleasantly, making Lily want to laugh aloud. At least they had learned their manners well. They gave not even the slightest hint that they had been discussing her and Nicholas intimately only moments ago.

"And this is Madame Patrice Claymore."

As for Madame Claymore, she looked several years older than Lily, with searching, expressive eyes. There was a knowing quality about her and a hardness in the set of her mouth that made Lily wonder just who she was.

"Won't you have lunch with us?" Charles said, pulling a chair out for Lily.

"Well, I . . ."

"Of course she will," Patrice answered with a haughty lift of her brow. "It isn't as if she has anything better to do." She smiled almost apologetically at Lily. "What I mean, of course, is that you hardly know anyone in Natchez. And unless I miss my guess, that husband of yours is off somewhere with his cotton broker, talking business."

Lily relaxed a bit. She was hungry. And she certainly had nothing to look forward to except spending a long rainy afternoon alone in her room. Besides, she was dying to learn if Charles Lydell might actually secure a horse for her to ride in the Pharsalia race.

"You know my husband then?" she asked, taking a seat.

"But of course," the woman exclaimed. "Everyone knows Nicholas St. James. He has quite a reputation." Patrice laughed and moved her head so that her raven hair fell away from her face and tumbled across her shoulders. There was a bold, brazen look in the woman's dark eyes.

Lily noted that Claudia blushed while her mother lifted her cup of tea and pretended she had not heard the remark. The two didn't quite seem to belong with the others and yet they obviously wanted to be here in their company.

Oddly, Lily felt sorry for them. And she supposed that was one of the reasons she stayed. And also the reason she risked Nicholas's wrath should he learn that she was here in such questionable company.

That afternoon was the beginning of a strange alliance between Lily and the unlikely group. Before she left, she had learned that Patrice was an actress on a riverboat that traveled the Mississippi, stopping in small towns and entertaining wherever a stage could be set. She would be here only for a few more days.

She learned that Mr. Gray had passed away a couple of years earlier; he'd been a businessman, but not a wealthy one. Lily had a feeling that every penny of Claudia's inheritance would be spent on finding herself a successful, if not wealthy husband.

After their meal, Jared broached the subject of horse racing with Charles Lydell.

Lily wasn't sure it was such a good idea to let the women in on her secret wish. Especially not the Grays.

But from the look of admiration in Claudia's eyes, she thought she need not have worried. She and her mother were much too interested in being a part of the delicious charade to put a stop to it.

Within moments, she had Charles Lydell's assurance that he would help her.

"That is if you're certain you're up to such a task. Horse racing requires great skill, not to mention strength and endurance." He let his shadowy eyes move pointedly over Lily's slender frame. "I couldn't take a chance on anything happening to a very expensive horse, despite my wish to help someone as charming as you."

"You have nothing to worry about. Lily is an excellent horsewoman," Jared said.

"Is that true, Mrs. St. James?" Charles asked.

"I suppose someone else would have to be the judge of that," she said. "But I have been riding since I was very young."

He laughed, a low, rough sound that sent shivers of apprehension racing over Lily's flesh.

"Then I shall take Jared's word on it. You must leave everything to me. I will want you to ride the horse beforehand of course. I'll take care of that and the other details.

"Then here's to Lily's race," Patrice said. She lifted her teacup in a salute toward Lily. "I find this most exciting. Please tell me that the race is to be held before I depart Natchez."

"It is indeed," Charles said, reaching across to touch her face. "The next race will take place this weekend, only a few days from now."

Patrice turned to Lily.

"In that case, I shall place a very large wager on you, Lily. What a wonderful trick it shall be if you win. I hope those arrogant men who dominate horse racing will soon be taught a valuable lesson."

Later, when Jared escorted her to her carriage, Lily was shaking. Even her insides were trembling.

"Jared, the race is to take place the same day as Mrs. Mireaux's summer party. How shall I ever manage?"

"But don't you see?" he said, laughing at her. "That's the perfect time. You'll have a million excuses to be away from the house that day—last-minute dress fittings, ornaments for your hair. All those mysterious things women do that drive the male species mad."

"I don't know. Now that the time has come . . ."

"Ah, Lily," he said, smiling crookedly at her, "don't tell me you're afraid. Certainly not of my boringly arrogant cousin? Nicholas might bluster about a bit, but believe me he would never do anything to harm a lady. He's quite used to their falling into line without his ever having to resort to physical violence. Though how he does it is a mystery to me," he added dryly.

Yet for all Jared's smile and teasing voice, there was a bitterness in his words. Lily was just beginning to realize the depth of resentment that Jared and his cousin felt for each other. And she wondered why.

"Of course I'm not afraid. Not of Nicholas. Nor of any man," she said, knowing even as she said it that she had fallen for his bait.

"Then don't worry," he said. "Nothing's going to happen. We'll go to the race. You'll have your friends there to urge you on to victory, which makes the charade all the more enjoyable. It should be quite the lark, don't you agree?"

What else could she do except agree, she asked herself as she sat in her carriage on her way back home.

It wasn't the first time Lily had done something because of stubbornness and pride. But this time she had to wonder at all the things she had to lose if Nicholas found out.

Chapter 16

Because of the heavy rain and standing water, the driver let Lily out at the front of the house. She hurried along the walkway, leaving her umbrella on the porch and brushing off her dress as she quietly entered the hallway.

The door to the study was open, and she was surprised to see Nicholas seated at his desk. He was so deep in thought that he had not heard her come in.

Lily's heart leapt briefly, then settled down to a slow, steady beat as she watched him. He sat with his elbows resting on the desktop, hands folded, chin leaning against his hands as he stared into space.

For a moment, Lily moved her head to one side, wondering at the somewhat pensive expression on his handsome face.

When he looked up and saw her standing at the door, his face changed, becoming for once almost welcoming. He stood up and walked around the desk.

"Lily," he said. "Come in. Where have you been?"

She could hardly believe that this time, there was no demand in his question. No anger or accusation.

"I . . . I thought since it was raining that I'd visit Madame Duvall's dress shop . . . have a new summer wardrobe made."

He nodded and a brief smile flickered about his sensuous mouth. His gaze quickly moved over her.

"You're wet," he said. "Let me have Mrs. Lloyd bring you something warm to drink or—"

"No," she said staring at him through narrowed eyes. She hardly knew what to make of the change in him. The last time they'd spoken he'd been furious with her. She thought he hated her. She'd even been certain that he'd made the ride in the rainstorm last night with a whiskey bottle because of her.

"No, I'm fine," she repeated. "I'll just go up to my room and change out of these wet things."

There was this sweet pensiveness about him. A mysterious sad expression in his eyes that she couldn't quite fathom.

Oddly, it made her want to put her arms around him and hold him.

"Lily," he said, his voice urging her to stay.

"Yes?" she said breathlessly, turning to meet his gaze.

"I'll be leaving for Live Oaks early in the morning. I really need to be there when the cotton crop is planted. I've asked Mrs. Lloyd and Clemmie for an early dinner tonight. And I had hoped you'd feel like joining me."

Lily stared at him, hardly knowing what to make of such a quiet, polite invitation. It wasn't what she was used to from him.

"I'd appreciate your company," he added. "I've come to hate dining alone."

Lily shrugged, unwilling to let herself believe what she was hearing. Was there something he wanted? Some reason he was being so nice to her?

"Of course," she said coolly. "I'd be happy to join you."

His eyes today were so intense, so compelling, that she

found it hard to pull her gaze away. She actually had to make herself move down the hallway and up the stairs.

That evening she dressed very carefully, making sure her hair was just right and that the dress she chose was flattering and elegant.

Why she should try to please Nicholas after all that had happened between them, she didn't know. But she had to admit, if only to herself, that was exactly what she was doing.

When she walked into the dining room, he was there, looking dashing and handsome in black, his white stock tied perfectly beneath his strong chin. Just the sight of him made her catch her breath in her throat.

What was it about him tonight? What was the cause of the sadness that lay in his eyes? She could swear there was even regret hidden behind there as well.

For a moment, she felt a lurch in the pit of her stomach. Had he somehow found out about today? About her meeting with Jared and his less-than-reputable friends?

Impossible as it seemed, might he even know about her intentions to race at the Pharsalia racecourse?

"You look lovely," he said, stepping forward to take her hand and lead her into the dining room.

No, of course he didn't know. Nicholas would not pretend to be so sweet if that were true. She knew better than anyone that he didn't waste time trying to mask his true feelings.

"You're shaking," he said as he led her around the table to her seat.

"I . . . I guess I'm still a bit chilled from the rain."

"Shall I have Burton light a fire in the fireplace?"

"No," she said. "I'm fine . . . really."

Nicholas watched her, recognizing the look of doubt and confusion on her beautiful face. He couldn't blame her for being confused about his changing behavior. He'd been as confused as anyone.

The other night, after being with Jeanette, he'd realized

just how empty and meaningless his life had become. But he could hardly admit that to his wife. He supposed he'd gone along blindly before, thinking he had everything a man could want.

But that was before Lily came home from Boston. Before he became entranced by her beauty and charm and before he had a dream with which to compare the reality of his life.

He knew what he wanted now. He wanted Lily. And for the first time in his life, he knew he had something to lose if he was less than honest. With her and with himself.

As Lily sat across from Nicholas at dinner, she thought she'd never enjoyed a meal more. She could hardly believe the difference. But what had happened to make him behave so differently toward her?

"Nicholas," she said, "there's something I need to tell you."

His eyes met hers and he put down his fork, leaning forward slightly as if intent on giving her his full attention.

"I . . . when you found me with Jared yesterday down at the waterfront, I told you that I'd explain why I was there."

"You don't have to," he said, his voice deep. "I was angry. I came there to find you with every intention of being patient. But when I saw you with Jared . . . laughing and obviously enjoying yourself, well, I . . ."

"No . . . I want to explain. I can't bear for you to think that Jared and I . . . that I would . . ."

Nicholas's eyes narrowed, and he turned his head, watching her from beneath his brows. He didn't speak and seemed to have no intention of trying to help make her explanation easier.

"I realize what it must have looked like, but the basket was not for us," she said, her voice a whisper. "I hadn't intended a picnic or some secret rendezvous."

Suddenly the room was so quiet that she could hear the candles fluttering softly in their silver holders. She became aware of the rain dripping from the eaves of the house and of the sound of her own breathing.

"Go on," he said quietly.

"Still, I . . . I knew you wouldn't approve, and that's the reason I didn't tell you, not because I intended doing anything wrong. I knew how you felt about my being there."

"What are you trying to tell me, Lily?" His voice was still skeptical, his look cool and waiting.

"I took the food and supplies to Miss Fran. Do you remember her?"

Nicholas shook his head and made a quiet grunting noise in his throat.

"Of course I remember Fran. I haven't seen her for years. But how did you—?"

Lily explained quickly about her first meeting with the woman and how poor her life had become.

"It sickened me, seeing her that way. I'm so worried about her, Nicholas. The man she was with treated her very badly, and looked as if she rarely has a decent meal."

Nicholas's look was incredulous.

"And there's something else I want to do," she continued. "You're not going to like it, but I feel it's my responsibility to do this. She was so kind to me and my mother." She took a deep breath and continued. "I want to let Miss Fran live in our old house and see that she has money of her own. Only on the condition, of course, that that odious man not be allowed near her. I'll pay him to go away if I have to but—" She had rushed through the words, as if wanting to have them over and done with. But something in Nicholas's look made her stop. Made her feel breathless and warm.

Suddenly Nicholas shook his head and laughed aloud. It was the first time since she'd come home that Lily had heard him laugh that way—free and easy, as if the whole world belonged to him.

For a moment she was stunned. But more than that she was fascinated.

"You. . . you're not angry with me?"

"Are you telling me the truth, Lily?" he asked. His eyes still sparkled with laughter, but he had grown serious, looking into her face with genuine interest.

It was a moment before she could manage to speak.

"Yes," she whispered. "Yes, I am."

"Good," he said. Although his voice was rough, his look was tender and warm. "Good," he repeated softly. "I'm glad."

"Then you aren't angry? You don't—?"

"No, little one, I'm not angry. And I have no intention of stopping you. Do as you wish where Miss Fran is concerned. It's your house and your money. Actually I think it's admirable of you to be so compassionate."

She stared at him for a moment, hardly able to believe his words, or the sweetness in his eyes. Then she smiled and nodded, feeling suddenly shy beneath the steadiness of his gaze.

After coffee, they walked out onto the front porch, where Nicholas lit a cigar. Together they stood staring out into the rainy darkness as the wind pulled the cigar smoke away and sent it curling out into the night.

"You said you were going to Live Oaks," she said finally. "You will be home in time for the party on Saturday, won't you?"

Without speaking, he stepped to the front of the porch and flicked the cigar out into the darkness. The tip of it flared, then faded as the rain hissed against it.

When Nicholas turned, he came very near to her, reaching out and touching the skin of her bare shoulders with the back of his hand. He laughed quietly when she shivered.

"I wouldn't miss it," he said. "Because if I did, I'd miss seeing you in your new gown, and everyone's reaction to my beautiful wife. And that's something I'm looking forward to.''

"Really?" she asked, her voice breathless.

"Really," he said.

Suddenly, as if on impulse, he bent his head and Lily closed her eyes, almost sighing as she felt herself pulled gently to him.

When his lips brushed against her cheek, she felt the disappointment bursting inside her chest like a physical blow.

She wanted him to kiss her mouth. To pull her tightly against him and kiss her the way he had in the barn.

Lord, but her feelings were wanton and desperate where he was concerned. To her surprise, she was learning that was something she seemed to have very little control over.

"This has been a very nice evening, Lily." he said, murmuring quietly against her ear. "When I return from Live Oaks, I hope we can spend more time together . . . like this. Perhaps . . . even start all over?''

He pulled away, looking down at her there in the darkness, his eyes questioning and warm.

"Do you . . . do you mean that we . . . that you and I . . . ?'' she whispered. She was trembling from head to toe. Unable to speak or breathe. Unable to think of one intelligent thing to say in response to his whispered suggestion.

Was he actually proposing what she thought he was? That finally they become man and wife?

"Is it so unappealing?" he asked, his voice teasing.

"No," she said quickly. "It isn't that."

Lily bent her head, shying away from the intensity of his look.

"Lily," he said. "My little river bride . . . you can be so sweet and so delightfully guileless. I think it's one of the things I like most about you." He touched her face, tracing his fingers down her cheek and stopping just at the corner of her mouth.

"I won't rush you. We will continue only if it's what you want, too," he said, his voice becoming more serious.

She felt breathless . . . speechless with delight, as he took her hand and led her into the house. They walked up the stairs, his hand touching her lightly at the waist.

She wanted him, and yet she hardly knew what it was she wanted. She thought she might die if she had to wait these last few days until the summer party for him to hold her and kiss her.

For a moment as they stood in the hallway outside her door, she thought he felt the same way. And that he might even sweep her into his arms and pull her into the room to make her his wife this very night.

Instead, he took a deep breath and deliberately stepped back away from her.

"I haven't been the most patient man in the world where you're concerned Lily. I know that. I've never in my life taken a woman by force, and I certainly never meant to make you fear that from me. I want you to be sure about where our future will lead us," he said. "Being apart for a few days will give you time to think. And to decide what it is you want. I don't want to pressure you."

She wanted to ask him about Jeanette Mireaux. Did he intend giving her up now? And if so, what had made him decide such a thing? But she dared not hope it, much less say it aloud.

This unexpected chance for a new beginning between them was so sweet and so fragile that she couldn't bring herself to say anything that might spoil it.

That night, as she lay in bed, she could feel her insides trembling. She went over every word Nicholas had said. She relived every look and every touch until she began to wonder if she had dreamed them.

Was she expecting too much? What if he still had no intention of giving up his mistress? What if he actually thought he could still have them both? She silently berated herself for not making her feelings clear to him about that.

For long moments she lay staring at the lamplight flickering on the ceiling and walls. How could she have so quickly forgotten all her vows, all her solemn promises that she would never let a man who kept another woman possess her? And now when Nicholas expressed a desire to make their marriage a real one, here she was ready to give in.

In the bedroom across the hall, Nicholas pushed the sheets off his legs and got out of bed. He felt hot and restless. He glanced from time to time toward the door, thinking more than once that perhaps he would walk across to Lily's room and make her his once and for all.

It was what she wanted. He thought he'd seen the proof of that in her emerald eyes tonight.

And it was what he wanted. He didn't know how it had happened, but heaven help him, he did.

He'd never wanted another woman as fiercely as he wanted this one. Last night with Jeanette had confirmed it. Her lovemaking, so expert and calculated, had left him needing something else.

And he knew that need had begun the day Lily came home.

But he had to admit something else as well.

He might make love to Lily, claim her as his wife, but he had a feeling that he'd never truly possess her. She was like the wind, like the river. There was some part of her that she held away, some untamed secret part that she seemed afraid to share with anyone.

And that was the one thing he wasn't sure he'd be able to change.

Chapter 17

Lily didn't see Nicholas before he left for the plantation. He was already gone the next morning when she came down for breakfast.

She tried not to let that fact disappoint her. But she couldn't help wondering if he might have regretted making the kind of commitment he had made last night.

Perhaps, like her, he'd been lulled by the intimacy of their evening together, as the rain had closed them into a cozy cocoon. Perhaps it had been anything except the one thing she wanted it to be—that he might really be beginning to care about her.

She was deep in thought when Jared arrived, calling out "Mrs. Lloyd, I'll have breakfast in here with Mrs. St. James," as he bustled in.

Lily placed her cup in its saucer.

"Jared . . . what are you doing here?" she asked, frowning at him. He seemed unusually cheerful and not the least worried that Nicholas might find him here.

"No need to fret, my dear," he said, coming to sit across from her. "I waited until I saw Nicholas leave. And now

Burton tells me that he'll be at Live Oaks for several days. I can't think of anything more perfect for our plans.''

"Our . . . plans?"

"Lily?" he said, pursing his lips at her. He poured himself a cup of coffee and leaned back, savoring the aroma before he took a sip. He looked at her with an odd expression on his face. "What's come over you this morning? First I find you lost in some reverie and now you don't even remember the plans we made yesterday. The race?"

"Oh," she said, remembering the horse race with a jolt. "No . . . no, of course I haven't forgotten. It's just . . .''

"You hadn't mentioned any of this to Nicholas, have you?" he asked, pushing anxiously against the table as he leaned toward her.

"No. Heavens, no," she said.

Nicholas. He'd be furious with her if he knew Jared was even here, not to mention what he'd do if he knew his wife intended making a fool of him by dressing like a boy and riding at Pharsalia.

"As soon as we've finished breakfast, we'll go to Charles's farm just outside the city. No one will see you there, and you'll have a chance to ride the thoroughbred that he's entered in the race."

Lily frowned and chewed thoughtfully at her lower lip.

"You haven't changed your mind, have you? I must tell you, I intend putting down a sizable wager on you, and so does Patrice Claymore. You can't let us down now."

That was hardly any reason for her to continue this foolish game, she knew. Still, she couldn't deny the excitement that their confidence gave her. Or the sense of exhilaration she knew she'd feel just putting one over on the exclusive membership of the Jockey Club.

She should be feeling complete elation at such a prospect. The only thing that kept her from it was the thought of deceiving Nicholas.

But she could hardly tell him and risk his disapproval now that they seemed to have moved beyond an unhappy period of their lives. Now that they were perhaps about to take their first step toward something she knew in her heart she'd been wanting for years.

"Lily?" Jared said.

He was staring at her oddly, making Lily wonder how many times he had called her name.

"Oh," she said. "I'm sorry. I do seem to be a bit scattered today, don't I?"

"You haven't changed your mind? Please tell me you haven't. I'll admit I didn't think much of the idea when you first broached the subject, but now . . . actually I'm looking forward to it. I can't wait to see their smug faces when they realize a girl has beaten them at their own game."

Lily took a deep breath. It was something she still wanted, she had to admit. She couldn't explain why it meant so much to her. She only wished she didn't have to do it behind Nicholas's back.

"No " she said with a sigh of resignation. "No, I haven't changed my mind."

Mrs. Lloyd brought Jared's breakfast, sliding the plate in front of him with a look that indicated her disapproval. Lily smiled at the woman, thinking of how kind she'd been and how protective she was of Nicholas. There was a chance for them all to become a family. And it made her wish she didn't have to be so deceitful.

Jared waited until the housekeeper had left the room before speaking again, this time in a conspiratorial whisper.

"Charles has trousers and boots for you at his stables. Why don't you go get your things while I finish eating?"

Later, as she rode with Jared out toward Charles Lydell's house, Lily could feel her stomach churning with anticipation and doubt.

She didn't want to make a fool of herself. It *had* been a while since she'd ridden. And of course she'd never actually competed in a race before. But she didn't want to disappoint Jared and the others who were counting on her. She was grateful to Jared and to his friends. They seemed to welcome her into their circle without being judgmental.

She focused her attention on the land around Charles Lydell's farm. This morning it was covered by a low-lying mist that swirled and moved when they drove through it. Much of the area was hidden by dense brush and scrub trees. Poorly kept, only the land near the house and barn was cleared and well tended.

At the stables, she took the clothes that one of the servants gave her and hurried toward one of the tack rooms to change.

Coming back outside, she had to admit that the horse Mr. Lydell had picked was outstanding. She'd ridden beautiful, well-trained horses before, but nothing like the sleek-bodied, long-legged colt that he brought out and walked before Lily and Jared. This horse was in a class by himself.

"Lily, meet Satan, Lydell Farm's pride and joy."

"Oh, my . . . he's beautiful. Isn't he, Jared?"

"Splendid," Jared agreed.

"I paid top dollar for this beauty. He's been trained by the best and ridden only by the most experienced jockeys. He's spirited and a bit headstrong. Do you think you can handle him, Mrs. St. James?"

She had to admit, the task did seem daunting.

"I suppose there's only one way to find out," she said, taking a deep breath of air.

Feeling only a bit self-conscious in the baggy trousers, Lily stepped to the horse. Jared placed his hand beneath her knee and boosted her into the small English riding saddle.

The great horse skittered slightly to one side as Lily took the reins in her hands and leaned down to pat his neck and whisper into his upraised ears.

"It's all right, boy," she murmured. "You and I shall get along famously." It was more wishful thinking on her part than confidence, she thought.

But as soon as the horse began to move, Lily felt the rightness of their unlikely union. He felt strong and sure, his muscles moving like pure liquid beneath her.

When they were on the track, she felt an elation rising within her. She barely had to tap him with the riding whip for him to respond. It was as if he were born to race, as if the mere sight of the track spurred him on.

Lily knew instinctively that this horse would race even if she weren't clinging to his back, urging him on.

She felt the wind in her hair, pulling at the pins. She could hear it in her ears, whistling by as the scenery beyond the track blurred. She became completely lost in the joy of the ride, as she felt herself seeming to become one with the magnificent creature who stretched his legs out farther and faster.

When she'd finish one complete turn and pulled the reins to slow the horse, she didn't have to ask how they'd done. She knew. She could feel it in her heart and soul.

She leaned her head back and laughed, a sound of pure joy that rippled from her chest and bubbled up inside her until she could no longer contain her shout of pure pleasure.

"You were wonderful," she whispered to the horse. "But just between the two of us, you are no Satan. You are my own sweet Blackie."

"She'll do." Charles Lydell said with a hint of admiration. "Yes indeed, she'll do very well."

Jared looked from Charles to Lily, his eyes narrowed and speculative as he contemplated her flushed cheeks and ebullient shout of laughter.

Lily walked the thoroughbred around the track to cool him. And when she'd finished, Charles suggested that she continue riding other horses, just to get the feel of the saddle.

"Not too much today though." he said, before she trotted away on another horse. "We don't want your muscles to be so sore you can't ride Saturday."

Lily had to admit, despite the man's eccentricity, he did seem to know a great deal about horses. She also had to admit that she had loved every moment of the ride. And she couldn't wait for the race.

She wouldn't let herself think about what Nicholas would do if he found out. She simply wouldn't.

It would be the first and last time that she did such a thing, she told herself. And then, once she and Nicholas settled into a real marriage, she'd ride her own horses. Perhaps not in races, but . . .

Lily laughed and lightly tapped her whip against the horse's rump, giving in completely to the freedom and pleasure that she felt when she was in the saddle.

For the next few days, she indulged herself with the horses and with talk of racing. She met even more of Jared's friends, some of them decidedly unsavory, she thought.

But they welcomed her so kindly, enthusiastically even, into their circle. After all, these were very much like the kind of people she grew up with, and they didn't seem so bad to her.

The day before the race, Lily was so nervous she could hardly sit still. She rode again, hoping to work off the last of her stiff and sore muscles.

She wasn't sure if her nervousness was due more to the race or to Nicholas's homecoming. Whatever it was, tomorrow would be an important day for her. One of the most important of her life.

She had become very popular with Lydell's horsy set, something she didn't quite understand. She believed she was intelligent, and a passable conversationalist. But for the life of her she couldn't understand why they gathered around to talk to her. Or why the men's eyes followed her with such admiration.

But they had become her friends, and she appreciated their support. She even invited Charles Lydell and Patrice Claymore to the summer party, knowing full well that Jeanette would probably be mortified. Claudia Gray and her mother had already been invited.

Jared seemed surprised by her invitations.

"I don't care if Jeanette disapproves," she said. Lily thought it might be amusing to see everyone's expression when Patrice and Charles came in dressed in their usual flamboyant way.

"It isn't Jeanette Mireaux that I'm thinking about," he replied dryly.

"You think Nicholas will be angry?" She certainly didn't want that. But after the other night, she'd hoped he would be more tolerant about such things.

"I guess we'll just have to wait and see, won't we?" he said with a mischievous grin.

Chapter 18

The day of the race came too quickly for Lily. She wasn't sure she was ready. And she wasn't at all certain that she'd be able to pull off the charade.

But her body seemed to ignore her thoughts, and she dressed and prepared herself instinctively, knowing in her heart that she would go through with it. Her pride wouldn't let her do anything else.

She was surprised to see such a huge crowd gathered at the racecourse. And troubled to learn that it was already widely rumored that a mysterious woman would be competing in the race.

"Jared," she scolded, turning to him as they waited in the back of the stables.

Jared shrugged his shoulders and grinned.

"I swear . . . I had nothing to do with those rumors. But so what if people are talking—all they know is that it's a woman. After all, you want the Jockey Club to know that much. They don't know your name. And if we're careful, they'll never know."

"Well, yes, but . . ."

"Lily St. James," he said, taking her shoulders and shaking her slightly, "this is going to be fun. If it isn't fun, you shouldn't be doing it."

Finally, Lily smiled and nodded.

She wanted to have fun. And to pay back all those people who had looked down on her family and their kind. And if she won today, she thought she would have the satisfaction of knowing she had bested them, if only in her own mind.

She was so nervous as the horses lined up for the race that she actually thought she might be sick. She wore her hair tucked up under a hat that was tied beneath her chin. She couldn't take a chance on it flying off during the race. Her clothes were the baggy trousers and shirt that Charles Lydell had provided earlier. Still, the other riders looked at her askance. Did they know she was a woman? Had someone already told them?

But as soon as the gun sounded and the horses scrambled away from the post, Lily forgot everything. She forgot the crowd; even the sound of their shouts faded away and all she could hear was the wind whistling past her ears. She even forgot Nicholas and his disapproval.

She had to concentrate on staying atop her horse when the other riders pushed and jockeyed for position as they rounded the first turn. Lily had to hold on for dear life as she tried to restrain the big black horse.

She knew he wanted to run full out, but she had to hold him back. Had to make him save his energy for the last half of the race. She knew him pretty well by now. The black had such spirit and heart that even if there were other horses in the lead, he would outdistance them at the end, even if it killed him. Charles Lydell had made the exact same observation about the colt.

She could feel the reins sawing against her hands, already tender from so much riding. Even the gloves she wore couldn't mask the burning pain.

"Hold," she whispered against the horse's ear. The wind

stung her eyes and pulled at the hat strings beneath her chin, threatening to rip the hat from her head. "Hold, boy," she said again, louder this time.

One of the riders moved his horse against hers, threatening to pin them against the rail. She could feel her horse jerk away, causing them to lose valuable seconds. But at least they were free.

"Not yet," she whispered. "Not yet . . . only a few more seconds.

After they passed the halfway mark, she deliberately made herself count to ten before loosening the reins. Immediately the horse strained forward, and Lily grimaced as the leather strips tore against the tender flesh of her palms.

"Now, Blackie!" she shouted. Holding the reins in her left hand, she tapped the whip against the horse and felt him almost move out from under her in an incredible burst of speed and energy.

Chills raced over her arms and down her legs as she felt the big black stretching out. She could hear his breathing, as well as her own. And now she began to hear the shouts of the crowd as her mount slowly began to gain on the other horses.

They came from the back, moving past two, three, and four horses until finally there was only one left in front.

"Come on," she urged. "You can do it, boy. You can do it."

She didn't know how, but the thoroughbred managed one final, incredible spurt of energy that propelled them ahead of the lead horse just as they crossed the finish line.

Lily was laughing and crying at the same time, her arms in the air as she let the joy and exhilaration move through her. She thought she'd never known such complete triumph in her life.

Her heart was pounding, racing like mad, and she thought it might never slow to its normal rhythm.

Out of the corner of her eye, she saw the ecstatic crowd

of people begin to surge toward her and she realized they meant to surround her in a throng of congratulations.

"She won!" she heard some of them shouting. "The woman won!"

So, they did know. They'd known from the beginning which rider she was.

For a moment she felt panic grip her. She became disoriented, uncertain how she would get off the racetrack without being swallowed up in the mass of people. She couldn't risk having them learn her true identity.

Through the crowd, she saw Charles Lydell and Jared. Charles took the reins of her horse and Jared pulled her down from the saddle, spiriting her away toward the opposite side of the field as the crowd converged upon Charles and his winning thoroughbred.

Apparently Jared had already prepared for just such a possibility. His carriage was waiting, hidden in the trees.

"Get in and close the door," he said. "I'll ride up front. Your clothes are on the seat. Just pull the curtains and change. Then if anyone sees us between here and town, they'll think that we've merely been observers at the race."

Lily was grateful for the soft seats and the room to stretch out her trembling legs. She felt weak and shaky, and she could still feel her heart pounding.

By the time they reached the house, she was beginning to feel more normal. Jared didn't turn the carriage into the back courtyard, but stopped on the street nearby.

As Lily climbed out of the carriage, Jared tipped his hat, his smile, so like Nicholas's, warm with triumph.

"You did it, Lily," he said. "You actually beat some of the best riders in the South."

For the first time, Lily allowed herself to believe that it really had happened.

She smiled broadly at him, and bit her lip. Her eyes sparkled brilliantly.

"I wish there was time for us to enjoy this moment," he said "But I'll see you tonight. Save me a dance."

"I will," she said. At the moment she felt such gratitude toward Jared. He had helped her experience a day she'd never forget.

She hurried along the street, her legs still feeling weak. It was just past noon. There was time to enjoy a light meal, something she hadn't been able to do before the race because of her nerves. Then she'd soak her aching muscles in a hot bath and still have plenty of time to prepare herself for the party.

The way she felt now, she was going to need it.

Her lunch and a tepid, leisurely bath left her feeling completely lifeless and relaxed. Despite her earlier excitement, she found she could hardly hold her eyes open another moment.

She was sleeping when Nicholas came home.

Nicholas tapped at Lily's door, but there was no answer. Quietly he pushed open the door and was surprised to find the bedroom darkened; it wasn't like her to sleep past noon.

But then he saw the bathtub in a corner of the room and damp towels hung across the painted Chinese screen.

He smiled as he stepped to the bed and stared down at her. Her hands were beneath her chin, knees pulled up against her flat stomach. He thought she looked like a child, and yet she was an undeniably sensuous and desirable woman.

His woman-child. The woman who had vexed and tormented him from the moment she came back, all grown up and ready to fight a battle of wits with him.

He had actually enjoyed watching her come to the realization of what was between them. Although she couldn't have been any more surprised by it than he himself.

It had only taken him longer.

Nicholas laughed softly and reached out to touch a dampened curl of reddish gold.

Lily stretched and slowly opened her eyes.

Nicholas caught his breath at the look of welcome that moved over her face when she saw him standing there. A smile pulled at the corner of her full beautiful lips, and her eyes lit with a genuine joy he knew he didn't deserve.

"Nicholas," she whispered, her voice husky and incredibly sensual. "You're home. I'm so glad you're home."

She pushed herself up in bed, pulling her dressing gown together as she did.

Nicholas couldn't help but compare her to Jeanette and other women he'd known. He was only realizing with Lily how much more exciting modesty could be than blatant exhibitionism. How could he have ever thought differently?

"You looked so beautiful lying there asleep," he whispered. He sat on the bed, his arms on either side of her legs as he leaned toward her.

She smelled of flowers and clean, fresh air. Like no one or nothing he'd ever experienced before.

Lily moved forward, touching his face lightly as his lips took hers softly . . . tenderly. When he pulled away and stood up again, she sighed, wishing she had the courage to ask him to stay.

"I was surprised to find you sleeping. You aren't feeling ill—"

"Oh, no," she said quickly. She turned her hands over so that her reddened palms were hidden against the sheets. "No. I'm just tired. I thought I'd rest before the party."

"That's a good idea," he said.

Nicholas had to use every bit of strength he had to keep himself from going to her and taking her in his arms. Every inch of his body ached to make love to her, right here and right now. But he intended to make her first night of love perfect. A quick afternoon of lovemaking simply wouldn't do for this woman.

"In fact, I think I'll do the same," he said. He had to make himself turn away from her inviting charms and move toward the door.

"I'll see you downstairs," he said from the doorway.

"Yes," she whispered, her eyes sparkling with happiness. "I can hardly wait."

Chapter 19

The weather had finally cleared. There was a warm breeze drifting in through the windows, carrying with it a wonderful combination of scents. Lily could smell lilacs and roses mingled with the faint smell of wet grass and earth. She thought it would always remind her of this summer day.

She could hear the sound of carriages arriving and of people talking quietly and laughing as they entered the house. Below her room, the gardens were strung with lanterns and candles in glass hurricane globes, waiting for nightfall.

One of the servants had come up to help Lily dress.

"Mr. St. James say to tell you he'll be downstairs waitin' for you, ma'am," she said.

"I'm so nervous that I'm shaking." Lily murmured, more to herself than to the girl.

"No need to be nervous," the girl said. She helped Lily step into the black-silk dress that had been delivered only this afternoon. "Lordy, when them people see you they gonna hold they breath. That's for sure. This here's the prettiest dress I ever did see."

Lily stepped to the long mirror inside her armoire. The dress fit very tightly about her waist, so tightly that for a moment Lily wondered if she'd be able to breathe at all.

The bodice draped below her shoulders in a band of tiny pleats, caught between her breasts with one perfect red-silk rose. The full skirt fell in three layers, each squared at the corners and each layer caught up at the sides with red roses.

For a moment Lily was speechless.

Madame Duvall had been right. Black suited her.

Until now Lily had been having second thoughts about the dress, afraid that it might be too mature for a young woman. She'd worried that she might end up looking foolish and plain. But there was nothing matronly about this dress. It was as feminine and sensual as anything she'd ever seen. And she knew, without false modesty, that it complemented her creamy skin and reddish gold hair as nothing else could.

"Oh, ma'am." The girl beside her covered her mouth and stared with wonder as they both stood looking in the mirror.

Lily touched the material at her shoulders and ran her hand lovingly down the skirt.

"It is beautiful, isn't it?" she said. Her eyes were wide and filled with disbelief.

"Oh, yes, ma'am. Just about the mos' beautiful thing I ever seen."

Lily looked down at her hands. They still stung, and, despite putting Clemmie's special ointment on them today, her skin was red and blistered.

She stepped to the armoire and opened a drawer, pulling out a pair of black net mittens that left her fingers bare.

"There," she said, glancing in the mirror one last time. "Well, here I go. Thank you for your help, Sela."

The maid curtsied and, with eyes wide and sparkling with excitement, followed Lily out into the hallway and watched as she started down the stairs.

The house was filled with people. The sound of music and laughter drifted up toward her. At the top of the landing Lily stopped, taking one last deep breath and glancing down the wide hallway.

She saw Nicholas almost immediately, talking to a group of men. Beside him was Jeanette Mireaux, her pale hair gleaming beneath the chandelier.

Nicholas and Jeanette looked up and saw Lily at almost the same time. A few weeks ago, or even a few days ago, Lily might have been troubled to see them together. It probably would have spoiled the entire day for her.

But today, when Nicholas's eyes met hers and lit with a special fire, he made her forget the blond woman at his side. She forgot everything except him and the look in his eyes that she knew was for her alone.

Lily was not even aware that the hall quieted as people turned and saw her. She barely heard the collective murmur of admiration, or the hushed whispers as heads turned and men stared.

She saw Nicholas shouldering his way through the crowd toward her, and she began to move down the stairs, her gaze never leaving his.

At the bottom of the stairs he took her hand. He felt warm and strong as he pulled her toward him and put his arm around her waist.

"I think you are the most exquisite creature I've ever seen," he whispered.

There was no time for anything else as the people converged around them. Men and women alike crowded about, some of them renewing their acquaintance with Lily, others eager to introduce themselves to this woman who had married the most attractive bachelor in Natchez and who reportedly had a very unconventional union.

Lily could see Jeanette Mireaux out of the corner of her eye. She was aware of the woman hovering just within earshot, and aware also of those cool blue eyes focused on her and Nicholas.

There was one awkward moment when Jared arrived, complete with the entourage that Lily had become a part of the past week.

She felt Nicholas stiffen at her side and for a moment she thought he might even confront Jared right then and there.

Charles Lydell was dressed in one of his most garish suits, his mustard-colored jacket like a bruise among the sea of black that most of the other men wore. Mrs. Gray and Claudia quickly left the group to mingle with the crowd, as if they hoped people would think they'd arrived with Lydell by accident.

It was Patrice Claymore who helped smooth over the awkwardness of the moment.

"Lily, what a perfectly lovely dress," she said, coming forward to take Lily's hand. "And Nicholas," she said. The woman, dressed in red and wearing a heavy application of rouge on her cheeks and dark kohl on her eyelids, looked flirtatiously from beneath long lashes at Nicholas. "It's been a long time."

"Patrice." Nicholas said with a wry smile. "I had no idea you were in town."

"Well, I wondered why you hadn't been down to catch the play."

Lily watched them carefully. It was obvious from the looks between them that they knew each other very well.

"I've been at Live Oaks for several days. Just returned this morning." He turned and pulled Lily closer. "You've already met my wife?"

Lily realized that she was holding her breath, and her shoulders felt tight and stiff.

"We met at the dress shop," Patrice said smoothly. "You're a very lucky man, Nicholas," she added.

"Yes, I know." he replied, with a smile at Lily.

"Nicholas, do you know Charles Lydell?"

If Nicholas seemed surprised by the man's presence, he didn't show it. Still, when Charles and Jared moved away without giving her a second glance, Lily breathed a quiet sigh of relief.

In the next moment Jeanette Mireaux was there, radiant in a white-satin gown trimmed with silver-blue braid and ribbon. The same color ribbons hung from a white lacy comb in her hair.

"Patrice." she said, her voice cool. "If I'd known you were in Natchez, I would have extended a personal invitation."

Patrice pursed her lips as her eyes became languid with disinterest. She obviously recognized Jeanette's remark as a rebuff.

"Oh, that's all right, Jeanette. I was invited by a member of the family."

Jeanette shrugged her round, pale shoulders.

"Of course I don't mind. It adds a certain spice to the festivities when we have guests who are as . . . well-known . . . as you and Mr. Lydell."

Patrice laughed aloud, the sound of her voice rising above the noise of the other guests. Some people turned to stare, while other women whispered behind their fans.

"Oh, my dear," she said, "that's quite a compliment from someone of *your* reputation."

Nicholas seized Lily's arm and led her away from the two women, sighing as he pulled her through the throng of people. "It isn't safe to be in between those two when they go at it," he said.

"I think they're both jealous," Lily said.

"Neither of them has a right to be," he said. "I hope you won't let them spoil your evening."

"I don't intend to."

They went into the main parlor. The doors between it and the ladies' parlor had been opened, and people were gathered there, some of them dancing to the music of a string quartet while others sat and talked.

Nicholas was attentive and polite, introducing her to so many people that her head began to whirl. She noted a certain pride in his voice, a certain possessiveness in the way his hand lingered on her waist.

When they danced the crowd stood away, watching them and smiling their approval. She saw Mrs. Gray and Claudia and smiled at them. Claudia made a little wave as she watched them enviously.

Lily actually felt sorry for the girl. She wasn't such a bad person, after all. Just lonely and sad and terribly desperate to find someone who would love her.

"What is it?" Nicholas asked, hearing Lily's soft murmur of sympathy.

"Oh, nothing" she said. "Just. Claudia Gray. I feel so sorry for her. I think she hides her loneliness with laughter and all those terrible gossipy things she says about other people."

Nicholas smiled. "Do you worry about everyone?" he asked affectionately. "I'll bet you were the kind of girl who brought home every stray cat she found."

Lily laughed.

"Yes . . . I confess I was. And believe it or not my mother always let me keep them. Much to the disapproval of my father, who swore that it was hard enough feeding a family, much less every cat that wandered down beneath the hill."

"Ah," Nicholas said, smiling at her. "Then I shall be forewarned if I begin to see cats gathering in my yard."

The afternoon seemed to fly by. Lily thought she'd never had such a wonderful time in all her life. Even the parties in Boston could not compare to this one.

Everything was perfect, the music, the wine, the flowers. And when it grew dark, the lanterns were lit about the house and in the garden, transforming the night into a magical scene.

Lily had agreed to Jeanette's party mostly out of pride, knowing that the woman intended to use it for her own purposes but determined not to show her jealousy. Now it seemed she'd been wrong in her opinion of Jeanette.

The party was elegant, and Nicholas' mistress stayed discreetly in the background.

When the guests were called in to the buffet dinner, Lily found that it too, was quite lavish and elegant. There were hams and pheasant, roast chicken, and lamb, not to mention trays of vegetables and fruit and another sideboard filled completely with elegantly decorated cakes and desserts. Fresh flowers overflowed silver bowls.

During dinner the conversation turned to the race and Lily held her breath, keeping her gaze downward as she pretended to eat.

"You should have seen it, St. James," someone said. "Lydell's horse is a beauty all right, and his jockey is said to be a woman. What about it, Lydell? Any truth to the rumor?"

"I'm sworn to secrecy," Charles said with a grin. It was obvious just how much he was enjoying being the center of attention at Natchez's most prestigious summer party.

Everyone laughed, including Nicholas.

Lily felt ill. She thought they would never stop talking about the race, or speculating about the winning jockey.

After dinner, she left Nicholas to his guests and sought out Jeanette Mireaux.

"I . . . I just wanted to thank you for the party," she said.

Jeanette seemed taken aback.

"Well . . . I wanted to do it. You've enjoyed it?" There was an awkwardness between them, and Lily supposed it would always be that way.

"Enjoyed it?" Lily sighed. "It's wonderful . . . perfect. I couldn't have asked for a more delightful welcome home."

"Then I'm pleased," Jeanette said.

Lily nodded graciously and moved away.

Jeanette watched her, noting the tiny waist encased tightly in black silk. The dress was perfect for her. Her slender hips moved demurely beneath the full skirt . . . just enough, Jeanette thought, to capture a man's complete attention. The girl was tall and stately; she carried herself like a queen, and yet there was a sensuality about her that she obviously didn't even know she possessed.

At one time, Jeanette would have said it was wasted on the girl. But now, seeing the way Nicky had looked at his young wife tonight, she wasn't so certain.

She was no longer the wild river girl with backwoods manners and a language to match. She had made her entrance this afternoon with the confidence of a woman who knew her worth, and in a matter of moments had managed to capture the attention of every male here. And yet, her demeanor was so sweet and gracious that the female guests seemed just as entranced.

Jeanette felt pain and bitterness rising in her so strongly that she wanted to cry.

She had underestimated Lily St. James.

Chapter 20

It was almost midnight and yet the breeze that wafted through the brightly lit house had cooled only the slightest bit. It was a perfect Mississippi summer evening.

After the supper that won raves from everyone present, couples strolled out to the gardens, or danced in the hallway and parlor. Some of them danced on the long front porch, declaring it much cooler.

Inside the house, Nicholas and Lily were still the center of attention. Yet she was hardly aware of anyone else around them.

All evening Nicholas had flirted with her. Teased her. Wooed her with all the romantic fervor of a man bent on seduction.

His attention had not been lost on the crowd, and now it seemed that every eye was riveted on this handsome couple who seemed so perfectly matched. And yet everyone murmured about the marriage that had been arranged. No one ever expected a match between these two very different people.

Was this real? Had they fallen in love? Those questions

and many others were whispered from one person to another throughout the house.

Jeanette watched, her eyes reflecting the pain she felt. This was not what she'd expected. She had expected the party to show her off to advantage, to reveal Lily as a hopelessly gauche child. Instead, not only was she forced to watch as the man she loved pursued another woman, but she had to suffer the further humiliation of having everyone know it was killing her. They were like vultures sitting on a rail fence just waiting for her to collapse.

"Are you all right?"

Jeanette turned to find Jared at her elbow. He looked so much like Nicholas that, for a moment, she caught her breath. When she blinked away tears, she felt Jared's arm, comforting and strong at her waist.

"Let's get out of here," he said, pulling her with him.

They were in the garden before either of them spoke.

"Thank you," she said. "I should have left sooner. I don't know why I stayed to be humiliated."

"I know exactly how you feel," Jared said.

Jeanette looked up at the young man beside her. His eyes glittered in the lanternlight, and his jaw was tightly clenched. She had wondered about his relationship with Lily, had hoped it would continue, even blossom, as a matter of fact. But Jared had such a reputation for gaming and paying court to disreputable women that she couldn't imagine he really cared about the flame-haired girl who had taken Natchez by storm. She'd suspected all along that he only did it to irritate Nicholas. It was no secret how bitterly Jared St. James resented his wealthy, more successful cousin.

"You're apparently as shocked by this turn of events as I am," Jeanette said.

"To say the least," Jared growled. "They're embarrassing, the both of them. Flaunting such intimacy in front of the entire beau monde of Natchez."

"They *are* married." Jeanette said. "I kept telling myself

that they were doing it for show. Until I saw the way they were looking at one another.'' She glanced from beneath her lashes at Jared. "I can see you're quite infatuated with her yourself. If you don't mind my asking, how did Lily behave when she was with you? Did she give you reason to believe that she might return your affections?''

"I had hoped," he exclaimed. "Especially after all I've done for her. What has Nicholas done except make his usual demands? Everything falls too easily into that man's damnable hands.''

"What do you mean, what you've done for her?" Jeanette asked, with interest.

Jared was almost trembling with his frustration and a sense of betrayal. "What would you think if I told you that Lily St. James was the woman everyone is talking about— the one who won the race today.''

"Lily?" Jeanette said frowning. "Surely not. She must have known how embarrassed Nicholas would be if she did such a thing. I can't imagine a woman doing that to the man she loved. And yet tonight, she seems completely mesmerized by him.''

"Exactly," Jared said. "But she had counted on my secrecy, just as she counted on me to arrange the entire matter.''

Jeanette's eyes turned bright with appreciation as she began to understand what he was saying.

"Jared St. James, you are a sly one." she said, laughing.

"And I haven't finished yet. When I'm done, Nicholas will be glad to send her away from him, and I, of course, will be there to *console* the poor girl.''

"I must confess, I'd like nothing better.''

"Yes," Jared whispered. "You and I would be a perfect team. And once our task is accomplished we shall both have what we want.''

"What exactly did you have in mind?''

"I'm not quite certain. But when I decide, I'll let you know. You will help, won't you?''

"Well, I . . . I don't know if I . . ."

Jared took her arm, pulling her closer. His hard grip bruised her flesh.

"Why should I take all the risks alone, Jeanette? You have as much to gain from this as I do."

Jeanette pulled away from him, rubbing her arm as she glowered up into his petulant face.

"All right," she spat. "As long as Nicholas never knows that I'm involved. What do you want me to do?"

"I'll let you know," he repeated. "You just be ready."

The guests were leaving. Nicholas and Lily stood on the front porch.

She could feel his body pressing against hers. The scents of the warm night air surrounded them, intoxicating and sensual. She could feel the heat of his body against hers, and was highly aware of every touch of his hand on her waist or the small of her back.

Did he feel it, too—this tension that lay between them like a living, breathing thing? Was he trembling with anticipation the way she was?

All night he had made her feel so special, so beautiful and desired. And now the moment had come. The moment when they would finally be alone in the house.

"You look exhausted," Nicholas said, bending his head low toward Lily. "Why don't you go on up, sweetheart? I'll make sure everything is in order down here."

His unexpected endearment took Lily by surprise. In fact she could hardly believe how that one lightly spoken word could fill her with such happiness.

She murmured her assent and left him there, turning once as she started up the stairs and found him watching her, his eyes dark and filled with a quiet desire that left her trembling.

Upstairs, she hardly knew what to do, or how to dress. By the time she heard Nicholas coming up the stairs, she had discarded the black dress and now wore only a silky cream-colored gown covered by a matching dressing robe trimmed in Belgian lace.

She was at her dressing table, about to take down her hair when Nicholas tapped lightly on the door and came in.

His eyes darkened when he saw her, and he came forward without a word, moving behind her.

"Let me." he said, his hands moving to covers hers where she had begun to unpin her hair.

Lily's flinch when he touched her scraped and blistered hands was involuntary.

Nicholas frowned and turned her hand over, holding her palm toward the lamp.

"Lily . . . what's this? What have you done?"

"Oh, I . . . I burned myself on the curling iron earlier." She could hardly meet his concerned gaze as she told the lie, and when he bent and placed a soft kiss against her reddened skin, she came very close to confessing what she'd done.

He turned her around in the chair, and Lily closed her eyes when she felt his hands in her hair. Small, delicious shivers ran down her back and arms as he gently loosened the pins. He combed his fingers through the gleaming curls before letting them fall down her back in one luxurious mass.

"You were the most beautiful woman here tonight," he said, bending to place a kiss against her neck. "I loved dancing with you."

"And I loved dancing with you," she said, her voice breathless.

"Then come here." he said, taking her hand. "Dance with me now."

Lily laughed and stood up, going into his arms as if she'd always done so.

As he pulled her against him, his hand moved slowly, provocatively up her back, beneath her loosened hair. The touch of him against her through the silken gown sent shivers over her already highly sensitized body.

But oddly she didn't feel afraid at what was about to happen. She had been so curious and had waited so long for him to care. And now that he seemed to, she was ready for his touch, and for this unknown intimacy that existed between man and wife.

She didn't want to appear too bold or brazen. Mary had often warned her about that. But she found it very hard to pretend not to feel the things she did.

Her heart beat faster when Nicholas pulled away and removed his jacket, then loosened the tie at his throat.

Through the thinner material of his shirt, she could feel his broad chest pressing against her. When he pulled her back into his arms, she could feel his thighs brushing against hers as he continued dancing her slowly about the room. His hand moved down lower, to the small of her back and just to the top of her hip as they moved to the sound of their own music.

She could hear his ragged breathing, and when he bent to kiss her, his lips were hot and urgent.

She could hardly believe this was happening. That this man who had been such an enigma, was holding her and kissing her. That he actually wanted to make love to her.

When he pulled away, she looked up into his heated gaze.

"Am I going too fast for you?" he asked, frowning slightly.

"No," she said, her answer immediate and certain.

To prove it, Lily reached up to unbutton his shirt. She thought she'd die if she couldn't feel his naked skin. When she slipped her hands beneath his shirt and closed her eyes, she heard him gasp and felt his hands against her hips, hard and urgent pulling her closer.

A ribbon of moonlight fell through the windows and across the room. When Nicholas danced her into the stream of light, she could see his face, dark and shadowed.

She reached out to kiss his mouth and heard his responsive groan.

"Perhaps," he whispered, "we've danced enough."

Without realizing it, Lily murmured a quiet little protest. She was enioying the moment, feeling his strong body against hers and realizing with amazement that she had the power to arouse him this way.

He continued kissing her, soft, teasing kisses that tormented her and made her want more. His teeth nipped at her full lips until she pressed herself close and forced him to kiss her completely . . . until their fevered breathing mingled and grew louder in the darkened room.

She hardly knew how they made their way to the bed. His kisses had left her so weak that she could hardly stand. And yet he continued kissing her, his mouth hungry, greedy, as his hands anxiously moved over every inch of her body.

"I want to see you," he whispered, his voice ragged with desire. "All of you."

He pushed her dressing gown away from her shoulders, and she shook it free. His mouth moved to her bare shoulders and farther down to the top of her breasts before his fingers impatiently pushed the material away.

"Oh," she whispered, feeling his lips against her burning skin.

"Tell me what you're thinking. I want to know what you're feeling," he urged.

"Oh, Nicholas," she sighed. "I . . . I—"

"Tell me," he demanded, his hands moving to cup her breasts.

"Hot," she murmured. "I'm so . . . hot . . ."

Nicholas ripped her gown off her shoulders and down her body until it fell to the floor around her feet.

For a moment as he looked at her, he stood unmoving, letting his eyes take in every inch of her in the pale moonlight.

Her breasts were firm and pink, swollen now from his

touch. Her waist was so slender he could almost span it with his hands. Her hips flared out gently and femininely and yet he could see the outline of delicate bones underneath her skin, skin that was soft and aglow in the moonlight.

"You are more beautiful than I ever dreamed," he said softly, letting his eyes move lower and taking in every inch of her all the way down to her toes. "Breathtaking."

Lily felt a moment of self-consciousness, and then it was gone. How could she not want him to see her, when he looked at her this way?

"I . . . I want to see you, too," she whispered, becoming shy again.

Slowly, still looking into her eyes, Nicholas stripped away his clothes until he stood in the darkness before her.

Lily had never seen a man unclothed, but she thought he must be the most beautiful of men. She was shocked to see exactly what his arousal meant. And yet she was fascinated as well.

When he placed her on the bed, she wasn't sure exactly what would happen next. But she was ready. Whatever he wanted to do, wherever he wanted to lead, she was ready.

Still, he kept her waiting, creating an exquisite torture with his hands and his kisses until she thought she might actually die from this unnamed longing.

She loved him and she was burning with some mysterious need that even she did not fully understand.

"Nicholas," she whispered, moving almost frantically against him. Her small hands clutched at him, wanting something and yet unable to express what it was she wanted.

"I know," he whispered as he moved between her legs. "I know, angel. It's what I want, too. What I've waited for."

Lily was stunned for a moment by the searing pain she felt. She clung to Nicholas as he grew still and waiting, yet trusting his softly murmured reassurances, letting him soothe her and kiss her until the pain was gone.

She opened her eyes and looked up at her dark, handsome husband as he began to move in a slow, erotic rhythm. She found herself moving with him as he lifted her, guided her, and sent her quickly over the edge of some sweet, unexpected splendor.

When he whispered words of love—erotic, forbidden words—she thought she might shatter into a million pleasurable pieces.

Instinctively she wrapped her long legs around him, reveling in this new sensation of lovemaking. Her teeth nipped at his strong jaw, her hands moving from his shoulders down to his muscular hips.

She heard him groan and felt his shudder against her and she gloried in the fact that he was as lost in this moment as she was. That her strong, intractable Nicholas could be so vulnerable and so emotional in these last exciting moments of lovemaking.

"Nicholas," she whispered. "Oh, Nicholas, I love you. I love you."

Later, as she lay in his arms, feeling such awe and such raw emotion, she wondered how she ever could have dreaded this moment.

And in the back of her mind she knew that this night had changed her life forever. She belonged to Nicholas now. To her husband. She was his, body and soul.

This was what it meant to love a man.

Chapter 21

Lily lay sleeping, her head resting on Nicholas's bare shoulder. She slept like a child, with her bright hair spread about her head and tumbling over her shoulders before making a golden splash against the white linens.

Nicholas was wide-awake, his eyes troubled as he lay staring up at the ceiling. He hadn't slept. Had not even closed his eyes, though he was tired.

Every time sleep came, his thoughts pushed it away. All he could think about was Lily and her sweet, innocent surrender.

She had said she loved him.

"God," he muttered between his teeth.

Lily stirred and smiled in her sleep.

"Mmmm?"

"Shh, love," he said, smoothing her hair back from her forehead. "Go back to sleep."

Why couldn't he just enjoy the fact that she loved him? Wasn't it what most men wanted? How many men had wives like Lily, one who was beautiful and intelligent and as passionate in bed as he was?

But he felt himself drowning in an unexplainable sea of desire and need, and he didn't like it. He was used to living his life to suit only himself. Without the complications of a woman's love, without the ties of a wife. He was afraid he'd never be able to give her what she wanted or what she deserved.

Now, as she slept, her slender body warm and soft against him, she seemed even more sweet and innocent than before. She was so breathtakingly beautiful, and despite her anger at him before, Nicholas knew that deep down inside, Lily was also very trusting and good.

He had lain for a long time, looking at her, his eyes quietly studying every detail of her face and body. She was his. She had given herself so completely, holding back nothing of herself.

He reached out, letting his fingers trail over her shoulder and down to the curve of her breast. Unconsciously he pulled a lock of her hair up toward him, closing his eyes as he breathed in the scent that seemed to be hers alone.

He felt his chest tighten, and he shuddered. These tender feelings were troublesome and as foreign to him as another language.

Knowing that he was the first man to make love to her left him feeling oddly elated and remorseful at the same time. Living with her every day had become a torment, and had awakened a need that couldn't be ignored. She was like a fever, and their lovemaking was a much-needed relief. He knew he had taken her as his wife to satisfy his lust; not because he loved her the way she needed and deserved to be loved.

But did that really matter, he asked himself. How many times had he said that love wasn't important in a marriage?

He'd take care of her. See that she had everything she could ever want.

So what else could she possibly ask from him?

Nicholas slid his arm carefully from beneath Lily's shoulders and moved from the bed. When he turned to look down at her, his face was still dark and troubled.

Lying there with her hands beneath her cheek, she was as beautiful and innocent as an angel. And yet for him, she had been shameless and unafraid, meeting his love measure for measure. Wanting him and unashamed to let him know.

Nicholas raked his hands through his hair and cursed beneath his breath.

What in hell was wrong with him? Why did he feel so confounded by his own wife's guilelessness and by her pronouncement of love?

He couldn't remember ever feeling this way with any other woman. Hell, he'd never have *let* himself feel this way. Had prided himself, in fact, on always remaining aloof. That was why his liaison with Jeanette had lasted so long.

Jeanette. She was going to be another problem.

He grumbled beneath his breath and searched the floor for his clothes, pulling them on quickly. As he was leaving, he turned once at the door, letting his gaze take in the outline of her there on the bed with the moonlight glinting softly against her pale skin.

Lily smiled in her sleep, then slowly opened her eyes. The sun was up, and her room was beginning to grow warm.

She stretched and turned onto her side, still smiling as her hand reached out to where Nicholas had been sleeping.

She sat up quickly and glanced around the room.

"Nicholas?" she whispered, even though she could see that he was not there.

She lay back against the pillows, frowning as she tried to remain calm and reason with herself. Perhaps he had gone back to his own room, thinking he might disturb her sleep.

Lord, she hoped he wouldn't be one of those men who insisted on sleeping in separate rooms. She loved sleeping in his arms, waking him and feeling him there beside her. Being in his arms was like coming home.

Lily could feel her face growing warm just thinking about last night. Nicholas had been passionate and tender. After their initial lovemaking, she had slept so deeply, waking to feel him touching her, arousing her again with his hands and his kisses.

She'd been surprised and pleased, then stunned by her own body's need for him. Nothing Mary had ever said could have prepared her for the wonder of it. This was something that a woman had to experience for herself to know the depth of emotion it brought. Lily knew in her heart, with a maturity that was beyond reason, that it could never have been so wonderful if they didn't love each other.

True, he hadn't said he loved her.

And yet hadn't he proved it with his looks, his touch? With his strong, perfect body?

A light knock at the door pulled her from her reverie and she sat up, pulling the sheet up and tucking it under her arms.

"Yes," she said. "Come in."

When she saw Nicholas push open the door and step inside with a breakfast tray in his hands, her face brightened. Relief and happiness washed over her in a warm rush and she found herself wanting to laugh out loud.

"Are you hungry, Mrs. St. James?" he asked, his voice teasing and light.

"Starving," she said.

She looked into his eyes and saw only warmth and tenderness and for a moment, the relief she felt was overwhelming. She watched him walk across the room and place the tray on a table near the windows.

She'd been so afraid that Nicholas had left her, that

he'd been disappointed somehow. She'd been wrong to doubt him. Thank God, she'd been wrong.

"This is very nice, but I'd hoped to have breakfast with my husband," she said, suddenly feeling shy. This was a special morning for her. Was it not the same for a man?

Nicholas took her dressing gown from a nearby chair and held it while she pushed her arms into the sleeves. Then he pulled her from the bed and toward the table where the tray was. Whisking away the white linen cloth that covered the food, he gave a mock bow.

"And I would like to have breakfast with my wife. That's why I brought breakfast for two."

"Oh . . ." she murmured, glancing from the tray up into his eyes. "Oh, Nicholas."

Nicholas took a warm, wet cloth from the tray and, without speaking, reached for her hands. Gently he moved the cloth over her tender palms and up her arms, releasing a clean, fragrant scent into the air.

"I'm glad to see that your hands are better this morning," he whispered.

Lily sighed and closed her eyes.

"This is heavenly. I feel completely spoiled."

"You're heavenly," he murmured. He bent and kissed her soft lips, then pulled a chair away for her to sit in.

Lily found that she could hardly stop smiling as they ate their breakfast.

"The entire household must know by now what happened last night," she said, glancing at him from beneath her lashes.

Nicholas looked at her for a moment over his cup of coffee, his eyes crinkling as he smiled.

"Does that bother you?" he asked.

"No," she said with a shake of her head. "Well . . ."

Nicholas laughed aloud and put down his cup. He reached to take her hand, leaning across the table and pulling the tips of her fingers up to his mouth.

"We're husband and wife," he reminded. "What happened between us is normal and healthy."

"Oh," she said. "I know that. I didn't mean to imply anything else. It's just . . . I can hardly believe that you . . . that you and I . . ."

The look in Nicholas's eyes changed. He stood up from his chair and pulled her up to stand in front of him, sliding his arms around her waist and holding her close.

"Unbelievable, I agree," he whispered as he kissed her. "Incredible that my little river urchin has turned into this beautiful woman . . . this creature who tempted and beguiled me all night long."

Lily buried her face against his neck, breathing in the clean masculine scent of him. She could feel his body hard against hers, and when she looked into his eyes, she saw his desire and his need reflected there.

Seeing her look, he cocked his head to one side and laughed again.

"As much as I'd like to stay here with you all day, I'm afraid I have an appointment. One I made long before I knew what this morning would mean."

Lily murmured her quiet disappointment. But she let him go.

How could she not, when he left her with such a look of promise in his gray eyes.

She spent the rest of the morning pampering herself and lazing in the tub. While one of the maids changed the bed and brought out one of Lily's new dresses, Lily wrote to Mary. She wanted to tell her everything. How very happy she was. How she'd been right about Nicholas.

"This dress, ma'am?" the young girl asked.

Lily barely glanced around. She didn't care what she wore. Anything would be beautiful to her today. She saw only that it was a delicate froth of yellow material spread atop her bed.

"That will be fine," she said.

Later, as she walked in the garden, she moved her hands

down over the soft daffodil-colored material. Actually it had been the perfect choice since it seemed to reflect the way she felt this morning.

New and bright as the morning sunshine. Happy. Joyous.

She was so lost in thought that she didn't hear anyone approaching. At a touch on her arm she whirled around to find Jared staring at her, his brows knitted together in a disapproving frown.

"Well," he said. "You seem exceptionally pleased about something this morning."

His look was so intense that Lily had to turn away from his curious stare. Surely he didn't expect her to discuss such intimate things as what happened between her and her husband last night. Besides, how could Jared even guess? Did she look so different today?

"It's a beautiful morning," she said. "And I love this garden. It pleases me very much."

"Oh, I'd say it's something much more than the garden that has pleased you."

Lily felt a moment of apprehension. She'd never heard Jared speak to her in this tone before. There was something harsh and hateful in the way he said the words, as well as the way he continued to stare at her.

"What is it, Jared?" she asked, moving away from him. "Nicholas will be home soon, and you know he won't be pleased to find you here."

"Oh, so that's the way it is now?" he said through gritted teeth. "You've no time for me?"

He reached out and grabbed Lily's arm, forcing her to turn and face him.

Lily caught the scent of liquor on his breath, and she frowned.

"Jared . . ."

"You listen to me," he said. "I don't enjoy playing the fool and I don't enjoy being used."

"But I haven't . . . I don't—"

"I was perfectly good company as long as your husband

wasn't around, is that it? A lark. Someone to take you here and take you there and to make arrangements for your childish little schemes."

Lily pulled her arm out of his grasp and took a step backward.

"And now that you and he are together, there's no longer any room for me, is that it?"

"Why are you behaving this way?" she asked, trying to remain calm, even though her heart was pounding. "There's no reason for you to say such things to me. Nicholas is my husband and he—"

"Nicholas!" he said, the name bursting forth like a bullet from his curled lips. "Always Nicholas. Well, we'll see what Nicholas thinks about his sweet wife once he learns that you were the girl in the race yesterday. Everyone in town's talking about it, you know. And from what I hear, she's considered by many to be trashy and ill-bred. Wouldn't they be surprised to learn that this brazen hoyden is the wife of one of Natchez's most respected businessmen?"

"Jared, no," she said. "You promised you'd never tell. If I'd known how Nicholas . . . if it were now, I'd never do such a thing without telling him. Everything's different now. Nicholas is different and I—"

Jared's expression was hard and ugly.

"Different is it?" he snarled. "That's too bad, because we aren't finished with you yet. You must race for us again, Lily."

"No." she said, her eyes reflecting her horror. "You can't ask me to do that—not now."

"But I can," he said. "In fact. I demand it. Do you realize how much money was made yesterday on that one race? Do You have any idea how much Charles and I could make if you raced one last time after we discreetly spread the rumor that the female rider is back?"

"Don't ask me. Jared, please don't do this."

"Why?" he growled. "Because you plead with me so sweetly? Standing here with your mouth still swollen from your night of lovemaking? Don't pretend you didn't know how I felt about you, Lily. How I hate seeing that insipid look of love on your face! I'm actually sickened by it."

"How dare you speak to me this way."

At his too-intimate words, Lily clenched her teeth together and whirled around, intending to push her way past him.

But he was too quick. She could feel his fingers bruising her delicate flesh as he pulled her against him, his face very close to hers.

"You owe me, Lily. And you owe Charles. Did you think we did this favor for you for nothing?"

Lily's face was pale, and she was trembling when he pushed her away and sent her stumbling on the uneven walkway.

"I'll let you know when the race is scheduled," he said. He stared at her one last moment, the look of hatred still burning in his eyes. "Don't disappoint me. You know I have the information it would take to ruin everything for you. I can make you sorry you were ever born. And I think you know I'm not bluffing—I won't hesitate a moment to do it."

She stood staring after him, her cheeks hot and flushed with anger. Jared was drunk, she was certain. But still, was that reason enough for him to behave this way?

The ache in her heart told her the answer. She'd been fooled by Jared's good-natured facade. Lulled by his attention and his flattery, by his eagerness to grant her every request.

Nicholas had warned her about his cousin, but like a willful child, she hadn't listened. Jared had used her. How could she have been so gullible and so foolish?

And how was she ever going to get out of the mess she'd created?

Chapter 22

Lily was still shaken from her encounter with Jared when she got back to the house. But she hardly had time to think about him or his threats for almost as soon as she stepped inside the hallway, Nicholas was there.

Touching her. His eyes filled with laughter, his smile happy and teasing. Bright enough to light every corner of the house.

"Where've you been?" he asked. "We have things to do, woman. Get your hat."

Despite her distress over Jared, Lily couldn't keep from laughing with her handsome husband. Being a part of his life, having him look at her this way, was all she'd ever dreamed it could be.

"Where are we going?" she asked.

"It's a surprise," he said, giving her a gentle push toward the steps. "Now go get your hat. I don't want the sun ruining that beautiful skin of yours."

Out of the corner of her eye, Lily saw Mrs. Lloyd coming out of the dining room. There was a bright smile on her face, just as there had been on the faces of all the house servants this morning when they looked at Lily.

But it didn't embarrass her, as she thought it would. Instead it had warmed her, knowing they all accepted her and were happy that she and Nicholas were together. At last, she felt welcome and cared for. She felt as if she were home.

Later, as their carriage pulled out of the drive, Lily sank back against the seat, sighing as she allowed herself to enjoy the beauty that surrounded them and the contentment she was finally beginning to claim as her own.

The sun was warm overhead and just a hint of breeze stirred the tree limbs that met and intertwined over the street above them. The air was fragrant with the scent of sweet shrub and lilacs. Birds sang and darted across the road in front of them. And from the direction of the river they could hear the low moan of a ship's horn.

Nicholas pulled the reins, turning the horse toward the road leading down to the river.

Lily glanced at him, wondering what he was up to.

"Where are we going?" she asked.

"We'll be there in a minute."

She laughed with pure joy for the moment and the way he made her feel so light and happy. She saw his eyes change and suddenly, with a move that took Lily by surprise, Nicholas pulled the carriage to the side of the road. With one arm, he reached over and pulled her to him, kissing her hard and thoroughly on the mouth.

"I've been wanting to do that since breakfast," he said, his voice low and seductive.

Lily shook her head at him, and he laughed, then clucked to the horse and pulled them back onto the road.

In a matter of minutes they were at the front of her old home. Lily looked at Nicholas and at the mysterious smile on his lips, but she said nothing as he lifted her from the carriage and took her hand, leading her toward the house.

The door was unlocked. Stepping inside, Lily saw Miss Fran in the living room.

When the woman turned and saw them, her eyes filled with tears, and she put her hands up to her face.

"Oh, Lily," she murmured, coming forward. "I can't believe you have done this. Or you, Mr. St. James. How can I ever thank you?"

Lily accepted Miss Fran's embrace and raised a questioning eyebrow at Nicholas over the woman's shoulder.

"It's the first real home I've ever had. Since I was a little girl."

Lily's eyes widened with pleasure and surprise.

"Nicholas," she whispered.

"Oh, look," Miss Fran said, going to the front door. "They're here with the furniture. Oh, I can hardly wait to see what they've brought."

Lily went to stand in front of Nicholas and slide her arms around his waist.

"I can't believe it either," she said. "You've made my wishes a reality. And you've even furnished the house! That's what the Boston Sisters would call full measure and running over."

"I hope you don't mind that I went ahead without discussing it with you."

"Mind?" She reached up and kissed him, her eyes bright with unshed tears. "Of course I don't mind. It's one of the nicest things anyone's ever done for me. Thank you."

"I wouldn't have done it if I'd have known it would make you cry," he teased.

"They're happy tears," she said shakily.

Nicholas wiped the tears from her lashes and kissed her, his mouth warm and tender.

"I don't ever want to make you cry again," he said, touching his chest. "For any reason."

Was it an apology? A promise for the future? Lily didn't know. All she knew was that his pledge, given so sweetly, made her feel happy and warm. Made her feel loved, even though he had never said those words to her.

They spent the entire afternoon there helping Miss Fran. Nicholas stepped into the street, finding enough men to move the furniture in as Lily and Fran inspected each piece and decided where it would go.

All of the heaviest pieces were in place when Nicholas came to Lily.

"We probably should be getting home. Mrs. Lloyd will have dinner, and she'll be wondering where we are."

"This old place never looked so beautiful," Lily said, taking Miss Fran's hands. "I hope you'll be happy here. As happy as I was when I was a child."

"I will be," Miss Fran whispered. "How could anyone not be happy here? I can see the river, and all my friends are here."

"And I want you to be safe. I didn't like the way that man treated you."

"Don't worry," the woman said. "That's been taken care of too. That old man won't be botherin' me anymore, ain't that right, Mr. St. James?"

"If he so much as shows up within a mile of this place," Nicholas said with a determined nod, "I'll know about it."

Driving back up the hill, Lily sat close to Nicholas, clutching his arm against her body.

"You did this for me," she said.

Still driving, he glanced down at her, his smile sweet and mysterious.

"You find that so hard to believe?"

"I'm finding all of my life right now hard to believe," she said, laughing.

"Yes, sweetheart . . . just for you." he said finally. "I decided I could learn something from your generosity and your caring nature."

"Thank you," she whispered.

It was one of the happiest days of Lily's life. And yet it was dampened a bit every time she thought about Jared and his earlier threats. She only prayed he wouldn't do anything to ruin the happiness she'd found at last.

Perhaps it would be easier just to make the ride than to try to argue with him. She certainly couldn't tell Nicholas. As furious as he would be if he knew how Jared had treated her, worse would be his disappointment at how she had betrayed his trust.

She loved her husband. Lord, but she never thought it possible to love anyone as much as she loved Nicholas St. James. She couldn't lose him now. And she knew that whatever she had to do to keep him, she would do.

Early Saturday morning, just as dawn had begun to spread its golden light over the Mississippi, Lily woke. Feeling Nicholas's arms around her and his breath against the side of her neck, she smiled and turned to press her body against his.

"I need you," he murmured.

"Oh, Nicholas," she whispered. "I never knew life could be this way." The past week had been like a blissful dream. She loved him so much, and their lovemaking was so powerful, so overwhelming that sometimes she could hardly believe it.

He kissed her, his mouth warm and seductive. She lowered her head as he lifted her gown up and over her head, then tossed it onto the floor.

When he took her breasts in his hands and trailed hot kisses over her skin, she groaned and arched against him, feeling the heat of his body, throbbing and hard.

He knew just where to touch her, just what to do to arouse her until her mind was in a spin and her body aching for him. When she pushed herself against him, she heard a quiet, deep growl in his throat.

"You're driving me crazy," he whispered against her ear. "Do you know that? Do you know how much I want you? Every moment of every day?"

She answered him with a kiss. Hungry and hot and demanding.

With a groan, he moved over her, taking her body quickly in a passionate hot rhythm. With their need and desire ruling them, they moved together, their lovemaking becoming urgent. For the first time, they found release together, giving in to the forceful, timeless ecstasy of fulfillment.

Lily thought it was the most wondrous thing she'd ever experienced.

Nicholas held her against him, never wanting to let her go. His face was against her neck as he breathed in the warm, provocative scent of her skin. When she snuggled against him, whispering love words in his ear, he laughed as he felt his body responding to her yet again.

They both laughed together, and he turned to look into her eyes as the morning sun threw soft, filtered light across them.

"You're going to be the death of me," he teased. He pushed his fingers into her hair and brushed it away from her forehead. "But what a lovely death it would be, my love."

They were sleeping when Burton knocked and slipped a small sealed envelope under the door. Lily lay watching from the bed, smiling and enjoying the sight of Nicholas's magnificent body as he stretched and got out of bed. He opened the note and read it, and a line appeared between his brows. When he glanced across the room at Lily, his face had a closed look, almost the way it had been when she first came back home in the spring.

"Nicholas?" she asked. "What is it?"

"Nothing important," he said. "But there's something I have to do today." He came to the bed and bent to kiss her. "Do you think you can manage to entertain yourself while I'm away?"

Lily's heart skittered wildly when she realized that this was probably Jared's doing. His demands and her deceit had intruded on this most glorious of mornings. On one hand she was relieved that she'd be able to pay her debt to Jared and Lydell. But on the other, she felt a terrible fear and guilt gripping her heart at having to lie to Nicholas.

"Of course I can," she managed lightly.

Nicholas had been gone no more than fifteen minutes when Burton came back to the room.

"Mr. Jared's downstairs, ma'am," he said. "He say he need to speak to you right away."

Jared was in the library when Lily entered.

"I should have known," she said. "You're the one who sent Nicholas the note, just to get him out of the house so I could ride in the race today."

"Well, I didn't actually send the note," he drawled, his eyes glittering. He seemed especially pleased with himself. "But you can rest assured that he will be away most of the day."

"What did you do?" Lily asked. Her chest tightened as her apprehension grew. "Nothing will happen to Nicholas," she gasped, as fear filled her eyes.

Jared laughed.

"God, no," he said. "Not that I would shed any tears if it did. But no, my dear, I'm not stupid enough to do something so drastic in a town he practically owns."

"Promise me," she said. Without thinking, she marched to Jared, and grasped the lapels of his suit "You must promise me nothing will happen to Nicholas," she said, shaking him, "or I swear I'll leave your wagers riding high and dry. I'll lose the race deliberately, Jared, I swear I will."

Jared's brow arched as he looked at her in surprise. Her eyes glittered emerald fire, and her cheeks were flushed with anger. She was like a little wildcat.

Jared took her small hands and tugged them away from his suit. His look was cool as he brushed at the wrinkles.

"All right . . . I promise," he said dryly. "Nothing will happen to your precious Nicholas. All I want is my money. After that, you and he can do as you please. Have a dozen babies and live in dreary monogamous boredom for the rest of your life. I assure you, it's nothing to me."

Lily was so upset that she was shaking. She stared into his eyes, trying to decide if he meant what he said. Slowly, she stepped away from him.

"I'll meet you at Pharsalia." she said, clenching her teeth. "When this is over, I don't care if I ever see you again. Until then, I'd prefer it if you left my home."

Without another word, she whirled and stalked out of the room.

This time, she let the big black horse have his head far back, even before the halfway point. She didn't want to take a chance on losing the race and giving Jared reason to want her to ride again. By the time she crossed the finish line, she was several lengths ahead of the nearest rider. The finish was not as exciting for the crowd, but she didn't care. All she wanted was for it to be over.

Lily hardly felt any elation at winning this time. All she felt was relief.

Now, nothing could stop her from being with the man she loved, and spending the rest of her life with him.

Lily reined in her horse, letting him cool down and move toward the winner's area. As before, the crowd surged toward her. But this time, Jared's carriage was not there to whisk her away to safety and anonymity.

She looked around in panic as she suddenly found herself being hauled down from the horse.

"Jared!" she cried. "Let me go. What are you doing?"

Before she knew what was happening, they were in the winner area. And as the crowd cheered, Jared pulled her hat from her head, letting her hair tumble around her shoulders as he pulled her roughly against him.

"To my lady" he spouted as Lily stared at him in disbelief.

He took her face between his hands and kissed her, his

mouth hot and devouring . . . as Lily, humiliated, struggled
to pull away from him.

Seeing the passionate kiss and the red-gold tumble of
hair, the onlookers shouted and cheered. Then there was
a patter of unsettled laughter as she was recognized and
her name moved with a loud murmur through the crowd.

For a moment, she stood frozen, knowing the sting of
complete betrayal and shame. Her eyes scanned the crowd,
and she recognized some of the people from their summer
party.

Then she saw him. Saw the look of horror and disbelief
in those beautiful, expressive eyes that she loved so dearly.
Saw his smile change to a look of pain and anger and
betrayal.

"Nicholas," she whispered.

He was with Jeanette, the one who had—no doubt—
sent the note. He had gone to her. One word and without
a moment's hesitation, he'd been ready to leave Lily for
his mistress.

Lily watched, her heart shattering into pieces as Nicholas
pushed his way through the crowd toward her, his eyes
never wavering from her ashen face. A wave of silence
moved with him, until by the time he'd reached her and
Jared, the entire area was filled with a deadly quiet except
for the stamp of the horse and its heavy breathing.

Without a word, Nicholas swung his arm out with swift
and violent accuracy before anyone realized what was happening. The blow sent Jared sprawling in the dirt, and
when he managed to push himself up on his elbow, there
was blood trickling from his nose.

"You bastard," Nicholas said, standing over him with
his legs apart.

Lily thought her heart might actually stop when he
turned that cold wrath toward her. His eyes glittered with
contempt as they swept over her trembling mouth and
down to the disheveled men's clothes that she wore.

"You lied to me," he said, his voice soft, but deadly.

"God, I can't believe I was fool enough to put my trust in you."

"Nicholas," she said. "Let me explain. Please."

Some of the bystanders helped Jared to his feet.

"You'll pay for this, Nicholas," he said, wiping blood from his face. "Do you hear me, you'll pay! As an honorable man, I must ask for satisfaction. Choose your weapons."

To Lily's horror, a low murmur of delight swept through the crowd. She wouldn't have been surprised if they'd begun wagering right then and there on which man would live and which would die.

"No," she said, moving toward Jared. "Please, Jared, don't do this. Nicholas is your cousin." She turned to her husband. "Nicholas!" she said, her voice pleading. "Please, let me explain."

The look in his eyes was filled with disgust. And pain. She thought she'd never forget the pain she saw there. If she lived forever, she'd never be able to forget it. Or to forgive herself for being the cause of it.

"Pistols," Nicholas growled, still not moving his gaze from Lily's face.

She reached out for him, but he moved past her, brushing his arm roughly against her and pushing away her hands.

Lily had paid little attention to Jeanette until that moment. But now as they stared at each other, she saw her own stunned disbelief reflected in the other woman's blue eyes. She might have been feeling triumphant at first, but now as the man she loved agreed to a duel against his own cousin, Nicholas's mistress seemed as horrified as Lily.

On Jared's face, however, was a look of pleasure and satisfaction. He had what he wanted. Lily knew with a sudden clarity that he had planned this all along, with the intention of goading and humiliating Nicholas into a duel.

And God help her, she had played right into his deceitful hands.

Chapter 23

"I'll take you home." Jared moved beside Lily, his eyes glowing with an odd light.

Lily turned on him, her entire body trembling with anger. "How could you do this?" she asked. "And how could you ever presume that I'd allow you to take me anywhere after what you've done?"

Ignoring his protest at her words, she began pushing her way through the throng of people.

"Lily . . . come this way."

She looked up and through the veil of tears that blurred her vision, she saw Patrice Claymore. Despite the woman's small stature, she was forcing her way through the crowd, ignoring some of the men's suggestive remarks and the women's looks of disapproval.

Lily bit at her lip and reached for Patrice's outstretched hand.

Perhaps they were more alike than Lily had ever wanted to admit. Neither of them deemed quite good enough for the Natchez elite, both of them ostracized—not for what they were, but for what people thought they were.

In that moment as she took Patrice's hand and moved with her away from the crowd, Lily felt both defeat and defiance. But she also felt an overwhelming surge of gratitude for this woman's kind rescue.

"Here," Patrice said. "Get into the buggy. My driver will take us to your home."

As Lily climbed in the buggy and felt it begin to move, she was stone-faced, refusing to let the pain in, refusing to give in to the agony she felt. She tried not to let herself think of anything.

But she was aware of Patrice's concerned gaze as they drove along the tree-lined road toward Natchez.

All Lily could think about was Nicholas. The way he had looked when he came through the crowd. The bitterness she'd seen in his beautiful eyes.

Those eyes that had finally begun to look at her with affection and understanding.

Now it was over . . . before it ever really had a chance to begin. She couldn't imagine he would ever look at her that way again.

"Jared," she muttered in disgust. He was the cause of this. She had trusted him . . . confided in him as a friend. And what pained her most was the fact that he'd used that trust against her deliberately. He'd used her to seek some kind of revenge against Nicholas, and she'd been too blind to realize it.

"Lily," Patrice said. Her voice was low and filled with sympathy.

She moved closer to Lily and put her arm around her shoulder. Lily could smell the scent of some exotic perfume. She glanced down at the brilliant blue material of Patrice's skirt and frowned when she saw several small splashes of darker color. She hadn't realized she was crying until then.

She felt the sobs moving up with agonizing rapidity from her chest, causing her throat to ache and burning her nose and eyes until finally she could no longer contain her grief.

She collapsed against Patrice, giving in to the tears and the self-pity that washed over her. She covered her face with her hands, hearing her sobs and thinking that she sounded like a lost child.

"I . . . I'm . . . sorry," she gulped. "I . . . I can't seem to—"

"Shh," Patrice whispered, stroking her hair. "It's all right to cry. Of course you can't help it. You've been betrayed by one man and hurt by another. What woman wouldn't cry."

Finally, Lily wiped at her eyes and sat back against the seat.

"I'll take you home," Patrice said. "We'll get you cleaned up and have Mrs. Lloyd make us a hearty pot of tea. We'll talk and decide what it is you are to do. All right?"

"Yes . . . all right," she said dully, giving in to Patrice's kindness.

She was so used to being on her own. Even after she came home to Nicholas, she had never really felt a part of his life until the past few days. Now, not only had he rejected her, but for Jeanette!

She thought it was that, more than anything, that broke her heart.

Jeanette had never seen Nicholas this way. As soon as they were inside her house, he walked to the cabinet where she kept liquor. Without a word, he poured himself a glass of bourbon, gulping it down with a self-destructive fierceness that made Jeanette murmur a quiet protest.

He wiped the back of his hand across his mouth and eyes and poured another.

"Nicholas," she said, moving to him. "Chéri . . ."

When she placed her hand on his arm, he jerked away and drank down the amber liquid.

"What a damned fool I've been," he said, slamming his

hand down on the cabinet. Crystal decanters rattled, and the glasses jumped and settled back down with small quiet thuds.

He hadn't said a word about the note she sent this morning asking him to come to her. Thank goodness he hadn't connected it to what happened at the race. Jeanette knew that he had come to her out of loyalty and concern. She had made him think she was despondent. And when he came she had convinced him that a day out would make her feel immensely better.

That much was no lie, at least.

But now, seeing him this way, she thought if she had known the depth of his feelings, the agony he'd felt at Lily's betrayal, she might never have agreed to help Jared. She certainly had no idea he meant to challenge Nicholas to a duel.

Not that she need worry about Nicholas in that respect. He was a deadly shot. Her husband had always said that Nicholas had the most accurate eye under fire and the coolest head of anyone he'd ever seen.

Jeanette had seen that coolness many times. Had despaired of it on more than one occasion in fact.

And it killed her knowing that today, when that coolness left him and was replaced by this bitter yet passionate fury, that it was not for her.

Jeanette knew he'd never have behaved this way except for a deep and true love.

He loved his wife. And Jeanette thought he probably still hadn't admitted it to himself yet.

"Nicholas," she said, putting her arms around him. She started to unbutton his jacket, reaching up to kiss his strong jaw at the same moment. "Darling, let me love you. Let me help you forget all that has happened today."

She felt Nicholas stiffen. He pulled his head back, out of reach of her searching lips. When he looked down at her, his eyes were dark and troubled, glittering with fury and the effects of the bourbon.

When he pulled her roughly into his arms and kissed her, his mouth was hard and punishing, his hands biting into the flesh of her arms. But just as quickly he pulled away, cursing quietly and turning to pick up the crystal decanter of liquor once again.

Nicholas remembered the last time he'd tried to erase Lily's memory in Jeanette's arms. It hadn't worked then, and, despite his pain and anger today, he knew it wouldn't work now.

"Nicky . . ."

Nicholas felt such bitterness rising in him. He wanted to smash something . . . anything. "Don't," he said, without turning. "This isn't the time, Jeanette. Not now."

He was being as honest as he could. And the truth was he couldn't possibly make love to her. Now now. Perhaps not ever again.

The memory of Lily was too near. Too real. How could he make love to any other woman after knowing the intoxicating sensation of having Lily in his arms? After her body and its sweet surrender had left its imprint on his heart and soul forever. Had any of it been real? Had he let himself be fooled because he wanted her so much?

What a damn fool he'd been to trust her. Better to have remained the way he was—making love to many women, but loving none. Always detached. Always free.

He had no idea what to do about Lily. His muddled mind wouldn't even let him think about it now. But one thing was certain.

Because of her betrayal, he was going to have to kill his own cousin.

Patrice stayed with Lily all afternoon. They sat on the gallery upstairs sipping tea and watching the traffic drift slowly down the river.

"I can't thank you enough for bringing me home," Lily said. She couldn't keep the little sob out of her voice when she spoke, any more than she could seem to keep the tears from filling her eyes every time she thought of that terrible, humiliating scene at the racecourse.

"I've been so stupid," she said.

"You are not stupid," Patrice replied, squeezing her hand.

Patrice had always seemed so sophisticated, so aloof. Lily had not seen her in this kindly, almost-motherly way before. And she realized that the woman, though older, was not much different than she was.

She had lived a hard life, pulling herself out of a poverty-stricken childhood in New Orleans and capitalizing on her beauty and charm. She'd become celebrated as an actress. She'd met royalty, dined with kings and princesses.

Patrice told Lily she'd even married a duke, only to find in him the same abusiveness that she'd known from her own father. She'd lost a child, and struggled for years to pull herself up from the dark, tortuous melancholy that came afterward.

And then she had struggled to come back and be even more successful and independent than before.

Lily had never heard any of this until today. Knowing Patrice's background made her much more real and human. And she knew that Patrice had told her all this to bolster Lily's own confidence and let her know that things were not always as bad as they seemed.

But how could she believe that when her heart was breaking? When it seemed that life held no meaning without the man she loved.

"I've lost Nicholas forever," she said quietly.

"No, no, darling," Patrice said. "Nicholas is a proud man, and he's hurt. But I know in my heart he loves you. How could he not? Just look at you. Those eyes . . . that face. Not to mention you are as sweet and kind as you are beautiful."

"No," Lily said. "He's never said he loved me. Not even when . . . I mean . . ."

Patrice's smile was knowing. "Men are like that," she laughed. For them, love is a surrender, while we women seem to run toward it with open, welcoming arms. Never looking down or even caring of the treacherous pathway beneath our feet."

Lily smiled weakly and nodded in mute agreement.

"Tell me the truth," Patrice said. "Did you ever . . . care for Jared? Or was this friendship between you all his idea?"

Lily's eyes flashed. "I swear I've never been intimate with Jared. I made it clear from the beginning that I was not interested in . . . that kind of relationship. He respected that, or so I thought." She explained quickly how Jared had befriended her when she first came back to Natchez. How she'd been lonely and desperate for friendship, after Nicholas's cold behavior.

"Men can be such fools with it comes to love," Patrice said. "And even the magnificent Nicholas St. James is no exception. But if what you are telling me is true, then things cannot be so bad. Once you manage to explain everything to Nicholas, it will be all right. He can be proud and arrogant, it's true, and he would probably never admit that he could be hurt by any woman. But he is an honest man. And a fair one."

"You . . . you seem to know him very well," Lily said, her voice quiet and questioning.

Patrice laughed softly.

"He once rescued me from a very drunk, very nasty man. And I was grateful in the only way I knew how to be." Patrice's eyes were gentle and filled with a quiet honesty. "There was no more to it than that, and it was before you came along, Lily."

Lily nodded, letting the explanation suffice.

"He was with Jeanette today," Lily said. "I know it's my fault this time, but I don't think I can endure it if he keeps going to her?"

"He's angry right now," Patrice said. "And his pride has been hurt. But believe me, he does not love Jeanette.

If he did not care for you, he wouldn't have reacted the way he did today. It's not like him to lose control."

Lily bit at her lower lip. She let her gaze move out toward the river, feeling only the slightest bit of hope in her heart at Patrice's reassuring words.

She'd thought about going to Jeanette's house and forcing Nicholas to listen to her explanation. But perhaps Patrice was right. Perhaps she should allow time for his anger to cool before she tried to explain anything.

Could he really believe after what they'd shared together that she'd prefer Jared to him? That she would ever look at any other man?

If he really thought that, then he didn't know her at all.

Chapter 24

Lily had Mrs. Lloyd bring a light supper to the upper gallery. She knew that Patrice would have to leave soon, but there was more she wanted to ask her.

"Patrice, do you think Nicholas and Jared will go through with this duel?"

"Hmm, it's hard to say," Patrice said with a lift of her brows. "I'm sure it isn't what Nicholas wants, but circumstances and honor, you know . . . But if it happens, I do know Jared will be at a distinct disadvantage. He has neither the nerve nor the skill to defeat a man like Nicholas."

"Tell me about Nicholas," she said. "Why is he the way he is? He wants everyone to think that he's cold and unfeeling, that he doesn't care what anyone thinks of him. I believed it at first, but now I know better."

"It was his mother, I think, and what happened to her," Patrice said, her voice soft and thoughtful. "Of course Nicholas never told me personally . . . but one hears stories. His mother married beneath her station and as a result she was sometimes not treated very well by the Natchez elite. She was a sweet, fragile woman, and they say that some days she'd have to take to her bed. Nicholas was just a boy then, and of course it was troubling to him, seeing his mother so sad and lonely. Jared used to taunt him about his mother, saying she was crazy. You know how children are. But I think Nicholas never forgot, or forgave. And I think he still has a great deal to prove because of it. Has he never mentioned it to you?"

"No, never," Lily said. "But his sister Mary has. She lived in the same house and witnessed the same thing, but it didn't seem to affect her that way at all."

"Young men are often very protective of their mothers and their sisters," Patrice said. "I think it was one of the things I always admired about Nicholas . . . that quickness he has to defend a woman."

"The way he did you," Lily said.

"Yes," Patrice replied. "The way he did me."

Lily sighed. "I can see now that was exactly what he meant to do when he warned me about Jared. But he was so overbearing that it made me resentful and defiant. I only saw a man trying to rule me, and I couldn't bear it."

The sun dropped lower toward the line of trees across the river, and Patrice stood up to go.

"I wish I didn't have to leave you alone like this," she said. "But tonight is our last performance in Natchez. As soon as it's over, we'll leave for New Orleans. And I confess I can't wait to be home again. I must be getting old, for I swear sometimes I actually ache to see the city again."

"I know," Lily said. "It's the same way I feel about Natchez." She stood up, still feeling a bit awkward about this new, unlikely friendship. "I wish you didn't have to go either," she sighed.

"Come with me to the performance," Patrice said. "It's a very funny play. It will cheer you up and make you forget today's fiasco."

"No," Lily said. "I'd love to see you perform, but perhaps some other time. I don't think I could stand being in public tonight, having people stare at me and whisper."

"I understand," Patrice said. "But promise you will write to me. Here," she said, handing her a card. "This is my address in New Orleans. In a few days, I wish to receive a nice long letter saying that Nicholas is safe and that you and he are back together again. And that things between you are better than ever."

Lily shook her head, smiling wistfully.

How she wished it were as easy as that.

Patrice kissed Lily's cheek quickly and, with a little wave, turned to go.

Lily was still sitting in the darkness when Mrs. Lloyd came out to take away the dishes.

"Is there anything else you'll be needing, Mrs. St. James? Shall I light the lamps out here for you?"

"No, Mrs. Lloyd," Lily said. "But thank you. I think I'd prefer sitting here in the dark. And please thank Clemmie for supper—it was delicious."

She was aware that the older woman continued to stand before her, and Lily glanced up.

"He'll be back, you know," Mrs. Lloyd said.

"Oh, Mrs. Lloyd," Lily whispered. "Don't tell me that you've already heard about what happened at the race today." Her voice was ragged with humiliation. She stood up and walked to the rail, staring out over the darkened trees, where fireflies flickered and moved. "I suppose everyone in Natchez knows by now."

"Gossip tends to travel fast in a small community, especially when it's about one of its most prominent families."

Lily winced at being the subject of such talk.

"You must think I'm very foolish," she said.

Mrs. Lloyd placed the dishes back on the table and came to stand beside Lily.

"You're being much too hard on yourself, my dear," she said. "No one in this house thinks you're foolish or anything of the kind. Nicholas St. James was not an easy man to live with when you first came back. No one knows that better than I do. In his stubborn way of trying to protect you, he pushed you directly into Jared's path. A decidedly treacherous one, too, if you don't mind my saying so.''

Lily took a deep breath and turned to look at Mrs. Lloyd.

"Thank you for saying that," she said. "But I can't blame my actions on Nicholas."

"I mean it," the woman said. "He will come home. One day both of you will look back on all this and laugh. It's probably something you'll tell your children and your grandchildren. Why, I'd think any woman would be proud to have beaten the best riders in the South at their own game. You're becoming something of a heroine among Natchez women, my girl." There was a sense of pride in the woman's voice as she reached out and squeezed Lily's arm.

Still, despite everyone's attempt at reassurance, Lily couldn't sleep. She stayed on the gallery until well past midnight when she heard the low moan of a ship's horn. She smiled wistfully as she stared into the darkness.

Patrice would be leaving now. Going home to her beloved New Orleans.

Lily went inside and prepared for bed. She was well and truly exhausted, and despite her troubled thoughts, she soon drifted off to sleep.

She woke with a start, her heart beating rapidly, and realized someone was pounding on the front door.

"Lily! Lily!"

It was a woman's voice, and, for a moment, she thought Patrice had come back. But even in her sleep-filled mind she knew it wasn't Patrice.

As she shook herself awake, she realized the voice that called so frantically to her was Jeanette's. And there was a sense of panic in it that struck at Lily's heart.

She ran barefoot out onto the front gallery, bending over the rail and trying to see down onto the shadows of the front porch.

"Jeanette?" she called. "Jeanette, is that you?"

"Lily!"

She saw Jeanette step out from beneath the edge of the roof and look up toward the gallery. Moonlight filtered through the live oaks and across her pale skin and hair.

"Oh, Lily, thank God. Get dressed. You have to come with me. You have to come now. It's a matter of life and death."

The breath left Lily's lungs, and for a moment she could not speak, could not move.

"What's happened?" she managed finally. "Has something happened to Nicholas?"

Please, God, she prayed silently. *Just let him be all right. Don't let anything happen to him. Not now. Not while we're apart this way and he is filled with such anger and despair.*

"He's all right, at least for now. But I must speak with you."

"Come up," Lily said. "The door is unlocked. I'll bring a lamp to the landing to light your way."

Jeanette was panting softly as she reached the top of the stairs. For a moment they stood staring at one another, their eyes wide in the glow of the lamplight.

"What is it?"

"I'll tell you while you get dressed," Jeanette said, nodding toward the bedroom.

Lily felt a moment of apprehension, and she hesitated. She couldn't think of one reason why she should trust this woman. Or why she should do anything that she asked.

But there was that quiet desperation in Jeanette's voice that shook Lily to her very soul. That and the little glint of fear she saw in the woman's pale eyes.

Lily knew that it would have to be something serious to make her humble herself this way and come to Lily for help. She was obviously genuinely frightened.

Lily turned toward her bedroom and Jeanette followed, speaking softly but quickly.

"The duel has been set for this morning at dawn."

"What?" Lily whirled about to face the woman. "But how can that be?"

"Jared sent a messenger to the house late last evening, while Nicholas was sleeping."

Lily recoiled.

Jeanette didn't know why she should feel sorry for this girl. But when she saw the look of pain that leapt to her green eyes, she hurriedly explained, "He only stayed because he drank too much. But the point is, he agreed readily to the duel."

Lily hurried into her room, going behind a screen and scrambling to dress.

"Where?" she asked.

"At the dueling tree across the river. My driver is waiting outside. If we hurry, we can make it before dawn."

Lily stepped from behind the screen, her hands trembling as they fumbled with a long row of buttons up the front of her dress.

Why should she believe anything that this woman told her? Jeanette had every reason in the world to hate Lily, to want her dead even. How could Lily be certain that Jeanette was not spiriting her away with the intention of doing her in? What if she was still conspiring with Jared?

"How do I know I can trust you?" she asked, her hands falling to her sides and suddenly becoming still.

Jeanette took a deep breath of air and looked directly into Lily's wide, questioning eyes.

"You have every right to ask that," she said, her voice quiet. "I love Nicholas. I admit that freely to you tonight. But it's because I love him that I came here to see you."

Lily turned her head to one side as if she didn't quite understand her meaning.

"After Nicholas left, I had a very long time to think," Jeanette said. "A long time to consider all the things I'd done wrong. I'm not a bad person, Lily, despite what you might think of me. It's true that I agreed to help Jared. You must have guessed by now that I'm the one who sent

Nicholas the note. I'm also the one who was to make sure he was at the race to see you with Jared."

Lily gasped softly.

"It was a terrible thing to do and I regret it." Jeanette's full pink lips trembled ever so slightly, but she never pulled her gaze away from Lily's. "You have to understand that I loved Nicholas desperately, long before there was a real marriage between the two of you. And all I could think about was that I was losing him."

Lily's lips parted slightly and she frowned.

"You're the only one who can stop this, Lily," Jeanette said, taking a step forward. "Do you understand? The only one he will listen to. It's because I love him that I came. Nicholas is an excellent duelist, but I know Jared. He's deceitful and filled with hate. He'll stop at nothing to get what he wants, and I have a very bad feeling about this. I would rather lose Nicky to you than see him die!"

Lily hugged her arms about her body and shivered. She turned away from Jeanette's desperate eyes and walked around the room as thoughts rushed and swirled about in her head.

"We don't have much time, Lily," Jeanette cautioned. "Please . . . I'm begging you."

Lily turned and looked once more into Jeanette's troubled eyes.

"I believe you," Lily whispered. "God, I must be the most gullible fool on the Mississippi, but I believe you're telling me the truth."

She could see the relief wash over Jeanette. It softened her features and relaxed her tensed shoulders. When Lily saw the woman's tremulous smile and her blue eyes sparkling with unshed tears, she knew she'd made the right decision.

By the time they'd driven to the ferry and wakened the ferryman, it was very near dawn.

Lily could feel her heart pounding with anxiety and fear.

What if they were too late? What if Jeanette was right and the bad feeling she had was a portent of disaster?

If something happened to Nicholas without Lily having a chance to ask for his forgiveness, she thought she would die, too.

As soon as the ferryman pulled the planks down on the opposite side of the river, Jeanette urged her driver on. They drove off with a clatter, the rough movement throwing them about in a teeth-rattling jumble that forced them to hold on to the seat and to each other.

When they reached the dueling tree they could see the outline of other carriages in the damp mist that drifted in from the river. In the faint half-light beneath the trees, several horses stamped and snorted.

"It hasn't happened yet," Lily said, jumping quickly from the buggy.

As they reached the huge old live oak known as the dueling tree, the sun was just coming up over the bluffs of Natchez. They hurried forward and were met by a group of men.

"You can't come any farther," one of them said, frowning at the intruding women. "You must be quiet."

When Lily looked out into the fog-enshrouded meadow, she saw the reason why.

Nicholas was there, his tall form straight and proud as he stood with his back against Jared's. Each of them held a dueling pistol near his cheek, barrel pointing up, as someone in the misty light began to count.

"No," Lily sobbed. "God, Jeanette, we're too late. We're too late."

She felt Jeanette's hand grab hers. Felt her holding on as if for life itself while both of them stood staring at the two men on their field of honor.

When the counting stopped, the duelists turned and slowly lowered their pistols, each aiming at the other across the meadow.

"Fire!"

After the shouted order, the silence was stunning. Every-one in the meadow seemed to be holding their breath.

There was a quiet, metallic click of a firing pin and then Lily heard Jared's voice swearing through the gloom.

"Jared's gun has misfired," someone whispered.

Nicholas had not used his shot at all.

Jared cursed and threw his useless pistol onto the ground. Then he straightened, throwing his shoulders back and his chin out as he faced his cousin.

Nicholas's pistol was still held in his outstretched arm, pointing straight at Jared's chest. He seemed cool and perfectly still, while everyone could see Jared's coattails moving and shaking in the light morning breeze.

The seconds ticked by; still Nicholas did not fire.

Finally, Jared made a quiet noise and his legs buckled, taking him to his knees. "Shoot, damn you!" he shouted. His voice was filled with the humiliation of his body's weak-ness. "Just take your shot and be done with it!"

"Yes, shoot," someone else muttered in the crowd of men nearby. "Now's your chance, St. James."

For what seemed like hours they all stood there, staring at Nicholas and waiting for the sound of his pistol shot. Was he making Jared suffer deliberately? If he was, Lily thought, it was probably a fate worse than dying.

Suddenly Nicholas raised his weapon above his head and fired it into the air. Then slowly he lowered it back down to his side as he made a slight bow toward Jared.

"I consider the matter between us settled, cousin," Nich-olas said, his voice reverberating over the meadow in a quiet rumble.

Lily closed her eyes and breathed a quiet prayer of grati-tude. The relief she felt turned her legs to jelly, and if she hadn't been clinging to Jeanette she thought she might actually have fallen.

When Nicholas turned toward the group gathered beneath the trees, he saw Lily and he stopped.

Lily pulled away from Jeanette and stepped out from

beneath the tree. Her gaze met Nicholas's and held. He was all she could see, all she could think about as she moved toward him.

When she heard a shout, she wasn't quite sure what or who it was. She did not see Jared leap to his feet and move forward, seize another man's arm and struggle with him for a moment.

Nicholas's eyes were troubled as he continued on toward Lily. She thought in that moment that she even saw the possibility of forgiveness there.

But she could never be sure. For in that same moment she heard the gunshot. Saw Nicholas's big strong body recoil as the bullet found its mark. Saw the pain and surprise in his eyes before he slumped over onto the grass in front of her.

"Nicholas!"

She wasn't even aware that the voice was her own. And she wasn't sure how she forced her legs to move. All she knew was that she was running . . . running toward the man she loved, who now lay bleeding on the ground.

Chapter 25

There was a moment of stunned silence before shouts erupted and people began to run forward to help. Lily only had a second to see Jared as he stood in the mist with the gun in his hand, its barrel still smoking. For a moment she thought he meant to kill her, too.

But then he turned and ran, pushing his way past the man whose gun he had taken, before leaping onto a horse and galloping away into the surrounding gloom.

Lily fell to her knees beside Nicholas. Others were there, too. Stronger, surer hands helped her turn him over.

"Here's the doctor," someone said. "Let him through." A man dressed in black knelt in the grass across from Lily.

Nicholas looked so pale, so lifeless. She held her breath as the man examined Nicholas, and when the doctor looked into her eyes, she fully expected to hear the worst.

"Are you his wife, ma'am?" he asked.

"Yes," Lily choked out.

"It's very bad," he said. "I'm sorry. Unless I miss my guess, this bullet has entered very close to his heart. He probably won't make it through the day. My advice would be for you to take him home and try to make him as comfortable as possible.''

''Make him comfortable?'' Lily asked. Somehow her mind was not functioning properly, and she could not seem to grasp what the doctor meant.

She was aware of Jeanette standing behind her, weeping softly.

''Jeanette?'' she said, turning to look up at the woman.

''What he's trying to say is that Nicholas is dying, Lily.'' Jeanette's voice broke as she spilled out her own grief and longing.

''No,'' Lily whispered, her entire body filled with disbelief. She turned back to Nicholas.

He was so strong and powerful. So full of life.

He couldn't be dying.

She fell against his body, aware of his warmth and the soft breath from his lips against her hair.

''No,'' she said again. ''This can't be.'' She touched his face and felt the wetness of her tears on his skin.

Suddenly she felt such fury sweeping over her. She felt like screaming at the men who stood staring so dispassionately. At the doctor whose sympathetic eyes now turned away from her.

''You're wrong,'' she said, turning her gaze on the silent crowd of men.

Her voice, though soft, quieted every murmur, every speculative word.

''He's not going to die,'' she said fiercely. ''I won't let him die.''

''Mrs. St. James,'' the doctor began. He reached across as if to comfort her.

''No,'' she snapped. ''Jeanette, have your driver bring the buggy around. We're taking him to Live Oaks. The trip across the river will take too much time.''

Lily didn't care how they looked at her or what they thought. She was reacting now purely by instinct. And something deep down inside would not let her admit that there was nothing to be done for Nicholas. She loved him too much to let him go without a fight.

Jeanette's lips parted, and for a moment she, too, looked at Lily as if she were demented from grief. Then her eyes brightened with hope, and she turned and hurried across the grassy area to where her buggy and driver sat waiting.

In a moment, she was back with the buggy, jumping down from the seat and rushing to Lily.

"Well, don't just stand there," Jeanette demanded, looking around at the crowd of men. "Help Mrs. St. James get her husband into the buggy."

Everyone there knew who Jeanette was: Nicholas St. James's mistress. And if they wondered how the two of these women came to be together, or if they were curious at the new, unlikely alliance between them, they didn't express it. Perhaps it was the diminutive Widow Mireaux's fierce demeanor as she stood with her hands at her waist, daring them to say something. Or perhaps it was the look of hope and faith on the young Mrs. St. James's lovely face as she silently implored them to help.

"Well?" Jeanette said.

Several men stepped forward, lifting Nicholas and moving him quickly to the waiting buggy.

"Mrs. St. James, I'd advise you against this," the doctor said. "But if you insist on caring for him at Live Oaks, then I'll follow along in my own carriage and do what I can for him."

Lily was standing now. Nicholas's blood had left a crimson swath across her stylish gown. But she lifted her head, gritting her teeth to keep away the tears.

"Thank you, sir," she said, much more calmly than she felt. "I'd appreciate that."

She would not break down in front of these men. If they and Nicholas cared so much about honor and pride, then she would show them a woman's honor and pride.

Nicholas's tall form took up the entire back seat of the small buggy, but Lily insisted on holding him. She sat on the floor with her arms around him while Jeanette climbed into the front seat beside the driver.

"You ready, ma'am?" the driver said. "I'll drive as easy as I can."

"I'm ready," Lily said, nodding firmly. "Just get us to Live Oaks as fast as you possibly can."

It was almost dusk that same day when Lily heard someone step into the room where Nicholas lay. She was so weary that she barely had the strength to turn around to see who it was.

"Jeanette," she murmured. "Come in."

"I've brought you a nice bowl of soup and a pone of Mama Jolie's corn bread."

Lily turned back to Nicholas, shaking her head.

"I can't possibly eat," she whispered. She reached out to touch him just as she'd been doing every few minutes for the past several hours. As if to reassure herself he was still alive.

"You have to eat," Jeanette said. She came forward, ignoring Lily's protests, and placed the tray of food on a table beside her.

"How is he?"

Jeanette's voice broke. She'd made no effort to stay with Nicholas, deferring to Lily's status as his wife. And suddenly, Lily realized how hard that must have been for her. Despite how she felt about the woman, the truth was that she did seem to love Nicholas. And she had humbled herself in front of Lily in order to save him.

"I think his color is better . . ." Lily said, her voice trailing away. Her words sounded so weak. Did she really think that, or was she deluding herself as the doctor had so bluntly suggested?

"Here," Lily said, pointing to another chair. "Sit down with me. You must be as exhausted as I am. Have you eaten anything?"

"Yes," Jeanette whispered. She pulled the chair close, glancing once at Lily with an almost-shy look of gratitude.

Jeanette reached out as if she wanted to touch him and Lily looked away. She felt such mixed emotions where this woman was concerned. She had thought at one time that she hated her. And yet today, seeing her grief over Nicholas, she actually felt sorry for her.

Still, it was an awkward moment, sitting so close to her and trying to pretend that she didn't care, didn't ache because Nicholas had loved this woman. Perhaps still did. After all, it had only taken a brief note to make him leave Lily's bed and go running back to the arms of the beautiful widow.

"I . . . I think you're right," Jeanette said. "His color does seem better." Her smile was self-conscious and tentative.

Only at Lily's insistence had the doctor finally agreed to remove the bullet, but he'd seemed more discouraging than ever that Nicholas would survive.

"It wasn't as close to his heart as I first thought. But he's lost a great deal of blood," the doctor had said, shaking his head. "I'm afraid there's nothing more any of us can do except tend to his wound and watch for infection. With a bullet wound and in this warm weather, that's almost a certainty. And when that happens . . ." The man had shrugged and solemnly left the room.

Someone tapped on the door behind them.

"Come in," Lily said.

The girl who came in was taller even than Lily, and her figure was strong and muscular-looking. Almond-shaped eyes were framed by long dark lashes, darker than the color of the girl's sepia-colored skin. She was a strikingly beautiful young woman whom Lily had met once before. She knew that she was the daughter of the Live Oaks cook, Mama Jolie, and that mother and daughter had come here from the bayou country farther south.

Lily's gaze fell onto the basket that the girl carried.

"Yes, Mae," she said. "What is it?'

Mae curtsied, her eyes wide as she stared at the two women sitting beside Nicholas's bed.

"I brought some new candles," she said. "Their light will keep away the death spirits."

Jeanette gasped and stood up.

"Death spirits!" she cried. "Good Lord. How dare you say such a thing?" Jeanette waved her hands at the girl as if to shoo her out of the room.

But Mae stood her ground, looking past the petite blonde toward Lily.

"It's all right, Jeanette," Lily said. "She only means to help. Come on in, Mae," she said, forcing herself to smile at the dark-skinned girl. "We can use all the help we can get."

Mae nodded, glancing briefly at Jeanette before moving with a strong purposeful stride toward the bed.

"Here . . . I put one at his head," she said, her voice soft. "And one at his feet."

Lily watched silently as the girl set about her task, placing the candles in various places around the room and lighting them as she went. In seconds, the walls and ceiling were aglow with candlelight, and their earthy beeswax scent filled the entire room.

Lily turned back to Nicholas, reaching out to slip her fingers into his big hand. It was an odd sensation, feeling so protective of this strong, powerful man. Nicholas had always been the one to protect her. The one to see that everything was done just right for her safety and comfort. He was the one everyone depended on. He'd taken care of Mary and then Lily. And not just his family, but Mrs. Lloyd and Clemmie and Burton and the others. And here at Live Oaks, there was grief and sympathy among the servants when Nicholas was carried into the house and upstairs to this room.

Nicholas was respected. But more than that, he was obviously loved as well.

She loved him too. And now it was her turn to care for him and protect him.

Tears filled her eyes as she listened to his shallow breathing and saw the small lines of pain etched across his brow.

"Oh, Nicholas," she whispered. "You can't leave me. You can't leave the people here who love you and need you. What would they do without you? Who would take care of them the way you have?"

She felt hands touching her shoulders and looked up to see Jeanette standing behind her. Her eyes were glittering with tears also as she nodded to Lily.

"You have to eat, Lily. You need to keep up your strength if you are to be any good to him at all."

There was a different look in Jeanette's eyes. If Lily hadn't known how the woman resented her, she'd have thought it was one of admiration. Whatever it was, it took Lily by surprise.

Without a word of protest, Lily pulled a chair up to the table where the tray containing the food rested. Jeanette nodded with quiet satisfaction and walked toward the door, glancing over her shoulder toward the bed as if she hated to leave.

"I hope you won't think I'm overstepping my bounds, but I've had one of the rooms prepared for myself. Just for tonight. The ferry is probably—"

"I don't mind," Lily said. "Please . . . I'd appreciate it if you did stay. I could use the company."

The two women nodded toward one another in mutual respect.

Chapter 26

The next few days went by in a blur for Lily. She slept and ate at Nicholas's bedside, refusing to leave him except for short periods of time. She didn't even realize that several days had passed until Jeanette came to her early one morning.

"I should go back to Natchez," Jeanette said, reluctantly.

Despite Lily's efforts to hold on to some resentment toward Jeanette, she'd found during the past few days that she could not. Jeanette had conducted herself as a lady. Even though it was obvious how much she loved Nicholas, she had done nothing to try to usurp Lily's place. In fact, Lily thought it must have been very painful for the woman to stay away from Nicholas as much as she had.

And if she couldn't yet bring herself to embrace the woman as a friend, at least she wanted to be fair.

"Do you really want to go?" Lily asked.

The look on Jeanette's face was cool and unreadable.

"It's what I should do."

"That isn't what I asked."

"Lily," Jeanette said with a heavy sigh. "Why are you so

nice to me? You should hate me for what I've done. Not just with Nicholas, but for my part in helping Jared."

Lily's eyes sparkled angrily at the mention of Nicholas's cousin. She thought she could kill the man herself if she ever saw him again.

The very idea of her strong, vital husband lying here helplessly infuriated her. Nicholas would hate it. He'd hate being waited on and tended to like an infant. And he'd hate the steady stream of visitors who came and stood at his bed, staring down at him as if he were already in his coffin.

The doctor had come back several times, and he'd seemed surprised to find Nicholas still alive. Others from Natchez came, some of them the same men who'd witnessed the shooting at the dueling tree that morning.

Lily welcomed them all and saw that they were properly fed and attended to, that they were given a place to rest if they wished. Some of them remained overnight, and she saw to it that Mama Jolie prepared elegant meals that Nicholas would have been proud of.

And although the work had occupied her, she'd spent most of the days lost in a weary fog. But the servants had come to depend on her and to respect her, and because of them, she couldn't let herself give in to the weariness she felt.

She hadn't realized how much she'd come to value Jeanette's knowledge and help. Until now.

She straightened her shoulders and looked up at Jeanette, bringing herself back to their conversation.

"You must know what a great help you've been to me," Lily said. She cleared her throat self-consciously, hardly knowing how to proceed. She never thought to find herself in such an odd situation. "I . . . I want you to know that I do appreciate it. And if you'd like to stay longer here at Live Oaks, I'd be pleased to have your company."

Jeanette's usually cool expression changed slowly. Her face seemed to crumple, and she bit her lip, frowning as she blinked her lashes quickly.

"You're a very kind woman, Lily St. James," she managed finally. "And I . . . I'm so . . . I'm just so . . ." She whirled around and hurried toward the door. "Excuse me," she said as she brushed past Mae.

"What's wrong with her? Mr. Nicholas ain't got worse, has he?" Mae asked, coming quickly to the bed.

"Oh, no," Lily said. "No, he's just the same. But that's good. I think the broth your mother made has strengthened him. He's moving his arms and legs more today, I think."

"That's good," Mae said. She carried several items in her arms and now she set them on a table beside the bed.

"What have you brought today?" Lily asked.

"Conjur man, he say Mr. Nicholas could be lost in the spirit world. Jest wanderin' and lookin', trying' to see his way clear back to this old world. And back to you, Miss Lily."

"And what does your conjur man say should be done to remedy the matter?" Lily asked, smiling gently at the girl.

"He give me some special water to clean his eyes with. So he can see his way better."

"Oh," Lily said. "Well, I suppose that makes sense."

After Mae gently washed Nicholas's eyes, she took something out of her pocket and rolled it with a metallic clatter onto the table. It gleamed a bluish gray beneath the lamplight and Lily shuddered.

"That's . . . that looks like the bullet that the doctor took from Nicholas's wound."

"Yes, ma'am," Mae said with obvious pride. "I asked if I could have it. Conjur man, he done oiled it up real good. Oilin' makes the bullet hole heal quicker."

Lily nodded seriously. "I see."

"And I brought some oil made from the Palm of Christian. If you rub it on him, it sure to take away the last of his fever. And conjur man, he done bored a hole deep into the sunny side of that old oak tree out front. When he blowed his breath into the hole, he plugged it up tight, so's the fever can't hurt Mr. Nicholas no more. I told conjur man we shoulda asked before he did it. That old tree might die now that it's got the fever locked up tight inside it."

At the conclusion of this speech, Lily leaned her head back, laughing for the first time since they'd brought Nicholas home to Live Oaks.

"That's quite all right, Mae. You tell the conjur man I'll gladly sacrifice the oak tree for Mr. Nicholas's return to health."

"Yes'm," Mae said, nodding enthusiastically. Her eyes were bright as she turned to leave the room. "He be happy to hear that. I go tell him right now."

"Oh, and Mae?" Lily said.

"Yes'm?"

"Would you look in on Mrs. Mireaux as you go? Make sure she's all right and please ask if she needs anything."

Without saying so to Mae, Lily hoped that Jeanette was not leaving. She'd been as surprised as anyone to learn that she actually enjoyed the other woman's company. Sometimes they sat in this room for hours, talking only rarely, Jeanette working on a piece of embroidery. It reminded Lily of her peaceful time with Mary, and the companionship, as strange as it was, had helped Lily cope with her fear.

Now she picked up the bottle of oil that Mae had brought, and removed the cork. She had no idea what Palm of Christian was, but she was surprised at the pleasant, spicy scent.

She glanced at Nicholas, wishing for the thousandth time that he would just open his eyes. That she could hear him say something . . . anything. Even if he hated her, she wanted him to wake up.

Was he wandering in some spirit world as Mae said? Was he a troubled, sad little boy again, alone and afraid?

She reached out and touched his face. He was so warm sometimes she couldn't understand why he continued in this unconscious state.

Dark lashes lay close against his skin. There was no expression on his face and his sensuous mouth was relaxed. At least the lines of pain had eased these last few days, and he seemed to be sleeping much better.

But there was the fever, and she just couldn't be certain if he'd ever come back to her or not.

"Oh, Nicholas," she sighed, bending over him.

Almost unconsciously, she poured some of the oil into the palms of her hands. She pushed back the sheets that covered his upper body and softly began to massage the oil onto his chest.

She closed her eyes, breathing in the pleasing scent of the oil and enjoying the feel of his skin and the taut muscles beneath.

In her mind's eye, she saw his face . . . his smile as it had been before. She heard his laughter and gave a quiet little moan as she remembered the urgency of his kisses.

She was hardly aware of the tears that spilled from her eyes and dropped down to mingle with the oil, warmed now by her hands.

When hard hands grasped her wrists, she thought for a moment that she had drifted off to sleep. That she was dreaming. But when her eyes flew open, she found herself staring into those familiar steely gray eyes.

"What the hell . . . ?" His voice was rough from days of disuse, and his gaze was confused and troubled.

Lily couldn't speak. Her hands, still covered in oil, were suspended in the air above his chest as she stared into his eyes.

"Nicholas . . ." she said finally. She struggled to catch

her breath and turned to put the cork back in the bottle
of oil, but with surprising strength, Nicholas pulled her
around to face him again.

"What are you doing?" he asked.

"Oh, Nicholas, I'm so happy to hear your voice. You
don't know . . . you can't imagine. Do you remember anything? The duel? You've been unconscious for several days,
and the doctor thought you wouldn't live." Tears filled
her eyes. She wanted to laugh and shout. She wanted to
take his beloved face in her hands and kiss him until he
was as breathless as she felt.

But the look in his eyes kept her from it.

"I remember the duel," he said, his voice slow and
deliberate. "Jared's gun misfired. And I remember seeing
you there beneath the tree."

She wiped her eyes, nodding to encourage his memories.
Still, she couldn't understand the anger she saw etched
on his face.

"What I don't understand is why you're here," he said.

Lily's heart sank, and the expression on her face
changed from one of happy relief to perplexity.

"What . . . what do you mean? I'm your wife. Where else
would I be?"

"With Jared, I'd presume," he said. He glanced around
the room, then down at her wrists, still imprisoned in his
tight grip. Deliberately he loosened his fingers, pushing
her away from him as he tried to sit up in bed.

Lily stared at him in stunned disbelief. Didn't he know
how she had sat by his side, telling him how much she
loved him? Talking to him every day and willing him to
come back to her?

Even in his unconscious state, she'd hoped he would
have sensed that.

"No . . . Nicholas," she said. "You don't understand. I
love you. I've always loved you. You can't really believe that
Jared and I . . . that we . . ."

His sardonic gaze stopped her words, and she stood up, moving away from the bitterness she saw reflected there.

"Get out of here, Lily," he said, his voice cold and filled with hate. "I don't ever want to see your beautiful, deceitful face again."

Chapter 27

Lily hurried out into the hallway, away from the cold accusation she saw on her husband's face. Shakily, she closed the door and leaned back against it, trying to catch her breath. Trying to forget the way he'd just made her feel.

She'd waited so long for this moment. And now it was spoiled. He hated her for what she'd done. And she thought he even blamed her for the duel that almost killed him.

She was trembling almost uncontrollably. But her eyes were dry. She had cried until she was empty of tears.

Enough of it!

As much as she loved Nicholas, she wouldn't shed another tear because of him and what he thought.

She was what she was. A simple girl from the river who'd always tried to do what was right, even when no one believed her.

Her ways might seem blunt and strange to people who had been raised to hide their feelings and cover up their doubts or misgivings for the sake of politeness.

She had tried. But being here at Live Oaks, close to the river, close to nature and the simple people whose lives were entwined with it, she felt happy. She felt as if she'd come home after a long, long voyage away.

She heard someone in the hallway and looked up to see Jeanette coming out of her room. Her smile, when she saw Lily, was genuine and warm.

"How kind of you to send Mae to ask about me," she said. She was brushing at her blue-taffeta skirt as she came down the hall. "And if you really meant it about wanting me to stay, then I wanted to tell you I'll be delighted."

She stopped in front of Lily, and the smile slipped from her lips .

"Lily? What is it? You look as if you've . . ." Her glance darted toward the closed door. "Nicholas isn't . . . ?"

"Nicholas is finally awake," Lily said, her voice flat and emotionless.

She winced at the light that leapt so quickly to Jeanette's eyes.

"Awake? Oh, thank God. Thank God." Jeanette closed her eyes and placed her fingers against her trembling lips. Her eyes were bright when she opened them again and focused on Lily.

"You should be ecstatic," she said. "What's wrong?"

Lily pushed herself away from the door with a sigh and stood in the hallway, her shoulders slumped.

"He blames me for everything," she said. "He doesn't believe that Jared and I were not lovers." She turned and looked into Jeanette's incredulous eyes. "He says he never wants to see me again."

"He doesn't mean that, Lily,"

"Oh, but I think he does mean it."

"Nonsense," Jeanette declared, glancing toward the bedroom door. "He isn't himself yet. Perhaps the fever—"

"It isn't the fever," Lily said, her voice filled with quiet resignation. "It's me. I have to face the fact that he has never loved me, and he never will."

Jeanette felt torn, hearing those words. There was a time when she'd have liked nothing better than to hear Lily confess that Nicholas didn't love her. But she knew him. She'd seen him when he was troubled and confused. And he cared much more about the girl than he was willing to admit. It had taken Jeanette a long time to see that and to accept it herself. She hated admitting it even now, because she loved him, too. Perhaps she always would.

But she was convinced that Nicholas was in love with this beautiful, spirited girl. And after getting to know her these past few days, Jeanette could understand why.

The problem was, should she take advantage of this rift between them? Try to win Nicholas back into her arms and into her bed?

"What do you intend to do?" Jeanette asked, her voice soft.

"Nothing," Lily said. "I may have been raised poor, but my parents always taught me pride. And I've danced to Nicholas St. James's tune far too long as it is. I don't intend to lower myself to begging, or even to trying to convince him he's wrong. If he doesn't know me by now, then he never will."

Lily stood there in the hallway, her slight figure straight and proud. There were no tears in her eyes, although Jeanette thought they were decidedly shiny and bright. Her fists were clenched tightly at her side like a defiant little girl's.

Jeanette shook her head, the smile on her lips soft and affectionate.

She loved Nicholas and wanted him more than she'd ever wanted any man. But she liked this girl. Dammit, she liked her too much to hurt her.

"Well . . ." Jeanette said, almost to herself. "That's certainly a departure for Jeanette Mireaux."

"What?" Lily asked.

"Nothing," Jeanette said. She reached out and touched the sleeve of Lily's gown. "Why don't you go downstairs and bring Nicholas some of Mama Jolie's nice broth? I'd like to go in and see him a moment if I may."

Lily gritted her teeth. What difference did it make if she did object? There was nothing she could do to make Nicholas love her. And there was nothing she could do to keep him and Jeanette apart if that was what he wanted.

Without another word, she turned to go downstairs.

"Lily . . ." Jeanette said.

Lily stopped at the end of the hallway.

"Don't be fooled by Nicholas's words. He's a shrewd gambler, and he's grown very good at playing the bluff."

Lily's eyes narrowed. "What are you trying to say?" she asked.

"What I'm saying, my dear, is that Nicholas is a stubborn, prideful man, unwilling to admit what's in his own heart. You, more than anyone I've ever known, have the power to change that. And I, for one, don't think you should let him get away with his pretenses any longer."

Jeanette smiled mysteriously and opened the door to Nicholas's room. Lily stood in the hallway for long moments, puzzling over Jeanette's words, before turning and going down the stairs.

The next few days were some of the worst Lily had ever endured. Nicholas didn't soften at all. And although she stubbornly tended to him, refusing to let him dictate to her, he made the moments when she was with him miserable with his stony silence and cold, unrelenting looks.

Lily found it hard to believe that Jeanette was willing now to give Nicholas up. Or that she was actually encouraging her to continue to fight for his love.

"I prayed diligently for Nicholas's recovery," Jeanette told her one night as they sat on the front porch of the plantation house. "And for the first time in my life, I actually made a bargain with God. Not that I'm sure I ever intended keeping it," she said with a self-deprecating laugh. "But . . ." Jeanette continued with a quiet sigh, "bargain I did. I told God that if he'd only let Nicholas live, I would mend my wicked ways . . ." Jeanette laughed again, but this time a bit of wistfulness crept into her laughter.

"Jeanette," Lily said softly, "there might have been a time when I'd have been the first to agree that you were the most wicked, wanton woman in all of Natchez. But not anymore. I hope you won't mind my saying so, but I've come to consider you a friend."

It was the first time Lily had found the courage to say the words, and she hardly knew how they might be received.

She felt Jeanette's hand reach for hers immediately and saw her eyelids blink rapidly.

"Thank you for that," Jeanette said. "Now, I know I've made the right decision in keeping my bargain. God has rewarded me with the friendship of one of the kindest, sweetest women I've ever known. I'm not surprised that everyone in Natchez thronged to your side. Or that half of the men fell in love with you on first sight."

Lily groaned, thinking of Jared and her gullibility where he was concerned.

"I could certainly have done without the attention of one of those men," she murmured.

"Well, if it's any consolation, Jared fooled me as well. And I have a considerable number of years on you, if experience counts for anything."

"I wonder where he went," Lily said. "Sometimes at night I wake up trembling, afraid that he might come back. That he might try to kill Nicholas again."

"Ah, no," Jeanette murmured. "Do not worry yourself about such a worm as Jared St. James. He will never come here to Live Oaks. There are too many people here looking out for Nicholas's welfare. No, Jared is too much a coward for that." Jeanette's voice grew as harsh as Lily had ever heard it. "He proved that by shooting Nicholas in the back. I've heard some say that he's probably in Mexico by now. I hope it's true, and that wherever he is, he's living a miserable existence.''

"With no money, he probably is," Lily said. "He depended on Nicholas for that, you know. For the first time in his life he'll have to work for what he wants.''

"Don't worry about him," Jeanette said. "He's out of our lives for good.''

A man stood in the shadows at the edge of the forest. Beyond him, in the moonlight, lay the great plantation house called Live Oaks. At the edge of the lawn and fields, the fence shone brightly against the darkness. It, like everything else here, was neat and excellently kept.

Even the slave houses were built up off the damp, Mississippi soil, their exteriors insulated with handmade brick, the split-hickory roofs snug and well tended to keep out the rain.

Sometimes, he saw Lily and Jeanette, dressed in their beautiful gowns, walking together and talking quietly as if they were the best of friends.

That was the part he didn't understand. He had plotted to use one against the other in order to exact his revenge. And since they were natural enemies, he'd expected it to work.

Jared cursed quietly, his eyes narrowed and suspicious as he stared through the gathering darkness at the house.

He'd been close enough sometimes to hear conversations and to learn that Nicholas was recovering. He'd even overheard the slaves mention Lily's name with affection. He had seen her ride out to the fields, taking her husband's place and seeming to advise the hands with a wisdom and expertise beyond her years.

And seeing her, even from this distance, with her redgold hair glistening beneath the hot Mississippi sun, still took his breath away. She was as beautiful and elusive as the golden butterfly that flitted about the hedges and flowers in spring.

She loved Nicholas, Jared was certain of that. And Nicholas had humiliated him on the field of battle that day, causing him to grovel on his knees like a coward. His cousin had taken the last remaining vestiges of his self-respect. And now, by God, Jared intended to take something precious from him.

"Soon," Jared whispered into the darkness. "Very soon, Lily."

Chapter 28

The next morning, Lily stood outside Nicholas's bedroom with a breakfast tray in her hands. She hadn't slept much last night, and sometime before dawn she'd decided that perhaps Jeanette was right. Perhaps anger and passion were closely related.

And yet here, in the light of day, she hesitated. What if she made a complete and utter fool of herself?

"It won't be the first time," she muttered dryly. Straightening her shoulders, she pushed open the door with the toe of her shoe.

Nicholas was sitting up in bed. The room was neat; all of Mae's candles and voodoo charms were gone now.

One of the manservants had already been in, leaving Nicholas freshly dressed and clean-shaven.

He looked across the room at Lily, frowning when he realized who it was who brought his breakfast.

"I don't know why you keep doing this—"

"I know you don't," she interrupted. She moved briskly to the bed, placing the tray across his lap and whisking a white-linen napkin from the surface and tucking it into the top of Nicholas's shirt. She patted his chest for good measure, gazing into his eyes with a mischievous glint.

"What the hell . . ." he muttered, glancing down at the napkin, and then up at Lily.

"Can you feed yourself, or shall I feed you?"

"Hell yes, I can feed myself. As far as that goes, I could probably make it downstairs to sit at the table."

"I'm sorry, but I can't allow that just yet," she said. She made a pretense of straightening his bed before standing back with her hands at her hips.

Nicholas's gaze moved slowly over his wife. From the top of her shining hair down over the cotton-print dress and white apron to the toes of her serviceable shoes.

"Why are you dressing like one of the servants?" he grumbled.

"Because it's comfortable, and I have a great deal of work, that's why. I could hardly do everything I need to do in a silk gown with layers of petticoats and ribbons and tiny slippers that fall apart when they become wet."

"I don't like it," he muttered.

"I don't remember asking if you like it," she replied.

"And what do you mean, you can't allow me to come downstairs?" he asked dryly.

"In case you haven't noticed this past week, sir, I'm in charge here now. It might interest you to know that while you've been ill, I was the one who bathed you and fed you, not to mention seeing to other more intimate functions." She ignored his frown and continued. "Besides that, I've planned our meals, greeted your guests, put them up when they wanted to stay and still managed to see to the cotton crop."

Despite himself, Nicholas laughed. Then he shook his head, still smiling at the little firebrand who stood so defiantly before him.

"And what do you know about cotton?" he asked.

"Not much," she admitted with a lift of her brows. "But I'm learning."

Nicholas began to eat, wincing slightly at the ache in his shoulder and chest.

"Better enjoy yourself," he muttered between bites. "You won't be in charge much longer."

"Good," she said, turning with a bounce toward the door. "Because I surely could use some help around here."

Lily stopped outside the door, taking a deep breath and allowing herself a quiet smile. Let him think about that for a while.

For the next few days, she moved in and out of his room as she pleased, and he made no further effort to stop her. She saw to it that Mama Jolie made all of his favorite dishes. She brought him newspapers and journals to read. And although she didn't tell him so, she was thrilled when he could sit up in a chair for an hour at a time and when he began walking slowly about the room. She deliberately irritated him, vexed him and made him laugh, despite his obvious determination not to.

One afternoon when she stepped into the room, Nicholas was standing at the window, staring out over the treetops. When he heard her, he turned quickly around, then caught his breath at the stabbing in his chest. The look of pain on his face made her hurry forward without thinking.

She was beside him in an instant, putting her arms around his waist and holding him tightly as she looked with concern up into his face.

"Are you all right? You should be resting—Mae tells me you've been up most of the day today."

She heard his intake of breath, and it frightened her. But when she looked up into his eyes, the look she saw there surprised her even more.

For the past week, Nicholas had been watching Lily. She worked from early morning until dark and still had time to make herself beautiful for dinner when she usually entertained guests who came over from Natchez to see him.

He hadn't missed the admiring looks of some of his

friends, just as he hadn't missed the admiration of the servants here at Live Oaks. Hell, even Jeanette liked her.

Lily had not said a word to defend herself these past few days. Even when he was tired and irritable, she listened to his grumbling and his accusations with quiet grace, but often pained silence—although sometimes she did lecture him quietly on his manners.

More than once he'd found himself smiling after she left the room.

But she hadn't touched him any more than was necessary to help him. Not until today. And he was finding it almost more than his weakened resistance could allow.

His mind was at war with his emotions. He couldn't stop thinking about that last morning they'd spent together. He couldn't forget the heat of her body and the intensity of her passion. His pride told him to push her away . . . insult her even, if that was what it took to keep her away from him and out of his heart. And yet another part of his brain urged him to pull her tightly against him, enjoy every luscious inch of her body against his and kiss those soft, warm, and willing lips.

It had been so long. So damnably long.

"Lily," he managed through clenched teeth. "If you know what's good for you, you'll get out of here. Now."

Lily knew what was happening between them. And she could hardly believe it.

"Haven't you noticed?" she whispered. "I've never really been good at taking advice. Or knowing what's good for me.

"You certainly know by now, it isn't me," he said, his voice gruff.

But his lips were so near. She stood in the circle of his arms, her mouth reaching for him, her eyes telling him that she was his for the taking.

"Why do you say that?" she asked. "Tell me why, Nicholas."

It took every ounce of strength he possessed to put her away from him. He turned away, not willing for her to see how her touch affected him, or how quickly he could become inflamed by her.

"Dammit, Lily," he muttered, moving back toward the bed.

"It isn't over between us, Nicholas," she whispered. "And you know it isn't."

"What do you want from me?" he asked, turning to face her. He stared at her across the room, his eyes dark and troubled.

"I want to be your wife," she said. "As simple as that. I thought at one time it was what you wanted, too."

"Simple?" he said with a soft sound of derision. "There's nothing simple about any of this."

"That's because you insist on making it difficult," she said. Seeing the look of resistance leaving his eyes, she started toward him.

"Don't do that," he said. "How can I trust you, Lily? How can we start over after what's happened?"

"You wouldn't let me explain," she said, frustration casting an edge to her voice. "So . . . you still blame me for the duel?" she asked.

"No," he muttered, frowning. "Hell, no. It was my decision to accept Jared's challenge. You certainly had nothing to do with his shooting me in the back." His eyes narrowed as he stared at her. "Or did you?"

Lily gasped, but her lips trembled only the slightest bit as she faced him.

"How could you ask me that? Don't you know what kind of person I am by now? Do you honestly think that I would want anyone murdered? And you of all people? The man I've loved more than anyone or anything? What does it take to get through to you, Nicholas St. James? For I swear, I don't know."

She turned quickly, her skirts whirling out gracefully around her legs as she moved toward the door.

"I'm tired of this," she said. "I'm tired of trying to prove myself to you. And I'm tired of trying to convince you that I love you. When you're ready to stop playing games and tell me what it is you really want, then perhaps something will change. Until then, I suggest you ask Mae for anything you need."

She slammed the door behind her, then opened it again, staring at him with a furious, warning stare.

"And don't you dare be rude to her. She's a sweet, gentle girl and she adores you."

After Lily had stormed out for the second time, Nicholas let the air out of his lungs in a loud whoosh. He raked his hands through his hair and turned around before kicking a nearby stool across the room.

"Damn."

When the door opened again, he turned toward it, surprised by the tingle of hope that rushed through his entire body. But this time it was Jeanette rather than Lily.

"Well," she said, standing with her back against the door. "I see you've made her cry at last. She swore she wouldn't, you know. Are you proud of yourself?"

"What the hell are you talking about?" he asked, frowning at her. "Of course she wasn't crying. Lily is as tough as new leather." He pointed toward the door. "She slammed out of here in a storm, madder than a wet hen. Hell, I don't know what she wants."

"You most certainly do know what she wants. She wants you."

He saw the wry twist of Jeanette's mouth.

"She wasn't really crying," he said quietly. "Was she?"

"Yes, Nicholas, she was."

He scratched his head and turned to move back to the window, standing with his back to Jeanette.

"I can't take it when she cries,"

"What did you expect?" Jeanette asked. He could sense

her moving into the room. "Do you think you can treat her so coldly . . . to heap guilt and blame on her head every day while she freely gives you her attention and her love? You know, Nicholas, I never took you for a fool. I thought you were just about the kindest, most honorable man I'd ever met."

"Jeanette . . ." he warned, still not turning around.

"Oh, don't worry, Nicky," she said softly. "I'm not about to throw myself at you. Whether you knew it or not, you made it clear, even before the duel, that your heart was with someone else."

He turned around slowly. "What the hell are you talking about?"

She laughed at the incredulous look on his face.

"Well," she said, "you're an even bigger fool than I thought. You couldn't make love to me because you were in love with someone else. And now you're letting your manly pride keep you from admitting that love."

Nicholas looked as if he'd been kicked in the stomach. His mouth opened, and he shook his head. Finally, he cursed and began to pace the room.

"I hope you aren't forgetting the matter of Jared," he growled.

"Jared wanted her, I've no doubt. But despite her education and her attempt at sophistication, Lily is still very much an innocent at heart, Nicholas. She had no idea that she could encourage a man simply by being herself, or by being one of the loveliest creatures God ever created. And if you hadn't ignored her, believe me, she would never have spent more than that first day with him."

"Now, you're blaming it on me?"

"Yes, I am," she said smugly. "You're afraid, Nicky, and I think you always have been. Afraid to let yourself love someone. Then Lily came along and made you love her whether you wanted to or not."

"I've never been afraid of anything in my life," he growled.

"Darling," she said, "you're going to have to make a decision. You're going to have to decide whether you want this lovely woman to be your wife again. Or whether you want to lose her forever."

His eyes sparkled dangerously as he looked at her.

"Because you will lose her, you know," she said.

"I find this rather odd advice," he drawled, "coming from you. "

"Yes, isn't it," she said with a pensive smile. "Oh, I still love you, if that's what your male ego is wondering. And I probably always will. But oddly enough, I've come to love Lily as well. And I want both of you to be happy . . . preferably with one another," she added dryly. "As for me," she said with a soft sigh, "I'm going back to Natchez tonight. And I'm going to start my life over, this time—I hope—with a man who wants and needs more than a mistress."

Nicholas's look was solemn. A muscle in his jaw tightened and released.

"You deserve that, Jeanette," he said.

Suddenly her blue eyes glittered with tears and her lips trembled slightly.

"I envy you, Nicholas. Do you know that? I want what you and Lily have," she said, trying to keep her voice steady. "Or could have . . . if you'll only stop being the biggest fool on the Mississippi."

Nicholas gave a quiet laugh and rubbed his hand over his face. He walked to Jeanette and brushed a kiss against her forehead.

"Get out of here, and go back to Natchez," he said fondly. "Find a man who deserves and appreciates you. I want you to be happy, too."

"Will you promise me that you'll—"

"I can't make any promises," he said, reverting to that

closed, stubborn look. "Whatever happens will happen,"
he said.

Jeanette pushed a slender finger against his chest.

"If you're as smart as I've always thought, you will *make*
it happen, *chéri.*"

Chapter 29

Lily stood at the end of the long porch that extended across the front of the house. The live oaks that shaded the house and gave it its name dripped their moss in ghostly patterns of silver. She always found watching the trailing moss soothing as it moved in the warm breeze.

The workers were just coming in from the fields, some moving toward their houses and some toward the barn to stable the mules and horses. Beyond the shade of the big trees, the sun still shone dimly, the twilight turning the meadows and the road that led away from the house to gold.

She wiped away the tears that had spilled from her eyes. She'd tried so hard to be strong, tried to put on a brave face and let Nicholas see that she wouldn't be intimidated.

But he was relentless in his rejection. And today she felt completely defeated.

"Oh, Nicholas," she whispered. "Why can't you be the man I know you are? That sweet, loving man I see inside of you sometimes?"

"Lily?" she heard behind her. Jeanette stepped from the doorway of the house. "Who are you talking to?"

Lily forced a smile to her face and turned to face Jeanette. Her gaze took in the woman's stylish riding dress of purple and the matching hat, with its jaunty black feathers.

"No one," Lily said. "Just talking to myself I guess. I see you're ready to go."

"Yes," Jeanette replied. The smile that moved over her lovely face was wistful and a bit curious. "I could swear you sound almost disappointed."

Lily nodded. "Actually, I will miss you. Funny, isn't it?

"Yes," Jeanette said. Her face softened, and she came forward, taking Lily's hands. "Lily, there's one thing I've never said to you. I want to say it now."

"Jeanette . . . there's no need . . ."

"Yes . . . please, just indulge me a moment longer."

Lily smiled at her, her look patient, even affectionate.

"I never realized how much you must have been hurt by my . . . liaison with Nicholas. Not until I came to know you, and then it became, well, personal."

Lily nodded. How could she explain that she felt the same way?

"Nicholas has changed since you came back from Boston," Jeanette said. "Because of you."

With a dubious lift of her brows, Lily moved away, hugging her arms about her body.

"He has," Jeanette insisted. "I know he seems impossible sometimes. But there are so many things that need to be settled between the two of you. Without my presence causing any awkwardness."

"You don't have to leave," Lily said.

"You are so trusting," Jeanette said with a shake of her head. "How could you believe so completely that I have no further designs on Nicholas?"

"Because you told me so," Lily said firmly.

"Ah, Lily," Jeanette laughed. "This is why I've grown so fond of you." She stepped forward and, after a moment's hesitation, hugged Lily. "So very fond of you. And why I must tell you about the day of the race . . . when Nicholas left with me and he didn't come back home.''

"No, Jeanette . . ." Lily pulled away, her eyes filling with pain as she looked at the other woman. "You don't have to tell me. I don't want to know.''

"You have to know this," Jeanette insisted. "Nicholas stayed with me that night, it's true, but he did not touch me. Absolutely nothing happened between us. In fact, he has been faithful to you since you came back home.''

She hoped God would forgive her that one small lie, for He knew as well as she did that the last time Nicholas made love to her, his heart was not in it. Jeanette had even come to realize that it had been a test for Nicholas . . . one of his own making, a way of proving to himself that he didn't need Lily and that he could have any other woman as long as it pleased him. And when the test had failed, Jeanette thought he must have been surprised beyond anything that had ever happened to him.

Lily didn't want Jeanette's words to fill her with hope. For in the end, nothing Jeanette or she or anyone else said would make a difference in what happened between her and Nicholas. That was something only he could change.

"I hope you believe me," Jeanette said. "It is very important to me that you believe me.''

"I do believe you," Lily said. "And I thank you for telling me." She stepped forward and put her arms around the smaller woman. "Promise that you'll come back to Live Oaks soon.''

Tears filled Jeanette's blue eyes for a moment before she blinked them away.

"You are a very special woman, do you know that? How many others would invite her husband's mistress to her home?''

"Just someone very gullible, I guess," Lily said, laughing awkwardly.

"No," Jeanette murmured. She reached out and

touched Lily's cheek. "Someone very good and kind. And very forgiving. You will never regret your trust in me, Lily. I swear that to you this very day."

When she went into the dining room that evening, Lily was surprised to see her husband there.

"Nicholas," she said. "What are you doing here?"

He turned and saw her in the doorway. For one brief moment he let his gaze take in the black gown she wore, the same one she'd worn at the lawn party. Seeing her that way brought back sweet, poignant memories that actually made his chest ache. Her mass of red-gold hair, swept up atop her head, seemed to rebel against its pins, some of the curls spilling around her face and neck. But she looked thin and tired, and there was a vulnerability in her eyes.

Jeanette's words about Lily crying had eaten at him all day. He'd been a fool—a prideful stubborn fool. And now all he wanted was to pull her into his arms and beg her forgiveness, bury his face against those fragrant curls. Lose himself in the softness of her body and the sweetness of her kiss.

But how could he expect such a thing after the way he'd treated her?

"Nicholas?" she asked, moving into the room. "Why are you staring at me like that? And what are you doing downstairs?" Her eyes moved over his elegant dark gray coat and the lighter gray trousers he wore. His white shirt looked fresh and bright and he looked as if the duel had never happened.

"I thought it was time I came down for dinner. And I think it's time my wife and I had a little time alone . . . to talk."

"Oh," she said.

She hadn't seen him this way in so long. She was afraid to hope that what she saw in his eyes was real. He was so changeable . . . moving toward her one moment, and retreating behind a mask of cold disdain the next. How could she ever know what to expect from this man?

She sat stiffly through the meal, listening to Nicholas talk about insignificant matters, about the tenderness of the roast beef and how much he'd missed being at Live Oaks.

"There's nothing better than eating vegetables from one's own garden," he said. "Don't you agree?"

"Nicholas," Lily said. She put her fork down in exasperation. "What is this all about? You made it very clear that you prefer not being in my company. Now you expect to have dinner and converse as if nothing has happened? I told you before, I'm not playing these games with you any longer."

"The games are over, Lily," Nicholas said, his voice deep and steady. He stood up from the table, carefully putting down his napkin before coming around and holding out his hand to her.

"Can't a man admit to being wrong once in a while? Come and walk with me. I haven't been outside these walls in weeks."

She stared up at him, her eyes like emerald glass, her look skeptical and distrustful.

"Please," he said softly. "I promise I will be a complete gentleman," he added, with a wry twist of his lips.

Lily took a deep breath and slowly placed her hand in his.

Go slowly, she warned herself. *Don't let yourself be fooled by him again, or you'll be spending another night in tears.*

Outside, they walked slowly. Nicholas, glancing sideways at her, noted that she kept her distance, refusing to let herself move too close to him.

Darkness had come early where the trees shaded the house. But beyond, the last vestiges of a summer sun sprinkled the treetops with light traces of gold. As they walked, they could see the glimmer of it through the trees, where it scattered its dying light like diamonds upon the river's surface.

"Perhaps we should go back," Nicholas said, finally.

They were near the row of brick slave cabins. Doorways stood open and light spilled outside. They could hear the sound of laughter, the cry of babies, and the bright squeal of the older children still playing in the twilight's glow.

"Of course," Lily said. "You must be tired." She glanced briefly at him, noting the strength of his shoulders and the way he carried himself. He didn't appear ever to have been wounded, but knowing him, he could be in a great deal of pain and would never show it.

"It isn't that," he said. "But without a lantern we might flush out a raccoon, or worse yet, a nocturnal rattler."

Lily shivered and moved a bit closer to him.

"And as far as I know, the authorities still haven't found Jared." Nicholas's gaze reached out toward the darkening forest, his eyes narrowed and searching.

"No," Lily said. "They haven't." She took a deep breath, stopping and placing her hand on his arm.

"Lily . . ."

"Nicholas . . ."

They both spoke at once and then Lily laughed shakily.

"You first," Nicholas said as they turned and moved back down the sandy road toward the house.

"I should never have become involved with Jared, or with a man like Charles Lydell. And I'm sorry I embarrassed you by riding in the race at Pharsalia." Lily's words came out in a tumble. She knew if she didn't say them quickly, she might never be able to say them at all. "I'll admit that the first time was a lark, just to prove something to myself. But the second time, Nicholas, you must believe me, Jared forced me. He said if I didn't race, he'd come to you and tell you. It was the day after the ball, the morning after we—"

Nicholas made a quiet noise deep in his chest, then he stopped in the middle of the roadway. For a moment as they stood there in the darkness, there was only the sounds of the forest and the nearby river to break the silence.

"What you say about Jared doesn't surprise me," he

said. "But did you think me such an ogre that you couldn't confide in me? God," he muttered in self-disgust.

"I couldn't bear to lose you," she said, her voice soft with pain. "And I thought that was what would happen if you knew. And I was right . . ."

He made no effort to touch her, but his nearness and the way he looked at her made her feel as if he had touched her.

"How can I make you understand the way I behaved?" he asked. "When sometimes I don't even understand it myself?"

"Try," she whispered. "Try and make me understand, Nicholas. That's all I want . . . to understand how you really feel." About me, she wanted to add.

"I'm a grown man. This is my world and I'm accustomed to it. But you . . ." He paused, and in the filtered light from the house, she could see him push his fingers through his thick, dark hair, the way he did sometimes when he was frustrated or impatient.

"When you came home from Boston, you were still an innocent in so many ways." At Lily's quiet groan, Nicholas smiled, and continued. "I don't mean that as an insult, believe me. I didn't want you to be hurt," he said. "Maybe I didn't know how to let you see that, but it infuriated me knowing that Jared was leading you down the garden path and that you might be scorned and ridiculed. I was afraid someone would hurt you so badly that you'd think your entire life was ruined. And that you'd change from a girl who sees good in everything to one who was frightened and hard. I've seen it happen before."

Lily stood in the darkness, unable to believe the sweetness in the tone of his voice. Unable to believe that this proud, arrogant man was actually attempting to apologize to her.

"Is that what happened to your mother?" she asked.

He sighed heavily and leaned his head back, looking up

toward the sky. She fully expected him to tell her it was none of her business.

"It wasn't the same thing, although my need to protect you certainly felt the same. Who told you about my mother?"

"Mary . . . a long time ago. She said you became a distrustful person because of the way people treated your mother."

"Perhaps."

Nicholas stepped closer to her, sending tingles of alarm and pleasure racing down her spine.

"You remind me of her sometimes."

"Do I?" she asked, surprise showing in her voice. "Is that why you married me? Because you wanted to protect me? The way you couldn't protect her? You . . . you felt sorry for me?"

"Would it hurt you terribly if that were the case?"

"I don't know," she said honestly. "It's . . . it's not as if I haven't thought that before. That perhaps you pitied me."

"Pity?" he said with a soft groan. He grasped her arms and pulled her toward him. "I might have felt sympathy when your parents died, and you were alone. But, sweetheart . . . don't you see how ridiculous that is now? You have everything—beauty, humor, intelligence. You have a style of your own. Mary told me how you completely charmed Boston and now, in a few short weeks, you've managed to do the same here in Natchez. Everyone loves you, Lily. And no one has a reason to pity you . . . including me."

How she wanted him to kiss her. But more than that, she wanted him to say that he loved her, too.

But he did neither.

Gently, Lily pulled away from him, looking up into his face and wishing she could see his eyes in the gathering darkness. Wishing she could see some hint of how he really felt inside.

"Thank you, Nicholas," she whispered. "For making me feel better about all the foolish things I've done. But now, if you don't mind . . . I think I'll go in."

She had to turn away before they reached the light and he could see the pain in her eyes.

Nicholas stopped, watching her turn and run away. He was stunned at the measure of emotion he felt watching her go. And at the deep instinctive need he felt to go after her. He wanted to forget everything that had happened between them before. Forget Jared and Natchez society. Here at Live Oaks they were safe, and he sensed that they could start a new life if only he would say the word.

He wanted to hold her and kiss her, take her to his bed.

Instead he let her go.

This time, he would be much more careful with his bewitching river bride.

Chapter 30

The next morning, Lily slept late. She hadn't slept at all well, thanks to her conversation with Nicholas—that and the fact that she could hear him in his room just across the hall.

She was still in bed when she heard the sound of a carriage coming down the entrance road to the house.

She jumped up, feeling a mixture of curiosity and reluctance that company was coming. She wasn't sure that she'd be such good company today.

But when she saw Miss Fran emerge from the carriage, she felt her heart leap with happiness. She hadn't seen the woman since the day she'd moved into Lily's old house.

There was a small girl with her, and the sight of her made Lily so curious that she hurried to dress.

She heard a tap at her door and then Nicholas's deep voice.

"Lily? May I come in?"

Without waiting for her reply, he opened the door and stepped into her room. Lily stood mutely before him, her cheeks burning as she watched his gaze move over her chemise and down her bare legs.

"We have company," she said, reaching for a dress that lay on her bed. She was determined not to let him unnerve her today. "It's Miss Fran," she said. "And she's brought someone with her."

"I know," he said. "Although personally I'd much prefer staying up here with you." His eyes sparkled in that old teasing manner she remembered so well, and his lips quirked appealingly.

Lily stepped into the dress, trying to ignore his remarks, and his look. He came forward without asking permission, gently turning her around and beginning to fasten the row of buttons at the back of her dress. His hands lingered for a moment, and Lily suppressed any reaction to the shiver that raced over her skin at the warmth of his fingers against her flesh.

Without speaking, she walked to the door, turning only to look at him over her shoulder.

"Are you coming?"

Still grinning, he nodded and followed.

In the hallway, they found Mae sweeping up a small pile of dust from a corner. Lily had often seen those little gatherings of dust, and when she'd asked Mae about them, she'd been told that it was bad luck to sweep the house at certain times. At those times, she said, the dirt must be swept into a corner and left to be carried out the next morning.

"Morning, Mae," Lily said.

Mae looked up and nodded, smiling.

"I suppose this is a good day for sweeping."

Mae began sprinkling something on the floor just in front of her broom. Salt, Lily knew, to sweep away the bad spirits.

"I tells Mama Jolie every day. Ain't no sense bein' so clean—we gonna sweep all our luck away. Got to be careful the conjur man say."

"A broom is a dangerous thing," Nicholas agreed, grinning broadly.

"I know you be teasin' me, Mr. Nicholas," Mae said, her look serious. "But it's the truth. Why, I could just sweep this old broom, like that ..." Dramatically Mae whisked the broom in the air just above the floor, being careful not to touch anything or anyone. "And if'n it touch your foot, why I could just sweep you clean on away from home."

Usually Lily would find Mae's superstitions humorous, but she couldn't explain the sudden shiver that moved over her this morning. Like someone walking over a grave, her mother always used to call the feeling.

"Please don't tease her," Lily said.

Mae nodded, her eyes bright.

"What happens if you're a little careless with that broom, my girl?" Nicholas asked. He wasn't taking either of the women seriously. His eyes still twinkled with amusement.

"Why someone could die ... don't you know that?"

"No," Nicholas said, laughing. "I don't believe I've ever heard that one."

"Yes sir. If'n you sweep your luck away, someone will die in the house 'fore the year be out."

"Oh," Nicholas said, nodding with mock solemnness. "Then, please, Mae, be very careful with that broom."

Lily moved on toward the stairs and Nicholas caught up with her. His hand touched her back, then he grabbed her arm, turning her around to face him.

"Lily," he murmured. "You're trembling. What's wrong?"

"Nothing," Lily said, her face innocent.

"Surely you don't take Mae's voodoo ramblings seriously?"

Lily's shoulders relaxed, and she shook her head.

"I don't know," she said. "I know it's foolish. Perhaps it's because of what happened to you. Maybe I'm still a little nervous about Jared being free to go anywhere he

pleases. But all of a sudden, I just had this terrible feeling."
She shivered again, unable to hide it this time.

With a low murmur, Nicholas pulled her into his arms.
She went willingly, needing his comfort. Needing the security of his touch and his soothing words in her ear. Forgetting her pride and just letting him hold her.

"It *is* nerves," he said. "That's all it is. You've been
under a strain since the duel, having to tend to me and
take care of the plantation. But that's all over now. Our
worries are all behind us."

As he ran his hand over her hair, Lily slowly put her
arms around his waist, tightening them and giving in to
the familiar rise of warmth and desire.

"Don't fret," he said, feeling the tremor that ran
through her slender body. He pulled away and looked
down into her eyes. "I'm here now. Whether you know it
or not, I would never let anything happen to you."

Lily sighed and nodded. Despite everything that had
happened, she did know that.

A slow, tremulous smile turned her lips upward, and
when he bent to kiss her, she didn't resist. And later when
she pulled away, he made no effort to do anything more.
He seemed different since the duel. Gentler and more
patient.

But it was amazing how much better she felt, just hearing
his reassuring words and having him kiss her.

Miss Fran was in the parlor, and, when they entered,
she stood up, her eyes bright with welcome. She came
forward quickly and embraced both of them.

"Oh, Mr. Nicholas, it's so good to see you looking yourself again. Why, you look even stronger than before. It's
a miracle, that's what everyone in town is sayin'. A pure
miracle. Some say our Lily is the angel that did it."

"Indeed," Nicholas said, his gaze warm as he looked at
Lily.

Lily noted Fran's new gown, in a subtle shade of rose.
It certainly was stylish. Nothing like the clothes she'd worn

before. Her hair was neat beneath a lovely straw bonnet. Even her skin seemed softer, and her eyes no longer held that tormented look of desperation and hunger.

The little girl with Fran was just as neatly dressed. But she sat silently, her eyes large in a small pale face as she watched the adults greeting one another.

"It does me good to see you looking so well, Miss Fran," Lily said. Then she nodded toward the little girl. "And who is this you've brought with you today?"

"This is Jenny," Fran said. Her face softened as she glanced toward the little girl, who looked to be no more than ten years old. "She's lost her parents, just like you, Lily. And someone brought her to me. I hope you don't mind, Mr. Nicholas, that I took her in at the house."

"Of course I don't mind," Nicholas said.

"Go over and say hello to Miss Lily and Mr. Nicholas."

The girl got up and came forward, her eyes still watching warily as she curtsied slightly. She bit her lips and turned her eyes down toward the floor.

"You two are just in time for breakfast," Nicholas said. "Come along with me, Jenny," he said, touching the girl's shoulder lightly. "Are you hungry?"

She nodded, finally glancing up at him with a shy smile.

"Well, good," he said. "Because our cook here at Live Oaks is Mama Jolie, and she's just about the best cook on either side of the Mississippi. Come on, I'll show you to the dining room." Nicholas bent and crooked his elbow at the little girl, who for a moment seemed confused. Then slowly her hand crept upward, moving around his arm as she smiled up at him.

Watching them, Lily felt her heart lurch in her chest. She'd observed Nicholas with children here on the plantation. He was so sweet and gentle. His patience with the shy little girl touched some inner part of her. It was that same kindness that had caused him to take her in after her parents' death. That same sweetness that had made him marry her and protect her. Not for convenience, as he'd often said. Not even for money, as others might have whispered.

But simply because Nicholas St. James was a decent, honorable man who believed in helping others.

She didn't know why she had never seen that so clearly as she did today.

"He's a good man," Fran said.

Startled, Lily turned. She'd almost forgotten the other woman was there.

"If you don't mind my sayin' so, Lily, it's good to see what's happening between the two of you. There are no two people in the world that deserve it more."

"I . . . I don't know what you mean."

" 'Course you do," Fran said. She put her arm around Lily's shoulder, laughing softly as they moved toward the dining room. "It's love that I seen on your face when you looked at that handsome husband of yours just now. And I've been around enough men to know that he loves you back."

But does he, Lily wondered. If so, why had he never told her?

During breakfast, Fran chattered away, telling them the news of the town and Under-the-Hill.

She told them how Jenny's mother had worked in one of the saloons and how she'd died of consumption.

"There's many more just like her," Fran said. "Some of 'em sleep on the streets, and they hardly have enough to eat. I had in mind a plan . . . there's another house for sale, just down the street a ways—it would be the perfect place for these homeless children to stay."

"And you want our help," Nicholas said.

"Yessir, I know it's a lot to ask, but if you could—"

"It isn't a lot to ask," Nicholas said. "But I'd like to leave the details of purchasing the house and furnishing to you, Miss Fran, since we're to remain here at Live Oaks a while longer. And you know Under-the-Hill as well as anyone."

"Oh, but Mr. Nicholas," she said. "I don't know . . . I've never done such a thing.

"Nonsense," Nicholas said. "Of course you can do it. You're very capable, and who better than you to know exactly what is needed? We could be here at Live Oaks into the fall, and it would help a great deal if you'd agree to manage the entire project."

Lily smiled when she saw Fran's expression. She fairly beamed with pride and pleasure. Smiling, she nodded her approval.

"How can I say no then, when you put so much trust in me?" she said. "Especially when I'll benefit more than most. I want you to know that you've changed my life, giving me a new home and a new start. I would be lying on the street somewhere, as lost and alone as I was that day Miss Lily came down there and found me. I'll never be able to thank you . . . either of you, for all you've done."

"No thanks necessary," Nicholas said, standing. "I think its a very admirable thing you're trying to do. Someone should have undertaken the task years ago. The least I can do now is contribute the funds. I'll write a letter to my lawyer right away for you to take back with you. I'll have him set up an account and you, Miss Fran, will have full legal responsibility. When we come back to Natchez, Lily and I will help you any way we can. If my wife agrees, that is." His look was patient and sweet, yet there was that little glint of challenge that always seemed to linger in his eyes.

Lily smiled.

"Of course I agree," she said. "I think it's a wonderful idea."

"Thank you. Thank you both," Fran said.

Lily hardly heard the other woman's words of praise after that. All she could think about was Nicholas. About how kind and generous, how completely trusting he was with Fran.

He'd been just as generous with her. Right from the very beginning. When she was only a child, with childish ways and rebellions. When she had tried his patience these past few weeks.

She loved him for that. In fact, she was beginning to realize that she loved him more with each passing day.

Chapter 31

Lily was delighted when Fran agreed to stay for a few days at Live Oaks. They spent hours walking about the grounds, talking about various flowers and shrubbery. And Nicholas, as always, took great pleasure in showing his guests the efficient workings of his grand plantation.

The weather was wonderful, hot and breezy during the day, but cooling nicely during the evening so that they were able to sit on the long front porch and watch the fireflies that flickered through the trees and the Spanish moss. It was so quiet here, so peaceful, that sometimes Lily thought she never wanted to go back to Natchez.

She would catch Nicholas watching her with an odd, enigmatic expression, his eyes dark and inscrutable. Sometimes he would smile quietly. Other times he would reach out to touch her, as if to remind her that she was no longer alone.

She knew she loved him. And she was certain he knew it as well. Yet he made no effort to return to their physical intimacy, even though she could see in his eyes that he wanted to as much as she did. She didn't know why he

waited—he was completely well now. Well enough even
to venture across the ferry and into Natchez one day,
although he would not tell her the reason.

"It's a surprise," was all he would say as he smiled that
teasing, mysterious smile at her.

And although she longed for the day when he would
come to her and make love to her, she enjoyed every
minute of their lives. She had learned to live from day to
day. To be content with the rising and setting of the sun
and the quiet peaceful sounds of the land that surrounded
the great, beautiful house.

She'd learned to take pleasure in the smallest things.
The quiet talk and laughter of the house servants as they
went about their chores. The smell of something good
cooking in the kitchen. The birth of a new baby in the
quarters.

It was Sunday morning and Fran and Jenny were going
back to Natchez. They had just walked outside when they
heard the sound of riders in the distance.

Lily shaded her eyes from the bright morning sun and
looked toward the road, waiting until she saw the rider
come into view.

There was only one rider, but behind him was another
horse—an unsaddled, riderless horse. Black as the Mississippi night, his head tossing with restlessness as he skittered
sidelong down the sandy road. Even from this distance,
she could see the excellent lines and the elegant way he
lifted his legs in a light canter.

The two horses came on, passing beneath the huge live
oaks that lined the drive. The dappled sunlight rippled
against the black horse's sleek coat.

Lily held her breath at the magnificence of the sight,
finally managing a quiet murmur of awe.

"Oh, Nicholas," she said. "Have you ever seen such a
beautiful horse?"

She turned and saw him looking at her, his eyes filled
with warmth and pleasure.

"Miss Fran," Jenny said. "Can I go see him? Can I?"

"Of course, child," Fran said. "Come . . . I'll walk with you. But you must be careful not to get too close. He's a very big horse."

As she and the little girl hurried away, Lily turned to Nicholas. There was the oddest look in her eyes as he smiled mysteriously at her.

"Whose horse is he?"

"Why he's yours, little one," he answered, his voice quiet.

"My . . . mine?" she gasped.

She turned, holding her hands up to her throat as she stared at the beautiful prancing horse again.

"Nicholas," she said, her eyes widening as the rider brought the horse nearer. "Nicholas!"

She began to run, and the man leading the horse smiled and handed her the reins.

"It's Blackie!" she shouted back at Nicholas. "It's the horse I rode in the race. But how did you . . . ? I can't believe Charles Lydell would ever sell his most prized thoroughbred. He's won races all over the South. Look, Jenny . . . Miss Fran . . . it's my Blackie . . . isn't he magnificent?"

The black horse lowered its head as Lily stroked his shining skin. She was certain he recognized her when he made soft, snuffling noises against the palm of her hand.

"Blackie, you beauty. Where have you been? Did you miss me? Oh, but I've missed you."

Nicholas walked up to her. He handed money to the rider and nodded up at him.

"You're welcome to go around to the kitchen for breakfast if you wish. Make yourself at home. And thank you for bringing the animal over to us."

"Any time, Mr. St. James," the man said. He tipped his hat at Lily and Fran and disappeared around the house.

"I hoped you'd be pleased," Nicholas said to Lily.

The look in his eyes made Lily want to throw her arms

around him. But all she could do was stand quietly gazing at him.

"Pleased?" she whispered. "Oh, Nicholas, I'm more than pleased. I can't believe you've done this."

"I'd do anything for you," he said. He reached out and pushed a strand of hair away from her eyes. "Don't you know that by now?"

Lily heard Fran cough quietly.

"Well, I hate to interrupt, but Jenny and me, we really have to be goin' if we want to catch the next ferry."

"Oh," Lily said. She'd practically forgotten that Fran and Jenny were there. She felt her cheeks growing warm as they all stood there smiling at her.

Nicholas called for one of the servants to come and take the horse to the stables.

"Rub him down well," he said. "And give him fresh water and some hay."

Lily walked with Fran and Jenny to their waiting carriage, hugging both of them.

"I'm delighted you came," she said. "You must come back again very soon. We're both so pleased that you brought Jenny and that you're making a home for her. I'll come to see both of you just as soon as we get back to Natchez."

Lily waved good-bye, then turned to face Nicholas again. She felt as shy and awkward as she had when she first met him so many years ago.

"Thank you," she said. "Not just for Blackie, but for being so generous and gracious with Fran and Jenny. And for being so kind and forgiving to me."

"You've made that easy, just by being you. There's something I should have told you sooner," he said.

"What?" she asked, her voice breathless as she looked up into his eyes.

"When I watched you ride that day at Pharsalia, I thought I'd never seen anything so magnificent. You were wonderful."

"Oh." She was hoping for a confession of another sort. But she had to smile at the light sparkling in his eyes as he paid her the unexpected compliment.

"So you see, kindness has nothing to do with it." He took her hand, bringing it slowly to his lips and gazing into her eyes as he softly kissed her skin. "I want you to be happy and I saw that day just how much you loved to ride a beautiful horse."

"I do," she whispered. "And you've made me happier than I've ever been in my life."

"Good," he said. "Now . . . let's go to the stables and see this very expensive animal I've just bought."

Jared stepped behind a tree as the carriage carrying Fran and the little girl drove past. Then he moved beneath the overhang of the tree branches, watching through narrowed eyes when Nicholas put his arm around Lily and they turned to walk arm in arm toward the stables.

"So," Jared muttered through clenched teeth, "that's the way it is now? Well, enjoy her, Nicholas," he growled. "For I swear, by all I hold sacred, you will not have her for long. And when I'm finished with her, you won't want her ever again."

That day was magic for Lily, a day that restored her spirits and her aching heart. It was spent just as she'd always dreamed—walking with Nicholas, talking quietly about the plantation and his plans for the future. He included her in those plans with a quiet ease, as if he didn't even have to think about it.

"I've always wanted to put a garden here," he said as they walked beneath the trees. "Perhaps we'll do that before the summer is over."

"A rose garden," Lily said, clasping her hands together with excitement. "I've always wanted a rose garden. One close enough to the house that you can smell the glorious scent of the flowers when the summer turns hot and humid.''

''Then a rose garden it shall be.'' he said. He stopped, bending his head to kiss her lightly on the lips. ''Just tell me what you want, Lily,'' he murmured, his breath soft against her mouth, ''and I swear, I'll move the heavens if that's what it takes to give it to you.''

''I want you,'' she said, without a moment's hesitation. The day's events and Nicholas's meaningful looks had given her the courage to say the words. ''Just you. All the other things are meaningless if I can't have you.''

His eyes darkened, and he pulled her close.

''I confess I can't quite understand your reasoning, given all the torment I've put you through. But, my little love,'' he said, I've been waiting for days to hear you say those words. And I'll admit, waiting hasn't been an easy task for a man as impatient as I am.''

When he pulled her tight against him, there was no doubt about exactly how he intended to show her what he meant.

''It's the middle of the day,'' she said, laughing up at him as she made only a mock protest.

''No one will ever miss us,'' he said. He took her hand and pulled her toward the house, both of them laughing as they went.

''Besides,'' he said, bending low to whisper into her ear, ''we can always put a broom across the threshold to our room. You know none of the servants would ever take a chance on stepping over a broom to disturb us.''

Upstairs, Lily found her courage faltering for a moment as he took her hand and led her into her bedroom. It had been so long, and so many things had happened between them. Sometimes she'd wondered if it could ever be the same.

But if Nicholas retained any resentment for the foolish

things she'd done, he gave no indication. He closed the door firmly and, with a look of purpose, locked it. He pursued her with his eyes, stalked her tenderly with his lips and hands, until she felt herself trembling with anticipation.

He helped her undress, cursing impatiently under his breath at the row of buttons on her dress. Lily laughed at him, touching his hands as they struggled with the tiny fasteners.

Once her dress was removed, she turned and unbuttoned his shirt, pushing his hands away when he tried to help.

"Let me," she said, sliding the material away and placing her hands against his bare chest.

His skin felt hot beneath her exploring fingers.

Nicholas found himself speechless, hardly able to breathe as Lily touched him. She bent forward, placing light kisses against his skin where Jared's bullet had left its mark. He drew in his breath and closed his eyes against her sweet, seductive assault.

When he felt her hands touching the buttons of his trousers, he opened his eyes suddenly and found himself staring into emerald, fathomless pools of love. Then Lily knelt before him, trailing kisses down his flat stomach to the waistband of his pants. Nicholas couldn't stop the involuntary flexing of muscles where her lips touched his heated flesh.

He groaned, and reached down, touching her hair, his fingers tangling in the silken mass of curls.

"God . . . Lily," he murmured.

Suddenly he couldn't stand her sweet assault a moment longer. His hands were on her shoulders, pulling her up and swinging her up into his arms. He carried her to the bed, standing for a moment and letting his gaze move over her creamy skin and the long, slender lines of her body.

She was so beautiful and so desirable. There was something about her mixture of sensuality and innocence that drove him wild. That made him want her as he'd never wanted any other woman. He thought if he made love to her every day for a million years, it would never be enough.

As she looked up at him, she hid nothing of her emotions. Not the desire written on her beautiful face, nor the love lying deep within her eyes.

"Whatever I've done," he said, "I never meant to hurt you, Lily. Never."

"And I never meant to hurt you," she said. She reached up for him, her smile one of sweet compassion, her slender white arms tempting him beyond endurance.

Nicholas could feel every muscle in his body grow taut with desire. Quickly removing his clothes and flinging them aside, he slid into bed beside her, pulling her to him and kissing her with a hunger he couldn't fight.

"There's one thing I want you to know," he said, his breath becoming ragged. "I have never wanted a woman the way I want you. And I swear to you, you will never have to wonder again where I am or who I'm with. For there will only be one woman in my life from this day forward. Only you . . . my sweet Lily."

"Oh . . . Nicholas," she whispered.

Their lovemaking was wild . . . ravenous . . . as neither of them could deny their fierce ecstasy any longer.

And when it was over, Nicholas drew her against him with a strangled breath, reluctant to let her go even for a moment. His breathing was hard as he stared with disbelieving eyes at the ceiling and let his hands linger over the soft curves of her body.

He thought for a moment that this was the day his life truly began. The day that Lily came so willingly, so sweetly back into his arms and his bed. She had offered him her body, and so much more. She had let him know in every way that this union was more than the duty of a wife toward a husband. In loving her, he had lost himself completely, and she had joined him with wholehearted desire and pleasure.

The past few days in this house, she had given him her heart, fully and without reservation. And today, in this bed, Lily St. James, his wild river bride, had given him back his very soul.

Chapter 32

Lily was amazed at how much Nicholas had changed. She thought she understood him a little better than she had when she first came home to Natchez. Understood his pride and his need for privacy. She was pleased and surprised that he shared as much with her as he did.

She didn't seem to have much pride left where he was concerned. She told him several times a day how much she loved him. And if he hadn't said the words to her yet, her confidence grew that one day soon he would.

It wasn't easy for him to trust anyone; she realized that now. She thought he probably hadn't trusted many women in his life. But Lily knew that he needed her and he wanted her. He didn't mind letting her know *that*—and quite enthusiastically, too, she thought with a smile. And that need and desire would just have to be enough for now.

They spent almost every moment together, exploring the forest, tending to the needs of the servants and field hands, supervising the cotton crop. Sometimes they trifled away the day, sleeping late, then walking to the river, picnicking beneath the old trees on the riverbank, or walking in the early-morning sunshine through the plantation's flower-strewn fields and meadows. Sometimes they'd ride, she on the big black thoroughbred and he on one of his favorite horses.

They were rarely apart, and Lily decided that was just the way she liked it. And the way she hoped it would always be.

She could hardly believe the happiness they shared. Or the love she felt for this extraordinary man who was her husband.

It was late one afternoon when a business acquaintance of Nicholas's came to call. The weather had turned quite sultry, and Lily felt a restless urgency to be out of the house.

She wanted to feel the wind blowing through her hair. She wanted to ride Blackie down to the river, where it was cooler.

Nicholas disagreed.

"I'd prefer you didn't ride out alone," he said. They were standing in the hall, and Nicholas kept his voice low and out of hearing of his guest who waited inside the parlor.

"Nicholas," Lily protested. She reached up and placed a quick kiss on his strong jaw. "You know I'll be fine. Blackie will take care of me." She smiled up at him, opening her eyes wide in a look of teasing entreaty. "Please?" she said. "It's so hot, and I do so love to ride down to the river. Just for a little while. Just until the sun goes down. You have your guest to attend to, and I promise I'll be back in time to dress properly for dinner."

"Lily," he groaned. "You know I hate to deny you anything, but sometimes you do sorely try my patience."

"Oh, thank you," she said. "I knew you'd say yes."

"On one condition," he said. He reached forward and lightly tugged at a lock of her hair. "That one of the stableboys rides with you."

Lily sighed.

"I'm serious," he said, shaking a finger in front of her nose. "You know that Jared could still be nearby."

"He hasn't been seen anywhere near here since the duel. Everyone says he's probably in Mexico by now."

"They don't know Jared the way I do," Nicholas said. "When he makes up his mind to do something, he's like a snapping turtle that won't let go."

"Oh, all right," she said. "If it will make you feel any better, I'll take someone with me."

"It would," he said growled. "But only just barely."

Lily laughed and reached up to kiss him before hurrying out the door.

Nicholas watched her go, his gaze filled with amusement.

"The girl has bewitched me, as surely as one of Mae's voodoo spells, " he said, with a shake of his head. Then he laughed softly to himself. "But what sweet beguiling witchcraft it is."

Jared was growing impatient. It had become harder and harder to remain close to the plantation house. Nicholas had some of the workers patrol the road and the riverbank, looking for him. Besides, his cousin never seemed to stray far from Lily's side for anything. They were constantly together, and the sight of them strolling hand in hand, laughing and gazing into one another's eyes sickened and infuriated Jared.

But in a way he had to admire his cousin. Nicholas was no fool. At least he had the good sense to know that Jared would never rest until this thing was settled between them.

It was growing late, and he had decided that he would have to come back another day to continue his surveillance. But just as he turned to go, he saw a flash of color at the front of the house.

He turned and watched with narrowed eyes as Lily hurried out of the house and down the steps. Holding his breath, he waited, expecting to see Nicholas follow her.

When he didn't, Jared crouched in the lush humid undergrowth of the forest. He had waited so long that he could scarcely believe his eyes when he saw Lily go into the stables alone.

Inside the stables, Lily called out.

"Hello?" she said. "Jess? Anyone here?"

She turned toward the stall where the black horse whinnied softly in greeting. She went to him and rubbed her hand down his nose.

"You're restless too, aren't you, boy?" she asked. "I promised Nicholas we wouldn't ride out alone. But I think Jess has probably already gone home to supper." She sighed with disappointment and walked around in the barn, shuffling her feet in the soft hay.

The big thoroughbred made another noise and she frowned.

"But we'd be very careful. wouldn't we?" she whispered, her voice conspiratorial. "We'd only go as far as the river and we'll be back long before dark. What do you say? Shall we risk trying Nicholas's patience just once more?" She laughed and pulled her saddle off its stand, then moved into the horse's stall.

"I think I can persuade him not to be too angry with me," she said. The thought of coming back to the house, of dressing for dinner and sitting so staidly and politely across from him, made her heart beat a little faster.

There was something exciting about entertaining guests while intimate, meaningful looks passed between herself and Nicholas. Each of them knew what the other was thinking, what they were anticipating, as soon as the formalities ended.

She laughed as she rode out of the stable and off toward the river.

Jared had to be very careful not to approach her too soon. If he failed in his attempt to take Lily, she would be able to tell Nicholas. And Jared knew that if that happened, his cousin would follow him to the ends of the earth to make him pay.

"Nicholas's justice," Jared snorted disdainfully. Over the years he'd come to despise his cousin and his high-handed ways. Some thought Nicholas should have disowned him years ago. But Jared was a St. James, too, and he deserved to share the wealth; why his father would have been a full partner if his uncle had done what was right. Now, after watching the house at Live Oaks for weeks, and seeing what went on between Nicholas and Lily, the hatred had begun to eat at him even more.

He had become more obsessed with Lily and was no longer certain if it was sexual or if his need to possess her grew out of his hatred and resentment of his cousin.

But possess her he would.

He watched impatiently from the shadows of the forest as Lily walked the big black horse along the riverbank. Jared knew he could overpower her. Pull her off the horse and drag her away. But he didn't want to risk her screaming.

He could hardly believe his luck when moments later Lily got off the horse and tied the reins loosely around a tree. Then she walked to the river and sat on a grassy knoll, wrapping her arms around her knees as she stared out at the water.

Jared moved quietly, crouching low and coming up behind her. Before Lily knew what was happening, his hand snaked around to cover her mouth and with his other arm, he pulled her up against him.

Lily was a tall girl, and strong. She struggled wildly,

kicking and launching herself back against him. When she moved her head around enough to see who he was, her eyes grew frantic and she began to thrash even more wildly, making small noises of terror in her throat.

Jared dragged her across the ground, ignoring the tracks her feet left in the sandy soil.

"Listen to me," he snarled against her ear. "You scream, or make any commotion, and I'll shoot the horse."

Lily drew in her breath, her eyes growing wide and silently pleading as she watched Jared fearfully.

"You think I won't?" he asked. Slowly he withdrew his hand from her mouth and pulled a pistol from his jacket. In two steps he held it against the horse's head.

Blackie's eyes rolled and he snorted, skittering nervously away from Jared.

"Please," Lily said, her voice breathless. "Don't . . . don't hurt him."

"Then behave yourself," he growled. "Why must you make this so difficult? Don't you know, my sweet Lily, that I'd never hurt you?"

Lily shivered as he held the cold barrel of the pistol against her cheek, moving it slowly down her face to the corner of her mouth.

He would kill her, she had no doubt. He had been so cold-blooded at the duel, shooting Nicholas in the back without a qualm. But for a moment, as she contemplated what he had in store for her, she considered whether she really wanted to live or not.

Then she thought of Nicholas.

A quiet sob escaped her lips, and she clenched her teeth against the ache that swept upward through her chest and throat. But she made no further protest as she lifted her head and stared with resentful acquiescence directly into Jared's eyes.

"Ah," Jared said. "A sensible choice. I've always been especially attracted to sensible women." His laugh was soft and low. Ugly.

   Lily was trembling when he took a handkerchief from
his pocket and placed it tightly across her mouth, tying it
at the back of her head. She wasn't sure how she managed
to make her feet move when he took her arm and half
dragged her into the forest.

Chapter 33

For some reason, after Lily left the house, Nicholas could not seem to get her out of his mind. He couldn't rid himself of the feeling that something was wrong. It was almost like a whisper in the back of his mind. Several times during his discussion with his guest, he would walk to the front windows and push aside the velvet curtains, gazing ouside into the growing shadows.

She probably took the entrance road, considering it would be an easy ride and one she could follow even after it grew late.

"Why don't we call it a day for now," Nicholas said finally, turning to the businessman. He couldn't keep up his pretended interest any longer. "I'll have one of the servants see you to your room. Dinner is at seven if that suits you."

"It does indeed," the gentleman said. "And I confess I can't wait to taste some of Live Oaks' famous cuisine."

"I promise you don't be disappointed," Nicholas said, nodding graciously.

As soon as his guest had gone upstairs, Nicholas went

out onto the front porch. Lily had been gone more than two hours now. It wasn't like her to stay so late—not when she wanted to make herself presentable for dinner.

Nicholas frowned, staring out at the lengthening shadows as the sun sank lower toward the flat horizon. Just then he saw one of the stableboys coming along the road from the barn.

"Jess!" he called out.

Nicholas jogged down the steps and out to meet the young boy.

"Jess, have you seen Miss Lily? Didn't she ask you to go riding with her?"

"No suh, Mr. Nicholas. Ain't seen her." His eyes were wide, and there was a look of worry on his dark face as if he might have done something wrong.

Nicholas felt the muscles tighten in his stomach as his gaze scanned the forest that surrounded the house.

"What about James? Have you seen James?"

"Yes suh, James be right in the stables, closin' everything up for the night."

Nicholas shook his head and touched the boy on the shoulder.

"It's all right, Jess. Go on home now. Your mama will be wondering where you are."

Nicholas watched the boy head toward one of the cabins, then he turned back toward the house.

"She's alone," he muttered to himself. "Why in heaven's name did she ride out alone?"

Nicholas walked restlessly out the road in front of the house, gazing into the distance, hoping against hope that he'd see the big black horse cantering toward him.

Finally, going back to the house, he paced the front porch, his gaze moving out toward the road time and again. Inside, his heart thudded against his chest as thoughts swirled through his head. He imagined every conceivable tragedy and then dismissed each one. But when Lily hadn't returned home by dinnertime, he knew with a grim, terrifying reality that something had happened.

Moments later, he heard the sound of hoofbeats and hurried out into the yard, hope welling up in his chest as his eyes scanned the dark toward the sound.

"Lily," he whispered, seeing her beautiful face in his mind. What would he do it anything happened to her? Now that he had finally opened his heart and soul to her, how could he go on without his Lily?

When he saw the big black horse come into view, the saddle empty, he felt as if his heart might actually stop. Quickly he ran to the horse and reined him in, running his hands over the thoroughbred's quivering sides as he searched for injuries or some clue that might tell him what had happened.

"Where is she, boy? I know you wouldn't leave her if she was all right." Nicholas's gaze scanned the distance worriedly.

Could his sweet Lily be lying somewhere injured, waiting for him to find her? Perhaps even . . .

"No," he muttered. "Don't think it," Grinding his teeth together, he hurried into the house, shouting to the servants as he went.

"The mistress's horse has come home without her. He must have thrown her. Go to the stables and have my horse saddled. Bring lanterns and have every available man out in front of the house in fifteen minutes.

They searched until well past midnight. Men slowly walking through the waist-high grasses with lanterns held high, others combing through the forest and the roads leading to the cotton field and out toward the Natchez ferry landing.

Nicholas drove himself harder than any of the others. He wouldn't let himself think. Wouldn't let himself even imagine the worst.

Finally he came back to the house, hoping that Lily might have come home on her own. Most of the men were there waiting. He was as exhausted as he'd ever been in his life.

"We've looked everywhere, sir," his overseer said. "It's so dark out there you can't see your hand in front of your face. I think it might be best if we wait for daybreak to continue looking."

"That isn't your decision to make," Nicholas snapped. He stared into the faces of the men. Some of them looked away; others stared at him with tired, red eyes, obviously as exhausted as he was.

These were people he valued. Some of them he had known since childhood. He knew them as well as he knew anyone, and he trusted them. And he knew they would search until they dropped if it was what he asked.

Deep down inside, that was exactly what he wanted.

But he knew, even as his fear urged him on, how impractical that was. None of them would be of any use to Lily if they were physically spent. Including himself.

They had absolutely nothing to tell them what had happened to Lily, and it was only a few more hours until dawn.

Nicholas sighed and slumped in the saddle.

"All right," he said. "Ask Mama Jolie to make plenty of coffee and hot biscuits. We'll start again as soon as it's light enough to see."

He went upstairs to their bedroom, thinking insanely that she might actually be there. That somehow this was all a nightmare that would end as soon as he saw her in bed.

Then he would crawl in beside her and take her in his arms. He'd tell her he loved her. More than anything in the world he wanted to be able to say those words to her.

Words he had held back, just the way he had withheld himself from her at first. He'd seen in her eyes how badly she wanted to know that he loved her. And yet he hadn't told her. Some deeply hidden, stubborn pride had kept him from it. It was something about himself that even he didn't understand.

He stepped into her darkened bedroom and lit one of the lamps. The pungent smell of the sulfur mingled with the sweet, lingering scent of Lily's perfume. It permeated the still air and made him catch his breath against the pain it brought to his heart.

He picked up one of the pillows from the bed, holding it against his face and breathing in the faint scent of her that still lingered there.

Nicholas swallowed hard and sank slowly down onto the bed, still holding the pillow in his hands.

"Lily," he whispered. "My sweet Lily."

He loved her. And yet he'd let all this time pass without telling her that.

Nicholas knew deep in the darkest reaches of his soul that if something happened to Lily, he'd regret that for the rest of his life.

Later he woke, still clutching her pillow. Glancing toward the window he saw that the sky was growing lighter. Quickly he pulled his boots on and made his way downstairs.

The men were already assembled in the front yard. One of them met him with a steaming cup of coffee and a leather bag filled with food.

Nicholas nodded, feeling a lump in his throat as he accepted the offering. They knew him well, and he never appreciated that fact more than this morning.

Nicholas was the one who went toward the river. He knew how much Lily liked to watch the great Mississippi drifting by. And he knew which spot was her favorite.

In the morning light he saw the marks in the sand immediately, and the sight of them sent bells of warning ringing inside his head. At first he feared she might have fallen into the river.

But something was not quite right. The marks looked as if someone had been dragged. And the direction was away from the river, not toward it.

He frowned and bent low, his eyes scanning the earth in the dim light of early morning. He saw a tiny patch of color among the grass and mud and leaves and reached to pick it up.

The blue silken flower felt like nothing between his fingers. Light and soft. Like Lily's skin.

He held it to his nose, imagining that he actually caught the scent of her perfume on this tiny scrap of material.

It had come from her dress; he was certain of that. And it proved to him that she hadn't drowned. She had been dragged away from here.

Then he saw the outline of a man's bootprint in the dirt. Nicholas cursed softly, his mind telling him what his heart already knew.

"Jared," he said.

His eyes, when he stood, were like ice. Cold and hard and clear. They belied the fury he felt inside. And the terrible, heart-stopping fear.

Jared had Lily. And God alone knew what he meant to do with her.

Pushing the small flower into his pocket, Nicholas quickly mounted his horse and rode back toward the house, shouting as he passed the searching men and telling them to come back with him.

Chapter 34

A few hours later, Nicholas rode off the ferry at the river landing below Natchez. He sat straight in the saddle as he rode Lily's black thoroughbred along Silver Street. There was something formidable about the dark-haired man astride the shining black horse. Something that made people stop and look back or simply stare with mute curiosity.

Of all the people who swarmed up and down the streets, Nicholas was the one who commanded attention. He rode slowly, with purpose, and with a hard look on his face that would make a man think twice before stepping out into his way.

The landing was busy that day. Everywhere he looked, Nicholas saw a variety of people, some dressed in bright colors, obviously from other countries. Around him, he heard the sound of other languages and the shout of men unloading barges and rafts.

Today many gazing admirers lined the bluff's edge and crowded the landing at the river as they watched for the arrival and departure of passenger boats. Perhaps some were hoping to see a quick sprint along this stretch of the river. It was not uncommon for some of the steamboats to race, even though it could be quite hazardous for the passengers, as the overheated engines sometimes exploded.

Except for New Orleans, Natchez was the busiest port along the Mississippi, and people often flocked to the landing.

Nicholas stopped in several of the taverns along the street, going inside and asking the same question.

"Anyone here know Jared St. James? Anyone seen him in the last day or so?"

When they answered no, Nicholas didn't bother to stop and converse further with any of the patrons, even the ones who'd heard about the duel and who inquired about his well-being.

There was no time. His purpose was simple and clear—to find Lily. Nothing or no one was going to stand in his way until he saw her again.

By the time he reached the office of the Natchez Steamboat Company, he felt frustrated and ill-tempered. The clerk in the office, a meek-looking bespectacled young man, looked up when Nicholas entered. He was new here—not someone Nicholas recognized.

"I'm looking for a man who might have booked passage on one of your boats," Nicholas said. "A man named Jared St. James. He might have had a young woman with him."

The young man coughed and glanced away.

"I'm sorry, sir, but we're not in the habit of giving out information about our passengers."

Nicholas clenched his teeth together and took one step toward the desk. His hand reached out and clamped around the man's coat, propelling him forward as if he were a rag doll.

"You listen to me," Nicholas said. "This man has kidnapped a young woman, and if you've seen him and know where he's taken her, then you'd damn well better tell me. Now!"

"Sir," the clerk gasped. He glanced nervously at a large ledger on the edge of his desk. "I . . . I can't—"

"You can and you will," Nicholas said, shaking him thoroughly.

Suddenly Nicholas pushed the man back into his chair, sending him sprawling against a wall. Then he picked up the ledger that the man had glanced at so furtively and thumbed to the first few pages.

The clerk stood up to protest.

Nicholas pushed him back down into the chair again, holding his hand out in front of him in a silent warning to remain where he was.

Quickly Nicholas moved his finger down the page, stopping at one signature and tapping the paper purposefully as he looked up and into the eyes of the frightened clerk.

"Here he is," Nicholas said. "He left last night on the *Bayou Queen*, heading for New Orleans. Were you here when the passengers boarded?"

"Sir . . ."

"Tell me, damn you!"

"All right . . . all right," the young man said, cowering away from Nicholas's upraised fist. "Yes . . . I was here. But Mr. St. James warned me that someone might come looking for him. He said he was taking the young woman away from a murderous husband. That she was afraid for her life. She did look afraid, sir," he added.

"She's afraid of him, you fool," Nicholas growled. He could feel his heart pounding against his ribs, and he felt as if his head might explode from the fury he felt at Jared's audacity. He hadn't even bothered to use another name, flaunting what he'd done right under Nicholas's nose and daring him to follow.

If Jared hurt her . . .

"What did she look like?" He asked the question, hoping against hope that he was wrong. But in his heart, he already knew what the man would say.

"She was beautiful, sir . . . if you don't mind my saying

so. Tall . . . almost as tall as I. With reddish gold hair and green eyes. Is that the young woman you're looking for?"

"Yes, and the young woman is my wife," he said. "I'm Nicholas St. James. Have you ever heard of me"

"Nicholas St. James?" the clerk said, his eyes growing wide as he obviously recognized the name. His gaze moved over Nicholas as if he'd seen a ghost. "Of course, sir. You own the ferry . . . and half of Natchez, they say. You . . . you're the man shot in the duel a few weeks back."

Nicholas could see the young man begin to tremble and he wanted to laugh. God, did he think he intended to kill him right here and now?

"That's right," Nicholas growled. "And the man I'm looking for is the one who shot me. And the only danger my wife faces is with him. He came to my plantation last night and kidnapped her against her will."

Nicholas reached out and grabbed the man's coat again.

"You get me a boat to New Orleans, and you get me one right now. I want the fastest one you have."

The clerk swallowed hard, his eyes glazing over with fear. "That'd be the *Natchez Belle*, sir. But the passengers won't be boarding for another three hours."

"To hell with the passengers," Nicholas said. "They can take the next boat." Impatiently he began shuffling money onto the desk. "How much?"

"For a ticket?"

"For the entire boat," Nicholas said. "I'll pay for every stateroom. As long as it can leave right now."

"Well, I . . . I . . ."

"And a thousand dollars for you," Nicholas added, throwing more bills onto the desk.

"I'll see to it, sir," the clerk said quickly. He raked in the money, his eyes growing bright with greed. "Let me round up the crew and talk to the captain. You can see the boat from here sir, if you'd like to go ahead and board."

Nicholas turned and walked toward the door. "I'll be taking my horse with me," he said as he went out the door.

"Yes . . . yes, sir," the clerk said.

Lily had never been so afraid or so heartsick in her life. All she could think about was Nicholas and what he must be going through at this moment.

Would he guess that Jared had taken her? Or would he doubt her as he had before and wonder if she went with him of her own free will?

"No," she whispered to herself. She'd made herself think of the wonderful nights they'd spent together at Live Oaks. Of Nicholas's words and the way he had made love to her. Slowly and deeply. All night long.

He had to know now at last that she could never deceive him, or pretend about something as wonderful and important as that.

She glanced around the stateroom where she lay, her arms and legs bound, a gag tied tightly across her mouth. Her limbs ached from lying in the same position, and sometimes she could feel panic rising in her, thinking that she couldn't breathe, and that she would surely die if someone didn't remove the gag from her mouth.

Then she would think of Nicholas and force herself to relive those nights with him. It was what had seen her through these past few days.

She had no idea where they were, but calculating the time and the sounds she could hear outside, she thought they might be in New Orleans. She had no idea what Jared had told the ship's captain about their not leaving the boat with the other passengers. Perhaps he intended taking her somewhere else. Perhaps even to another country.

Her heart skipped a beat at the thought, and she struggled anew against the restraints that held her.

She heard the door open and looked over her shoulder to see Jared enter the room.

He brought a tray of food and placed it on a table beside the bed.

His hands, when they untied the gag, were gentle, but the hot look of hunger in his eyes sickened her and made her look away.

"Don't look away from me," he muttered. " And don't think about screaming for help. There's no one left on the boat to hear you."

Lily turned on him, her eyes burning with anger.

"Are you foolish enough to think you can get away with this?" she asked. "Do you really think Nicholas won't find me, no matter where you go?"

"He can try," Jared said blithely. "But, since we left at night, I figure it took him at least two days to decide what happened to you. By the time he figures out you're with me, we'll be long gone. Here, you need to eat." He nodded toward a box that lay on a chair across the room. "And I've bought you a new dress."

"I don't want it," she said. "And I don't want anything to eat."

"Suit yourself," Jared said dryly. He reached out and touched her cheek, his eyes narrowing when she pulled away and spat at him.

"You little hellcat," he said. He wiped his face and reached for her, pulling her against him and shaking her hard. He was trembling as his fingers grabbed the bodice of her dress and ripped the material away with a loud tearing noise.

"Don't," she screamed.

He clamped his hand against her mouth, holding her tightly against him as he struggled with the ragged remnants of her dress.

Lily closed her eyes, squeezing them tightly against the

humiliation she felt as his hand crushed her breast. When his mouth clamped over hers, wet and hungry, she struggled to keep her lips closed, shuddering when she felt his tongue and tasted the bitterness of liquor.

She gagged and pulled away from him, crying out in pain as he twisted her arm.

He was furious, and she could feel the violence coiled in him. "Wait . . ." she whispered. "Please . . . Jared, not like this."

He hesitated, looking at her for a long moment, as if trying to decide what to do.

"Is there something you want to say?" he asked, jerking her tight against him.

"A . . . a woman likes a little gentleness. Surely you know that by now, considering all the women a man like you must have known."

She tried to keep her voice quiet and soft. Cajoling and nonthreatening.

"Quite a number," he drawled. "If I do say so myself."

"I . . . I must look a mess," she said, forcing a tremulous smile to her lips. "I hate this . . . having you see me this way."

Jared's eyes narrowed.

"What are you getting at?" he asked. "And if this is a trick, I swear, I'll—"

"It's not a trick," Lily said, her voice breathless with hope. If only she could make him think she would cooperate. If only she could distract him for a few minutes, perhaps she could think of something . . . anything to get herself out of this fix.

"It's inevitable, isn't it?" she asked. "Our being together . . . the way you want? It was meant to be."

His eyes glittered, and he bent toward her. She could see the spark of desire and the triumph. He was beginning to think he'd won. And that was exactly what she wanted.

"I just want to look my best," she said, moving away

from him. "And I'd love a bath. Please . . . is that too much to ask? Just a few more minutes while I make myself presentable." Her glance darted toward the box. "I'll wear the dress you bought."

"I'm not fool enough to leave you alone here," he growled.

"You can ask one of the maids to help me. You can even wait outside the door. I don't care about that. Just please . . . let me have these few moments. I promise, you won't be disappointed." Her insides quivered as she said the words and looked up to let her gaze linger on his face.

He was handsome. Amazingly like Nicholas. Except for the evil in his eyes. How could two people be of the same blood . . . so much alike and yet so very, very different?

Jared growled low in his throat, but the look in his eyes let her know his answer. She held her breath as he put the gag back into her mouth and tied her arms and legs. Then slowly he got up from the bed and walked toward the door.

"I'll find one of the maids to help you. And if you try anything, I swear, Lily, I'll kill you. And then I'll wait for Nicholas so I can see the look on his face when he finds you.

Lily wanted to scream at him, wanted to scratch and hit and claw. But she forced herself to remain silent. She could hardly breathe as she shook her head hard. Somehow she had to make him think she would cooperate. And somehow she had to convince the maid to help her.

The *Natchez Belle* made the trip to New Orleans in record time, partly because of Nicholas's generous pay to the crew and partly because there were no other passengers or cargo aboard.

It was very late and the streets near the docks were practically deserted as he rode the black horse down the boarding plank. He saw the *Bayou Queen* docked nearby, dark except for a few lights on the decks, and obviously empty.

He knew Patrice Claymore lived nearby, and he also knew she would help him if she could. It was late when he reached the Viaux Carre and found her house, and he was surprised to see the lights still shining downstairs.

When he knocked on the door, it was answered immediately.

"Nicholas!"

Patrice wore a dressing gown and her hair was loose, her eyes dark as if she'd been sleeping. Behind her, he saw a young woman dressed in a black servant's dress and wearing a gray cape to ward off the damp mists of the Louisiana night.

"My God, Nicholas, how did you get here so quickly?"

Nicholas stepped into the shadowy hallway and grasped Patrice's arms.

"What are you talking about?" he asked. "Do you know something about Lily?"

"I know where she is," she said breathlessly. She turned to the young woman. "This girl attends the ladies on the *Bayou Queen*. Quickly, child, tell Mr. St. James what you just told me."

"Is she all right?" Nicholas asked.

"Yessir," the girl said. "From what I could tell."

When she'd finished her story, Nicholas turned on his heel.

"Nicky," Patrice said, grabbing his arm. "Wait . . . you can't just go barging in there. Jared is armed and he's dangerous. Besides that, he has Lily. Do you know what could happen if she gets caught between the two of you?"

Nicholas took a deep breath and frowned. Every instinct in his soul urged him to go. Every minute that Lily was with Jared was a torment for him.

"I can't stand to think of her alone with him for another minute," he said. A muscle flickered in his jaw as his teeth clenched and unclenched.

"Let me go with you," Patrice said. "He won't be expecting me, and perhaps I can distract him for a moment . . . just long enough for you to catch him off guard."

Despite his impatience, Nicholas nodded, feeling the practicality of her plan.

"It could be dangerous for you," he warned. "Are you sure you want to—?"

"I'm certain," she said. "I love Lily, too, and I want nothing more than to see the both of you together again."

"Then get dressed," he said. "And quickly."

As Patrice hurried away, he handed the maid some coins and made certain he knew exactly which stateroom Lily was being kept in.

Minutes later, he and Patrice made their way slowly along the deck of the boat's upper level, pausing outside the room that the maid had pointed out.

Nicholas pushed his body back against the siding and nodded to Patrice, who took a deep breath and stepped forward, tapping lightly on the door.

When Jared opened the door, Nicholas could hear his curse of surprise.

"Patrice? What the hell? How did you know I was here?" Jared asked.

"Oh, news travels fast in New Orleans," she said. "And I hear that you have a beautiful red-haired woman with you. Don't tell me you finally convinced our lovely Lily to accompany you downriver?"

"And what if I have?" he growled. Jared stuck his head out the doorway, and Nicholas flattened himself against the boards in the darkness.

It took every ounce of self-control he could muster to keep himself from reaching for Jared.

"But darling, Lily is a friend of mine," Patrice said, her voice coy and teasing. "I've come to see her. And you, too, of course."

Nicholas heard Jared's low growl and saw his arm reach

out to pull Patrice into the room. She deliberately fell against him, allowing Nicholas to make his move.

He caught Jared's arm, pushing Patrice out of the way and pulling Jared out onto the deck at the same time.

He had expected Jared to have a weapon. What he hadn't expected was that the weapon would be a knife. He saw the glint of light on the steel blade in Jared's hand.

Quickly he leapt out of the way, closing his fists together and hammering them down hard against the center of Jared's back. With a grunt, Jared sprawled onto the deck. But he was up as quick as lightning. Nicholas had forgotten just how agile his smaller, lighter cousin was.

He saw the knife glint again as Jared lunged at him. Behind him he heard Lily scream his name. There was fear and warning in her voice. But the sound of it buoyed him, and all he could think was that she was here. And that she was alive.

That was all that mattered to him now.

Jared shoved Nicholas against the rail, pushing the weapon up to his throat. He managed to sidestep Jared and whirl around to catch his arm, twisting the knife back away from his own body. The knife was between them as each man struggled for control. Wrestling they rolled on the deck, and Nicholas slammed Jared hard against a barrel. He felt the knife give and heard Jared's gasp just as his hands reached out to tear at Nicholas's clothing.

Then slowly, with a loud sigh, Jared lay very still. Nicholas could see a pool of darkness spreading from beneath his cousin's body.

He bent over him quickly and placed his fingers at Jared's neck.

Despite their death struggle, Nicholas felt stunned. Somewhere deep inside, he had hoped they might end their battle without this. He should hate this man for what he'd done. But suddenly all he could feel was an overwhelming sadness and a sense of loss and guilt. In a flash, he saw the boy he had played with as a child, the son of his father's only brother, Nicholas's own flesh and blood and his nearest male kin.

"He's dead," Nicholas said to Patrice, who hurried forward from where she'd been hiding. "He fell against the knife."

"Nicholas."

At the whispered sound of his name, Nicholas rose and turned to see Lily standing in the doorway, the light from the stateroom reflecting through her hair like a golden halo.

"Lily."

Suddenly she was in his arms, her hands clutching at him desperately. He could feel her slender body trembling violently. She gasped when she saw Jared's body and hid her face against Nicholas's shoulder.

"Is he ... oh, God, it's my fault," she whispered. "I came between you and now because of me ..."

"No," Nicholas said. "There was bad blood bewteen us long before you ever came back home, sweetheart. Jared's mind was filled with hatred and bitterness and I'm afraid he saw you as just another possession of mine that he wanted." He held her tight, stroking her hair. "Don't cry, angel. It's all right. I'm here now. Did her hurt you? Did he ... ?"

"No ... he didn't ... he hasn't ..." she stammered, meaning to reassure Nicholas, yet unable to find the words.

Instead he took her mouth, closing away her words as his arms rocked her gently against him.

"Shh," he whispered. "It doesn't matter. I don't care. All I care about is that you're alive. And that you're coming back to me."

He felt Patrice behind him, touching his arm and embracing Lily at the same time.

"I'll send someone for the authorities," she said. She glanced quickly at Jared's body and shivered before hurrying away.

Nicholas nodded and turned his attention back to Lily. He pulled her inside the stateroom out of view of Jared's lifeless body.

"I was afraid you'd think I left with Jared of my own free will. That you'd be angry and hurt, and you might never even try to find me."

"Never," he whispered. "I didn't think that for a moment." His voice was actually shaking as he spoke and his big body trembled as he held her. "Do you know how afraid I was when I couldn't find you? I might have lost you forever."

"I know," she said. "I *do* know. I was afraid I'd lost you, too."

"I love you," he whispered. "I've loved you for so long and I've wished a thousand times these past few hours that I'd told you that."

"Oh, Nicholas, you . . . you mean it?" she whispered, her eyes sparkling with tears.

"Of course I mean it," he said. "I've had more chances with you than any one man deserves. Your love has made me feel like the most blessed man on earth, and I should have told you that. And from now on, I'm not taking anything for granted. I intend telling you every day . . . several times a day, just how much I love you. I prayed that God would give me just one more chance to make you as happy as you've made me."

"I am," she whispered. "Oh, Nicholas, my darling, now that you're here, I am."

"We'll put all this behind us, I promise. And life will be sweet . . . just as good as both of us ever dreamed. But first I need to take care of Jared's burial . . . he is still part of my family."

"I know, darling," she whispered, touching his face. "Of course you do. I'll help you. I'm so sorry it came to this and that you were the one who had to stop him."

"When it's over, all I want is to take you back home to

Natchez. I want to spend the rest of my life with you, Lily, loving you, making a home with you and the children we'll have one day.''

"It's what I want, too," she said. "I think it's all I've ever wanted."

Epilogue

October 1822
Live Oaks Plantation

"I'm so happy that you and Theodore could come to Natchez," Lily said, smiling at her sister-in-law.

"So am I," Mary said. She sighed as she glanced out over the trees and the new rose garden. "I've missed you and Nicholas so much, and I've missed the plantation. I love Boston, but there's nothing like Mississippi to me . . . nothing like being at home."

They were on the front porch, watching Teddy play in the yard while his baby sister lay sleeping in a cradle beside Mary. Mary laid her knitting aside and reached over to touch the baby's face with the back of her hand.

"I'm glad that the weather's cooperated," Lily said. "And that the trees are going to be especially lovely this fall."

She glanced up to see Nicholas coming across the yard toward them, and her eyes changed, growing warm and languid with pleasure. She thought she'd never grow tired of seeing her tall, handsome husband. Especially now, since the unfortunate incident with Jared finally seemed to be fading, and she and Nicholas could smile again.

Mary giggled softly. "Are you going to tell him?"

"Yes," Lily said. She caught her breath and pushed her own knitting into a large basket beside her chair.

Nicholas tousled Teddy's hair as he passed and stepped onto the porch, his eyes scanning Mary and going to Lily.

"Good morning, ladies," he said with a teasing bow. Bending, he touched one finger softly to the sleeping baby's cheek before leaning his hip against the porch railing.

"Well, sister," he said. "I think I've about convinced old Theodore to remain in Natchez and become a full partner in St. James Enterprises. I even took him downriver to show him that parcel of land that you always loved so much.

"Oh, Nicky," Mary said. "Do you mean it?"

"All he needs is a little encouragement," he said with a wink. "And you can start planning where you want the plantation house."

"Oh Nicky! Thank you!" She jumped up and threw her arms around Nicholas's neck. "If you'll excuse me," Mary said breathlessly. "I'll leave you two alone. Teddy!" she called. "Let's go find your father."

Mary glanced encouragingly at Lily and bent to pick up her sleeping child out of the cradle.

"Oh, don't disturb her," Lily said. "We'll watch her."

"Are you sure you don't mind," Lily said.

"Of course we don't mind," Lily said.

After Mary had gone, Lily lifted her mouth to kiss her husband, touching his face and watching him with adoring eyes when he stepped back to the railing.

"You love having the children here, don't you?" he asked, glancing over at the cradle.

"Oh, Nicholas," she sighed. "Aren't they wonderful? Little Teddy has grown so much since I last saw him, and

Catherine is such a sweet baby. She has the St. James hair and eyes, I think." She glanced up at Nicholas and saw that wistful look on his face whenever they discussed the children. She'd delighted in watching him with them and he hadn't been able to hide the fact that he'd like nothing better than having children of his own.

"I think you're right," he said, his face softening. "Although you must admit, they're both a bit spoiled."

"Oh, bother," she said, smiling. "That's what children are for. And *you* must admit that you and I have spoiled them as much as Mary and Theodore ever have."

Nicholas laughed. "That's true." He came to sit beside her, reaching out to touch her and brush her hair back from her neck. He still couldn't seem to resist touching her. "It's such a beautiful morning, I thought you'd be riding," he said. "You haven't ridden in several days now."

"No," she said. She reached down for her knitting, placing it in her lap as she smiled enigmatically.

"You're not ill, are you? Or, anything?" Nicholas stared at his wife. He could see for himself that she wasn't ill. In fact he thought he'd never seen her looking healthier or more lovely. There was a soft glow to her skin, and today her emerald eyes literally sparkled with happiness.

"Did I tell you that Mary is teaching me to knit?" she asked.

"No," he answered, looking at her oddly.

With a quiet sigh, she picked up the item she had in her lap and held it up for him to see.

Seeing the tiny white sweater, he frowned.

"Oh, don't tell me," he grunted. "Mary's having another child? Dear Lord, am I going to have to have a talk with that brother-in-law of mine?"

Lily heard his teasing and saw his forced smile as he tried to be happy for what he thought was his sister's news. At that moment Lily's heart actually ached with love for him.

"No," she whispered. "Not Mary."

His mouth opened, and he caught his breath, moving toward her and looking into her eyes as if he was afraid to believe what he was hearing.

"Lily?" he said. "Sweetheart?"

"We're having a baby, Nicholas," she said. "Sometime in the spring. Maybe April."

She heard his whoop of excitement and then his laughter, and suddenly she was in his arms, being held tightly against him as he swung her around the porch.

"Nicholas!" she exclaimed, laughing with him.

Gently he placed her back on her feet, kissing her hard on the mouth, before grinning down at her.

"You're not teasing?" he said.

"I'm not teasing," she said, grinning back at him. "We're really having a baby. Oh, Nicholas . . . are you happy?"

"Happy?" he said, his voice growing quiet with awe. "God, I never thought I could ever be as happy as I was when I brought you back home from New Orleans. But this . . . this . . ." He laughed and shook his head. "Will you listen to me? I sound like a blathering fool. I am happy, sweetheart. You've given me more than I ever deserved. I love you so much."

"And I love you." she whispered. "Oh, Nicholas, we're so lucky."

"Yes," he whispered, just before he kissed her. "Full measure, my darling, and running over."